Secrets of
The Carousel

A Story of Strong Courageous Women

Pursuing Their Texas Roots

Sussie Jordan

All Rights Reserved
Printed in the United States of America

ISBN # 9781690812975

Copyright ©2019 by Sussie Jordan

This book is a work of fiction. The characters, incidents, and dialogue are drawn from the author's imagination and are not to be construed as real. Any resemblance to actual events or persons, living or dead, is entirely coincidental.

No part of this book may be used or reproduced in any manner whatsoever without written permission, except in the case of brief quotations embodied in critical articles and reviews. For information, address: Sussie Jordan, Inc. 6080 South Hulen St, Suite 360, PHM 218, Fort Worth, TX 76132

Cover artwork & design: Consuelo Parra

Dedicated to Faith, Family, Friends and Fun

A Message to my Readers

There's an old song that I learned in Camp Fire Girls long ago. It goes *Make New Friends but keep the old; some are silver and the other gold.* How true that little jingle rings! There's a big difference between 'friends' and 'acquaintances.' Most of us have lots of acquaintances - people we know from our work, our neighbors and our social clubs. But friends are different. You might not see friends every day. You may only visit them occasionally. However, when you're with a friend, you can jump back into your last conversation without missing a beat. This is especially true of lifelong friends, the ones who have known you since you were young, so there's no bragging or putting on airs-they know the truth. They are absolutely Gold! New friends quickly find a common thread with you. You have similar ideas and enjoy some of the same things. You recognize new friends when you become comfortable sharing space in your relationship. Your mutual experiences lead you to trust each other. Over time, you rely on each other for support and pleasure. They are absolutely Silver!

In today's world of BFFs (best friends forever, in social media and television reality shows), friendship has been exploited to appear cheap and frivolous. True friendship is not cheap. It takes time and effort. It means you reach out to the friends when they are at their lowest and you encourage them. You celebrate the good things in their lives. You're not jealous of them. Friendship takes work, and it's a treasure to be cherished!

As we get older, friends become more and more important. We realize that our relationship with friends enables us to thrive and enjoy life in good times; and we feel their support in tough times. Friendships are the bonds that allow us to survive against loneliness and loss. They are the confetti showering us when we celebrate the good times.

This book is about one of the greatest gifts in this life, friendship!

True friends are those rare people

who come to find you in dark

places and lead you back to the light.

Facts and Fiction

FACTS: There are some places in the book that are historically true. These include Prague in the Confederate German States, Mainz in France/Germany, London, New York, New Orleans, Galveston, Indianola, Nassau Farm, San Antonio, Schulenburg, Austin and several other cities.

FACTS: Likewise, there are characters in the book who are real: Prince Carl Solms-Braunfels, John O. Meusebach, Samuel White, St. Cyril and St. Methodius.

FICTION: The rest of the characters, including the Kosovitsky family, the Moniac families, and all their friends in Cyril Hill and Gristmill and Austin, are purely the imagination of the author. The places such as Cyril Hill and Gristmill, Texas are fiction.

Thank you for taking your time to read this book. I hope you find something about yourself in these pages. If you wish to read more about friendship, Texas events, Alzheimer's Caregiver Support Groups and genealogy, then please join me at

www.sussiejordan.com

or Find me on Facebook:
www.facebook.com/sussiejordanbooks

I also invite you to Follow Me as an author at Amazon. Just go to the Amazon page for *Secrets of the Carousel* and click on Follow Me to receive notices of new book releases. You can also read my latest blog posts from my Author Page on Amazon.

If you enjoy Secrets of the Carousel, then you might also like my first book, Pink Bluebonnets. Same town and same characters on another adventure!

ENJOY,

Sussie Jordan

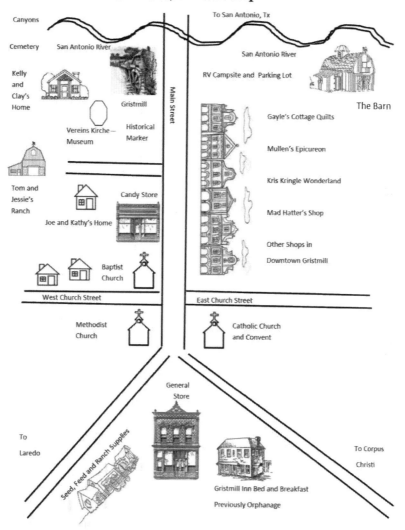

Descendant Chart for Sam Moniac and Betsy Weatherford

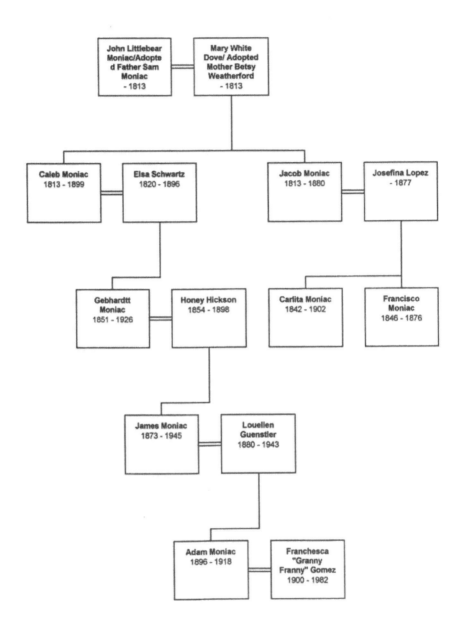

Descendant Chart for Hayden Moniac

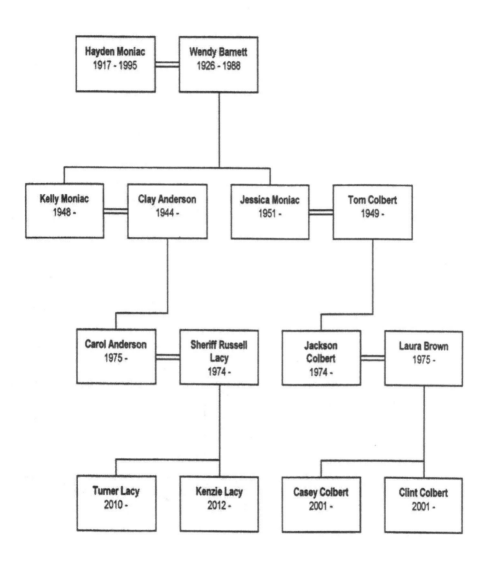

Chapter 1

"Damn, I just broke another fingernail and I know I'm going to find a snake back here," cried out Kelly as she pulled another piece of timeworn farm equipment from the back of the barn. Jessie just laughed at her complaining. Jessie and her husband were cattle ranchers, so this was everyday fare for her.

January in Gristmill, Texas could be freezing cold with sleet or a mild cool day. This was the latter. It was still chilly when they arrived at the barn shortly after sunrise. Looking north of the barn across the pasture, they could see the sun glinting off the San Antonio River that meandered through limestone banks shaded by overhanging cypress trees. A sudden rustle disturbed the silence as a flock of geese swooped upwards in one movement forming their perfect V shape for southern flight. The gentle background cooing of the mourning doves offset the eruptive rustle of the geese. The old barn was at peace as the short, scrubby velvet mesquite trees blew gently in the wind, with their twisted branches just daring anyone to disturb their domain. The sharp, thorny trees shared a nasty reputation in south Texas, one that might not have been deserved, accusing their deep roots of sucking the life out of the soil. The mesquite trees can become so dense that they prevent any grass from growing under them, thus killing a food supply for the cattle. If the mesquite is cut down and grows back, it grows out in every direction, morphing into a large bush. Farmers and ranchers face a vicious cycle, often cutting them back and then burning them. But today, the elusive mesquites sway from side to side, wispy dancers in the wind .

Looking at the mesquite trees, Jessie said. "Tom has spent his whole adult life cutting and burning mesquite trees on the ranch, but now he has decided to prune the mesquite trees around our house trying to make them look more like real trees. He says that telling a Texan to prune a mesquite tree is like advising someone to wash their garbage before they throw it out." The sisters smiled; only Tom could find something humorous about mesquite trees. Just then, a little road runner scampered in the brush, out to find a tasty breakfast from the insects hiding in the grass.

Earlier, Kelly and Jessie had to shovel the collected dirt around the base of the barn door before they got it open. Amazingly, the hinges creaked but still worked, even though it had been closed for at least 20 years. The inside of the barn was dark and musky and cooler than outside, but it felt good while they were working and building up a sweat. A visual inventory of the barn showed there was a tremendous amount of dirty, grimy work to be done if they planned to get it cleaned out for a possible new lease. Stacks of old lumber and wood were piled along the walls on every space of the dirt floor. This was obviously the final resting place for the old ranch and farming equipment: plows, tractor parts, planting bins, tools of every kind, as well as several tractor tires and an old tractor seat. Plus, there were several ancient motors that had outlived their usefulness. What a mess!

As the day progressed, they pulled lumber and junk to several piles. One pile would be burned and the other would be hauled away to sell or taken to the dump.

They were dead-tired from working all day, but the sun was setting early, so they needed to finish up quickly before it got dark. Jessie called from the back of the barn, "Hey,

Kelly, can you come and help me pull this out." They both grabbed the two faded white poles sticking out from under the old rotten blankets. Pulling hard, they fell backwards and found themselves facing a large wooden horse. "What in the world is that?" asked Jessie.

"It's an old carousel horse, but what is it doing in the back of the barn?" questioned Kelly.

Jessie was busy throwing old junk from off the top of the horse. She asked, "When do you suppose was the last time someone cleaned out this barn?"

"I don't know, maybe it has never been cleaned out. We have leased this land out for the past fifty years, maybe much longer. The farmer who leased the land never used this barn because he had a newer barn over by the road," stated Kelly thoughtfully.

"I'll get a flashlight so we can see better back here," said Jessie. When she returned, they scanned the pile of junk at the back of the barn. They found old pitch forks, rusted tractor parts and horse tack with dry hay scattered over it. Sticking its head up from behind a stack of old tires was another horse with a black head. Kelly and Jessie tugged it free and beheld a third horse, a copper-colored stallion.

The three carved horses lined up at the front clearing in the barn left barely enough light for them to examine the horses. They could see these were carousel horses beautifully sculpted. Even with the paint peeling and fading, they were exquisite. Each horse had a wooden spiral pole anchored at the front of its saddle. Each saddle was embellished with decorative ribbons and leather scrolling. The horses' manes blew as if in the wind and their eyes glared menacingly at being disturbed from years of slumber. The wood was worn with cracks and the paint was dry and deteriorated. Despite grim exteriors betraying days of glory gone by, they stood proud and striking.

Staring at their discovery, Kelly asked, "Where do you think these came from?" Examining them in the little daylight that remained, they found a small set of "HHM" initials carved on the rear flank of each horse. But, it was getting late and further examination would have to wait. Kelly and Jessie left their newfound treasure and locked up the barn.

They picked up fried chicken from the Crispy Chicken on their way back to Kelly's home, where they found Tom Colbert and Clay Anderson sitting inside by the fireplace. Clay was Kelly's husband who suffered from Alzheimer's disease; nonetheless, the family treated him with respect and often visited with him, reliving the old days when he was sheriff of the county. Tom Colbert, Jessie's husband, was as kindhearted as any living soul. He was a tough rancher who had spent endless hours riding horses or driving four-wheelers herding cattle. He knew that Clay enjoyed hearing about the ranch even, if he no longer could work on it, so he described the latest cattle encounters and breeding experiments.

The sisters came through the backdoor and could hardly hold their excitement about the carousel horses. Kelly described their mystery horses and Jessie filled in any gaps in her description. "We just don't know where they came from. That old barn has not been used in over 50 maybe even 100 years. Old Mr. Smith has leased it from as far back as I remember; and I think his father before him leased the property. They always raised grain or milo and never used that barn."

Tom laughed, "Now you're thinking Casey's idea of striking a match to the old barn might not have been a bad idea." Casey and Clint were Tom and Jessie's twin grandsons. They were seniors in high school and a big bonfire sounded like a lot of fun, compared to cleaning out the barn. Tom continued, "Do you really have no idea where the horses originated? Surely, in Granny Franny's family story book she must have mentioned a carousel."

"If Granny Franny had known, she would have told us some story when we were little girls, but I remember nothing like that," assured Kelly. Granny Franny had been the grandmother of Kelly and Jessie. Their own mother had suffered from bi-polar depression, which had left her incapable of giving them the attention they needed growing up. But, Granny Franny, who was widowed as a very young mother when her husband was killed in World War I, was a woman of grit with a baby son to raise and a cattle ranch to run. She became notorious in south Texas for promoting changes, such as bringing electricity to Gristmill, improving education, and introducing oil wells to their property. But Kelly and Jessie remembered her for the love, the stories and the fun she brought to enliven their youth.

Jessie picked up the conversation, describing the initials carved into the flanks of the horses. "Who is HHM?" asked her husband.

"We wish we knew," answered Jessie and Kelly.

"The painting," said Clay. They stared at him in astonishment. Clay's Alzheimer's usually prevented him from speaking a word. They always included him, but never expected him to take part in the conversation. As they looked in bewilderment, he continued. "The painting by Honey Hickson Moniac." Clay had been the sheriff of Gristmill for years before he developed dementia; sometimes his old talent of remembering details just popped up, but then moments later his memory would be gone again.

Kelly responded incredulously, "You're right, HHM could mean Honey Hickson Moniac."

Tom asked, "Who is Honey Hickson Moniac?"

Kelly began her thoughtful explanation, "Honey Hickson Moniac would be our fourth or fifth great-grandmother. According to the book that Granny Franny wrote about the ranch and our family – you remember, the one we used when we were working on the historical marker for Gristmill. Honey Hickson was married to Gebhardt Moniac."

The previous year, the State of Texas had bestowed on Gristmill, Texas an historical marker. The town of Gristmill was launched in 1838 by twin brothers named Moniac. The brothers were from the Creek Indian Nation of Alabama who had earned a land grant as Texas Revolutionary heroes. Over the next 150 years, Gristmill grew from a rough and dangerous pioneer ranching and oil town to a modern small Texas tourist town still supported by ranching and oil. The Moniacs remained a backbone family here. Kelly and Jessie were daughters of the last male Moniac descendent, Hayden Moniac. During the research for the historical marker, they found a book published by their great-grandmother, Granny Franny, essential to the town history. She and her friend, a newspaper publisher, had left a pictorial treasure of life on a Texas ranch. The book also offered a family tree for the Moniac family.

Kelly went in search of her copy of the book. Returning with the book and the page with the family tree, she pointed to Honey Hickson, a single name of an obscure woman listed as the wife of Gebhardt Moniac. Looking through the book, Kelly remarked, "There's no listing of parents for Honey Hickson and there're no stories written about her. But now that you mention it, the picture of our ancestor family portrait had the signature 'HHM.'" The absence of any information on the mysterious Honey Hickson stunned the group of four. Yet, if she was the creator of these carousel horses and the creator of the painting, she had been an amazing artist. Even more puzzling, she had been a part of their family, yet they knew nothing about her.

"A few months ago, I opened an account on that ancestry website but just haven't had time to work on it. Maybe we could go there for help," offered Kelly.

Jessie said, "Let's get the dinner table cleaned up and then see what we can find."

Logging on to the ancestry website and selecting their family tree, Jessie watched, sitting next to Kelly, and could see that Honey Hickson had no parents listed. Kelly's click on the little leaf, supplied only a census report of 1880 when she was married to Gebhardt. She wasn't listed on the census reports for 1870 or before. Even using her Hickson maiden name, they found no clues to her family. They continued to search several methods but no luck. Returning to the den where Clay and Tom were watching football and drinking iced tea, Kelly said, "No luck. We didn't find any information about Honey Hickson. It's as if she just appeared out of nowhere." Tom responded, "Not surprising, since Texas was a pretty rough country before 1880."

"Yes, but Granny Franny might not have known her personally because Honey Hickson died before Granny Franny married into our family, but Granny Franny knew Honey's husband, Gebhardt. Actually, Gebhardt helped her put the book together about the ranch. Seems he would have provided some information about his wife," mused Kelly.

"Tomorrow we'll finish cleaning out the barn. Maybe we'll find more clues about the horses and HHM," said Jessie.

Saturday morning, Jessie and Kelly met at the barn. Kelly had left Mrs. Brauder, a sitter, with Clay. He enjoyed watching game shows on TV and Mrs. Brauder would sit with him as they talked about the contestants. The barn clean-up was hard, dirty work but Kelly relished the time away from Clay's incessant questions. She loved Clay with all her heart, but his constantly repeating questions almost drove her crazy. The physical work of cleaning the barn eased her stress.

The stale, musty smell of mold and old oil soaked into the ground overcame the sisters as they walked into the barn. The dirt floor, packed from years of pounding by tractors and cows, darkened their path and displayed streaks of morning sun sifting through cracks in the worn, rotting boards of the high walls. Along the baseboards and in the corners were strands of dirty white cotton from bales long since gone to the cotton gin. On the ground lay debris from corn husks and wheat stalks, reminders that better days had passed through this shrine to ancient farming and ranching. The barn structure itself had withstood the winds of spring storms, but now looked shabby and tattered and just worn-out. Exhausted of life.

Kelly and Jessie again looked at the carousel horses and pondered their mysterious secrets. Their eyes mocked and dared them to guess their origin.

Turning away, an exasperated Jessie asked, "Where are those boys? I left them eating breakfast and told them to hurry and get the bobcat tractor down here to help us move this stuff. If we can push most of it out of the barn into a pile, we can set a controlled burn and get rid of it."

In the distance, they could hear the bobcat rumbling down the dirt road with Clint driving his pickup with a flatbed trailer behind it.

As Kelly and Jessie were putting on their work gloves, Clint and Casey hurried up to the barn, eager to see the carousel horses. The sisters lifted the horses from the back of the barn and carried them out into the sunshine. Intrigued by the delicate and distinct carving of the horses, they loaded them into the back of the truck for a closer examination at home.

"Let's get to work, I've got plans for later today," said Casey. Driving the bobcat into the barn, he began picking up piles of old trash, mostly old wood, and hauling it outside into the field in front of the barn. Kelly, Jessie and Clint continued to stack old rusted metal tools, which Casey would then haul to the trailer. The salvage yard wouldn't give them a rusty nickel for the tool trash, but at least they could get rid of it.

Even in the January cool air, they grew sweaty and filthy from the dirt and grime in the trash pile. After two hours, the pile was shrinking. Casey was making a round to pick up one of the final piles with the bobcat when his blade ran deep and dug into the dirt floor. He backed the bobcat up. Kelly shrieked, "Stop, stop, there's something here. I'm not sure, but it looks like bones."

Casey and Clint rushed to the spot and Clint said, "That looks like a leg bone. I've seen lots of deer bones and some cattle bones, but I've never seen a bone exactly like that."

Kelly responded, "I think you're right. It looks like a human bone to me."

The boys at once found an old shovel and began to dig around in the dirt and with little effort, they unearthed a skull. Jessie spoke up, "We'd better stop and not touch anything else. I'll call Russell and he'll know what to do." As the local sheriff, Russell Lacy would have legal authority to do something with the skeleton. Sheriff Russell Lacy was married to Kelly's daughter, Carol. Everyone waited as Jessie made the call, "Russell, we have a little problem out here at the old barn. I think we've uncovered a body, well actually just the skeleton that's left from a body. I think you'd better come now!

Chapter 2

Diary of Suzanna Kosovitsky – 1842 - 1844

I have never kept a diary, but my parents insisted that I should do so as my husband and I begin our journey to Mainz. They want to hear all about my travels when I return. So, this will be my full account of my adventure. My name is Suzanna Kosovitsky. My father is a university professor. My parents believed in education for their daughters so my father taught me to read and write. I recently married. My husband, Josef, graduated from Charles University just a year earlier with a degree in theology and philosophy. For the past year and while he was in college, he worked for his older brothers in construction. However, there is not a place for him in their family business, and his dream is to be a professor teaching theology. Joseph is the most interesting man that I know. He is brilliant teaching theology, but he is also passionate about painting art and studying the structures of old cathedrals. He claims they are as much art as oil on canvas! He recently received an offer for a full professorship at the University of Mainz teaching theology. I will also work there as a nanny for children of a widowed professor. So, now you know why we are moving and welcome to my world and my thoughts.

July 20, 1842 *I am so excited about our move to the great city of Mainz, on the banks of the Rhine River. But I'm also sad and heartbroken to be leaving my family behind. I've lived all my life in Praha in the Kingdom of Bohemia. How will I get along in the Confederation of German States? Even with a job near the University, I will know no one except Josef. This morning Josef and I went to our Orthodox Church of Saints Cyril and Methodius where we attended Mass. We asked Father Markovik to bless our journey. We lit candles, and the Father prayed for us. He said that we were journeying to new lands just as our Saints Cyril and*

Methodius traveled here to bring Christianity to the Slavic people over a 1,000 years earlier. I'm not sure I can make that comparison, but I do love to hear Mass in our Slavic language. That's one more thing I will miss dearly. Even though I understand Latin, and can understand the Catholic Mass, I will miss the melodious sound of our native Slavic scriptures being read.

I must get busy and finish packing. I have packed our clothes and personal items. Josef has packed his paints, brushes and architecture tools, including his compass, protractor, plumb bob, angles, hammers and his axes. I packed only a few of my books – my copy of the Chronicle of Dalimil that my parents gave to me and my Slavic Bible. Other books I can purchase in Mainz. I have packed all our quilts and linens and a few dishes. Tomorrow before we leave, we will pack our bed and our table on the wagon.

I must pack my travel bag with Vaclav Klicpera's most recent historical romance. He was so fascinating to hear when he spoke at the college about how he came up with his farcical plays and fairy tales. Maybe reading will take my mind off the five days of traveling by wagon to get to Mainz. Mother suggested I pack apples, some dried meat, some pastries and hard cheese. I don't know if there will be places along the way to purchase food or not.

Josef should be back soon. He has gone to meet with his father at his bank. Josef's father insists that we convert part of our money to Prussian thalers, because we can use them as currency in almost any part of the German Confederacy, but the bulk of our money will be in gold coins. Josef's father says that there is so much turmoil in Europe and Bohemia that no currency is safe. He has stressed over and over to us that we must be very careful on this journey to let no one know what we are carrying with us. For that reason, Josef's brothers are going with us. One of them will drive the wagon where I'll be riding; the other two brothers will ride horses alongside of us. Both will carry their guns for protection.

Since I can't do much about any of that, I'll concentrate on what I can manage. Tonight, we will have dinner with my parents and my sister, Ada's, family. This should be fun but melancholy. To think I'll not see Ada's children growing up breaks my heart.

Tonight, at dinner, my mother and father looked older, but they were still very supportive of my upcoming move. Father has been a professor at Charles College as far back as I can remember. Usually Father is very talkative about politics and the economy and the revolution that he believes is coming for freedom; but tonight he was very quiet, almost with tears in his eyes every time he looked at me. Finally, after dinner it was getting late, and we hugged and kissed before Josef and I returned home. It felt like a final goodbye, although I know I'll be seeing them again in a few years.

July 21, 1842 *Alex and Radomir, Josef's brothers, arrived very early. They put our trunks, the bed, and the table in the wagon; and we set off for Mainz. The trip is 545 kilometers and will take us about five days to get there. We soon passed St. Agnes' Convent and crossed over the Vitava River Bridge. Then, turning south, we traveled on to Pilsen where we camped outside the town. The brothers took turns sitting up to take watch. We were very uncertain about the people in this area. Around Pilsen, people from the farms who have lost their land are moving into the city to find work. Vagabonds and criminals infest the town. It was a bit scary at night, but we remained safe.*

July 22, 1842 *We left Pilsen early in the morning, and we found fresh water from a city well, along with some fresh meat pies. We continued west into the hilly area and then into the Bohemian Forest. The forest was cool and beautiful with tall trees and rolling hills. As we left the forest coming* *down from the hills, we camped a last time in the Kingdom of Bohemia and entered the German Confederation the next morning.*

July 23, 1842 *We made excellent time today; the road was in much better condition than the previous roads. There were other travelers moving along the roadway. We arrived in Nuremberg early in the evening and we found a room in an inn. We had a good meal and slept on very uncomfortable beds with a roof over our heads. Nuremburg is a busy, prosperous appearing town with much talk about their new railway. We enjoyed visiting with the people in the biergarten and listening to their music. Overall, this was a good day. And I'm too tired to write more.*

July 24, 1842 *After a hearty breakfast, we left Nuremberg headed toward Wurzburg. This is an interesting town because the River Main runs right through the middle of it. But most of the town lies on the east side of the river. We crossed the river and went a short distance out into the hills and found a nice place to make camp. The breezes off the River Main kept the temperature cool, so it is a nice night. Tomorrow we should reach Mainz!*

July 25, 1842 *We arrived in Mainz about mid-afternoon. It was Monday and the town was busy with many types of commerce and a bustling marketplace with venders hawking fruits, vegetables, meats, pastries and bier. We crossed the Rhine River and then traveled farther west to the university. Around the university is a village of older homes that are rented by students and faculty. We finally found our boarding house, and the landlady gave us a key. Our new home is nothing to brag about, but it is a home. We have two rooms. One a main room with a fireplace and a second room for a bedroom. We share an outhouse in the back for our toiletry, but there's a well in the garden so we can bring in a bucket of clean water for our room.*

We unloaded all our trunks, the bed, and the table. The trunks may not be unpacked, but at least they are in our flat.

I haven't had a bath in five days. I feel dirty and filthy. I think Josef sensed my need for some time to clean up. He fetched a bucket of water for our room and then invited his brothers to go with him to find food and bier. Oh, my love, Josef, I can't think how to thank you for this small private time! As soon as they left, I stripped down and washed myself from head to toe and put on clean clothes. After I bathed, I emptied our bucket of water and brought back another bucket of clean water. When the brothers returned, I excused myself to go down to the parlor of the boarding room to give them some time to clean up.

Tonight, we had roast chicken and root vegetables for dinner and, of course, bier. I think I shall learn to really enjoy bier. We celebrated our journey with a relief from stress that I'm not sure we all appreciated until then. Now, a bed and a good night's sleep. Delightful!

July 26, 1842 This morning, Alex and Radomir left to return to Prague. They were eager to get home. I suspect they did not like it here in Mainz. We hugged them and said goodbye.

Today, Josef and I went to the bank and deposited our gold coins. One cannot be too careful about keeping valuables at the boarding house, and the last thing that we want to happen is for our money to be stolen. Then we went in search of food that we can keep in our rooms, and prepare in the fireplace. During the summer, it would be too hot to build a fire in the hearth, so we had to find fresh fruit, bread, and dried meat. Luckily, in Mainz, this is in abundance. The Germans love their sausage much like the Czechs.

July 30, 1842 Josef and I have been exploring Mainz. We have walked to many of the different sites. My favorite place is the gardens near the university. We took a picnic lunch *there today, and we sat under a large oak tree on a blanket. Students are returning to academia after the summer and preparing for the fall term. It is interesting to watch them coming and going, often huddling together in small groups with great anticipation of what lies ahead. I remember those anxious days filled with apprehension.*

Josef has had time to paint. He truly loves his art. He has found a dealer in canvas who can supply him with most of his art supply needs. I often just sit and watch him paint and sometimes I read or write poetry. I have found the university library so there is no shortage of books to read.

July 31, 1842 *Today we attended Catholic Mass at St. Martin's Cathedral. The cathedral is beautiful. It was originally built in about 975 AD, but additions have been made, and it is now huge with all the outer buildings. Josef is fascinated by the nave with the white stone walls and the stone columns supporting the vaulted ceiling. He said nave means the section of the cathedral where the worshippers are seated and the front or the chancel area is where the high altar is located and where the priests sit. Another interesting point, nave or navis means ship. In the church, navis is a possible reference to "the ship of St. Peter" or maybe the Ark of Noah. If you turn a ship upside down over a building, the inside would look like the high-vaulted ceiling of the cathedral. This cathedral was so large that it had three aisles dividing the nave so there were lots of columns to hold up the ceiling. At the very top of the side walls were arched windows. The windows are magnificent with stained glass depicting all the stories in the scriptures. Josef told me that St. Martin's was built in the Romanesque style, but the bell tower is Gothic with a Baroque roof. I'm not sure that I understand those references, so I will check that out in the library; then I'll be able to recognize it in other cathedrals that we visit.*

October 1, 1842 *Finally, a day off, Saturday! The fall term began, and I have worked every day with the professor's children. Every evening Josef is preparing for the next day of classes. But the good thing is that we are working side by side in our new home in Mainz. The children are well behaved; and I enjoy being around them. Most of his students are enthusiastic about their studies.*

Last night, we attended a Freidenker Society Meeting. These Germans call themselves freethinkers or sometimes Latinists. They devote their discussions to German literature, philosophy, science, classical music and the Latin language. Well, this is their stated purpose, but really their discussions revolve around politics.

The group is made up of mostly professors and some older students. Bier was available to all, and it was a lively discussion. Father, you would have felt at home and enjoyed the evening.

For example, last night the discussion went along these lines. Can a Freidenker or a freethinker believe in God? One man stated, "No one can be a freethinker who demands conformity to a Bible, creed, or messiah. To the freethinker, revelation and faith are invalid, and orthodoxy is no guarantee of truth." You can only imagine the uproar this caused. Many of them shouted that one only had to look around to see that God exists in creation; and it was not a demand for conformity to accept the truth as freethinking. Some said that one could absolutely believe in God without accepting the restrictions of a creed or an orthodox religion.

The argument went on and on, until one wise older professor speaking in an authoritative tone stated, "What makes a freethinker is not his beliefs but how he holds them. If he holds them because his elders told him they were true when he was young, or if he holds them because if he did not he would be unhappy, his thought is not free; but if he holds them because after careful thought he finds a balance of evidence in their favor, then his thought is free, however odd his conclusion may seem." The meeting adjourned after this and everyone left as friends.

October 7, 1842 *The Head of the Theology Department asked Josef if he would enter some of his paintings into a gallery art showing. Josef felt so honored to be asked. They will hold the showing in Stephen's Hall next Saturday. I am so proud of Josef!*

January 5, 1843 *A strange thing happened today. A man by the name of Lewis Diedrich came to Josef's office after his classes. He said that he represented the Prince of Solms, Friedrich Wilhelm Carl Ludwig Georg Alfred Alexander, Lord of Braunfels, Grafenstein, Munzenberg, Wildenfels and Sonnenwalde. Can you believe that – he actually said all of that just to introduce the person he was representing? We've since learned he was talking about Prince Carl Solms.*

Someone from Prince Carl Solms' family saw Josef's paintings at the art gallery showing last October, and they wish to have a royal portrait painted of Prince Carl Solms. They want Josef to paint the portrait. Of course, Josef agreed. The man told Josef to come to Biebrich which is south of the city to a hall used by a group called the Adelsverein. Josef is to paint while Prince Solms meets with this group.

January 28, 1843 *Josef left immediately after his afternoon classes to go to Biebrich to start the royal portrait of Prince Solms. Since the commissioning of this portrait, we have talked to several professors about Prince Solms. They tell us he is well connected to Prince Frederick of Prussia, Queen Victoria, Czar Alexander I of Russia, King Leopole I of Belgium and Prince Albert of Saxe-Coburg-Gotha. At a recent reception for the professors, some of their wives told me that*

Prince Solms is very handsome, highly spirited and romantic. He was married to Baroness Luise von Schonau but recently got a divorce from her and their three children. He then became a captain in the cavalry in the imperial army of Austria. There are even rumors that a Prussian court martial sentenced him to several months in prison because of having absented himself from his command without leave.

Josef will not return home until tomorrow, but I can't wait to hear about his meeting with the intriguing Prince Carl Solms!

January 30, 1843 *When Josef returned, we stayed up almost all night talking about his meeting with Prince Carl Solms. Josef says the man talks incessantly, but with fascinating ideas. He talks mostly about a place called Texas. Carl (he gave Josef permission to call him Carl) says that he has read Charles Sealsfield's novel about Texas. Sealsfield's real name is Carl Anton Posti. He's a Slav who advocates German democracy, but he lives in the United States, and he has written a novel about a place just southwest of the United States called Texas. I plan to go to the library today to find his book.*

And Father, you will like this. Carl Anton Posti was born in Moravia; and he entered the Knights of the Cross with the Red Star in Prague, where he became a priest. He fled the repressive government of Prague to live in the United States. He's one of our Slavs!

Prince Carl also talked about a book by William Kennedy called Texas: Its Geography, Natural History and Topography. *This man is an Irish poet. He spent two months in the Texas Republic in 1839 and then wrote this book, which gives a very favorable picture of Texas.*

So. These are two books that I've got to go to the library to read – and also, where is this place called Texas?

February 10, 1843 *The weather could not be drearier. It is below freezing with snow two feet deep. We covered our mouths with our scarves to keep the frost out of our lungs but as cold as we were; we trudged on to the meeting of the Freidenker Society.*

There was so much discussion tonight about the actions of the repressive German Confederacy government. Many of the professors asserted that they felt in danger for professing their ideas of freedom of thought. Many of them avowed that they would leave the German Confederacy rather than succumb to the restrictions of a government that was not democratic. Others told them that those types of liberal ideas would definitely get them in trouble and that they should be secretive, if not silent, with their notions.

The old man who spoke so eloquently last fall stood and declared to them, "I love my country. It is my homeland, but I will not live in a society that shackles my thoughts and I will not raise my family in such a land. I have heard good things about the United States. It is a place founded on the principles of freedom and democracy. So, I plan to emigrate to North America at the end of this school term. 'Uber libertas, ibi patria,' Where there is freedom, there is my homeland, my country."

You could have heard a pin drop. The room was silent as everyone was awestruck by this man's conviction. His desire for freedom and future freedom for his family was so strong that he will leave his homeland for a place completely unknown.

March 3, 1843 *Friday at last! It seems the children are tired of being inside, day in and day out. I feel the same way. I can't wait for spring. Josef left again to continue work on the royal portrait. He should be back by Sunday evening. I found another book at the university library called* Texas, *a book of history by Mary Austin Holley. The only* *problem is that it is in English, so I'm having some trouble in reading it and translating it at the same time. I have been studying English in the evenings while not working as a nanny. English differs greatly from the Slavic and German languages, but I feel it is important that I learn to speak and read English.*

March 5, 1843 *Josef is back from Biebrich! He told me that Prince Carl is more intent than ever on taking a group of Germans to Texas. Prince Carl works tirelessly to promote the growth, finances, administration and political acceptance of the society that he and his friends call Adelsverein or the Verein zum Schutze Deutscher Einwanderer in Texas. Prince Carl is traveling daily to lobby with his many relatives throughout France and Belgium, all the way to the Isle of Wight, England. He feels that he has even secured the support of England, France and Belgium for the Texas colonial project, which is philanthropic, economic and political.*

The group has purchased undeveloped land from Robert Mills who has a grant of land in Texas. They are calling it Nassau Farm after Duke Adolph of Nassau. Two representatives from the Adelsverein society, Count Joseph of Boos-Waldeck and Count Victor of Leiningen, have traveled to Texas to develop Nassau Farm. From the news that they have received back from these men, they purchased slaves and supplies in New Orleans, Galveston and Houston. The slaves are already busy constructing a blacksmith shop, hay barns, living quarters, and smokehouses. Later this spring, they will start cultivating the fields.

It amazed Josef that there is a place that has no construction and is completely undeveloped. I was so excited to tell him about the Texas history book that I was reading. I told him all about the Texas Revolution in 1836, where Texas fought for independence from Mexico.

It all sounds like fables or imaginary legends filled with a new land, Mexican banditos, wild horses and Indians. We wondered if Texas was real or a romanticized dream backed only by a desolate territory.

June 24, 1843 The day of the unveiling of the royal portrait is finally here. At last, I got to meet Prince Carl Solms. He is as handsome as they said he was. Josef had painted Prince Carl with his pointed mustache and wearing his leather army vest and holding his helmet topped by a plume. I told Josef that he made Prince Carl look very prestigious. Prince Carl seemed thrilled with the portrait, and he invited Josef and me back to his villa for drinks and dinner.

The man is obsessed with Texas. No sooner than we sat down to eat than he started telling us about North America and its culture, commerce and geopolitics. He truly believes that the new Fatherland on the other side of the ocean will be Texas. He sees himself at the head of the migration of German artisans and peasants to Texas.

The next thing he said shocked us beyond speech. He is planning a trip to Texas in about six months to establish the emigration plans for the migration. He wants Josef and me to go with him so that Josef can paint pictures of the Texas land. He believes that pictures will enhance his offer for people to join the migration. He thinks when people see pictures of Texas, it will convey more meaning and the essence of the land than mere words.

Prince Carl explained that the head of the household of emigrants wishing to go to Texas would have to deposit 600 gulden. The Adelsverein would use half of this to furnish transportation from the German Confederacy to the projected colony, and housing once there. The other half was to provide a credit upon which the emigrants could draw for tools and farming equipment, also food rations to sustain them until the first harvest. Since we would travel at the service of the Adelsverein, we would not have to pay anything, and Josef would draw a salary during this time.

Josef and I said we would consider his offer, but now I'm not so sure. How can we even consider leaving the German Confederacy to go so far from our beloved, Prague? It is one thing to move 500 kilometers to Mainz – but across half the world to Texas, that's quite another thing.

Josef expressed a deep desire to go on this adventure. I'm probably more prone to stay in Mainz where we have a secure lifestyle and can start a family. But the excitement of traveling to a place where no one that we know has ever been is tantalizing. I know that once we have children, we may no longer be able to travel. I finally agree with Josef that this is a once in a lifetime experience and if we do not take advantage of it, we may regret it for the rest of our lives. Also, we will be gone only about a year, then we will be back to our lives in Mainz.

August 6, 1843 We met with Prince Carl Solms and several of the members of the Adelsverein to let them know that we have decided to make the trip to Texas. They agreed upon a grant for Josef's services and agreed that they would pay all our expenses. We signed a contract with the Adelsverein, and we're now so excited about the journey!

August 7, 1843 Josef informed the university that he will teach for the fall term, but he wishes to take a sabbatical for the next year of 1844 to make this trip to Texas. I spoke with the father of the children and explained I would not be able to be their nanny for the next year. I think I will continue to write my journal about our travels. My parents will want to know every detail when I return.

January 13, 1844 We attended a meeting today of the Adelsverein. Prince Carl spoke of their plans to bring several thousand emigrant families to Texas. He proclaimed the *purpose for this interest in sponsoring those willing to emigrate were to ease tensions resulting from widespread political turmoil, and to relieve dangerous pressures caused by economic depression and its accompanying high rate of unemployment. He said, "We shall encourage to emigrate persons known to be radical political activists. We shall very carefully choose those to emigrate so as to provide a balance of artisans, mechanics, physicians, farmers and representatives of all other crafts necessary for the success of communities established in a part of the world remote from the Fatherland." They applauded his comments and shouted cheers of acceptance.*

But then another man stood up to speak. He was Count Joseph Boos-Waldeck, the man who had been sent earlier to establish the first settlement called Nassau Farms. He seemed to be angry and agitated by the members of the Adelsverein. He counseled, "After purchasing the 4,428-acre plantation in Fayette county, I cannot in good conscience advise that a large-scale emigration to Texas start. First, the deposit that you are requiring does not come close to covering the expense of transportation and housing. This whole expedition is doomed to failure."

The members of the Adelsverein scoffed and jeered at his comments. The Count Boos-Waldeck became incensed that his knowledge of Texas was of no consequence in the minds of the Adelsverein. So, the man resigned his membership and left. Everyone seemed to think that Boos-Waldeck was a pessimist and had expected this all to be easy. Possibly, it will not be as easy as Prince Carl is suggesting, but the enthusiasm of the group is infectious. Josef and I are still excited about the journey. We will go and Josef will record Texas in paintings and when we return our lives in Mainz will be enriched beyond measure.

February 3, 1844 *Today, Prince Carl Solms was appointed Commissioner-general for the first colony that the*

Adelsverein society proposed to establish in Texas. In his acceptance speech, Prince Carl declared, "The eyes of all Germany, no, the eyes of all Europe, are fixed on us and our undertaking: German princes, counts, and noblemen...are bringing new crowns to old glory while at the same time insuring immeasurable riches for their children and grandchildren." All I could think was, "He's either a visionary or a fool." They also changed their purpose to be for the 'protection' of the German emigrants to Texas.

May 1, 1844 *We left Mainz by coach traveling to Hamburg where we boarded a transport ship to London. On my last journey from Prague to Mainz, I could take most of my belongings, but on this trip, they limited me to one trunk. Prince Carl had arranged a special acceptance for Josef to bring a second trunk with his painting supplies including paint, pigments, turpentine, a fine set of sable brushes plus an easel and a dozen canvases. Since the trunk was larger than he needed for his paints, he included some of his architecture tools. However, I packed our clothes as efficiently as possible. I almost laughed when I heard what Prince Carl had packed. He brought two cannons, table linens and a twelve-place setting of china.*

When we arrived in London, they delivered us to our hotel, and we had the night to ourselves to explore London. Prince Carl had a royal audience with the queen, or at least some of the royal family. The next morning, he seemed pleased with the previous night's affair. We met very early at the pier to board a much larger ship for our journey to America.

May 10, 1844 *It seems like we have been on this ship forever. Most days the sea is complete stillness, and the sun bears down on us scorching our skin with heat and the salt spray. Other days, the worst days, the waves are enormous and treacherous. They often swell high as a mountain above the boat and then crash down around us, splattering the whole deck with salt water. Then there are the days of* torrential rain. You feel like there is nothing between you and the depths of the ocean – water for as far as you can see and rain so thick that it's like a blanket smothering you. I have been sea-sick most of the trip. My stomach just turns over and over with nausea. There's nothing left to throw up because I haven't eaten in days. I usually just stay below deck trying to focus on anything to stop the seasickness; but the heat below deck is sweltering and the flies from the rotting food sting my arms and face. I feel miserable and often cry myself to sleep wondering, why did we do this?

Josef has not seemed to be affected by seasickness. He has been my savior, bringing me clean water to drink and bits of bread to settle my stomach. He tells me about the flying fish and the whales he has seen. He even sketched many drawings of the fish and the birds.

But today, there is no rain, and the sea is calm and still. The sun is shimmering off the water like brilliant little diamonds sparkling, and it feels good to be on deck and breathing the fresh air. The captain of the boat says we should reach land soon. I can only pray it will come soon.

May 12, 1844 I can see land! The captain says that the land we're seeing is the port of New York. I've read about New York and I can't wait to see it!

May 14, 1844 We landed at the port of New York about noon. The city is nothing like I imagined. It's not like Mainz or London or even Prague. The streets around the dock are muddy, grimy and bad smelling. It is crowded with people huddling together and yelling chaotically. There are many ships being loaded and unloaded with cargo. We were able to get a coach to take us into the City of New York. Once we were in the city, we saw there were more and more cobbled streets and brick buildings. Much like home, there were venders in the streets selling vegetables, fruits, and fish from their carts.

Josef was busy drawing sketches of New York. He marveled at the buildings and their new construction techniques. I spent my time admiring the window shops displaying hats and dresses. Maybe when we return, I'll be able to shop for at least a new hat.

May 16, 1844 *We didn't stop for long in New York. Today we left by stagecoach to Pittsburgh where we boarded another much smaller ship to travel westward down the Ohio River and then the Mississippi River to the Republic of Texas. The Ohio River is much smoother, and it is crystal clear. The water is unbroken by rocks and rapids. Josef and I stood on deck and watched the beautiful trees along the sides of the river. Josef sketches most of the day.*

Along the riverbank, I swear we saw some Indians. Their skin is much darker than ours, and they were wearing leather britches, but not shirts. I thought I would be terrified of wild Indians, but these men seemed completely unconcerned about our passage. They didn't wave or make noises; they just stared at us, and we at them.

May 25, 1844 *Our ship moved smoothly from the Ohio River into the Mississippi River. The Mississippi River is much larger than the Ohio, but it was still an easy trip south to New Orleans. We will not stop at New Orleans, where the Mississippi feeds into the Gulf of Mexico and we turn to go around the Louisiana and Texas coast toward Galveston. The transition from river to gulf was treacherous, but once we were clear of the sandbars, we set sail toward Galveston. Texas here we come!*

I met the most interesting man on our trip. He boarded our ship from a small transfer boat just before we passed New Orleans. He sells notions to stores in Texas. He's an old French bachelor, dark complexion with little round glasses and a white beard. I love the way he talks with the French lyrical 've ve ve.' He says that he was born in New Orleans to a French father and a black mother, calls himself a mulatta, and sometimes a Cajun. He said that he has traveled the south for many years selling buttons, hat pins, buckles, thread and fabric. His name is Basile.

Basile talked about New Orleans and Texas as if things happened yesterday. With both hands flying in the air, he regaled, "Galveston was the home first of the Karankawa Indians. They were a fierce group of Indians. The Karankawa were a physically imposing race, strongly built and magnificently formed. The Karankawa had distinctive tattoos, a blue circle tattooed over each cheekbone, one horizontal blue line from the outer angle of the eye toward the ear, three perpendicular parallel lines on the chin from the middle of the lower lip downward, and two other lines extending down from under each corner of the mouth. Their women also were tattooed but in such a way that a gentleman would not describe to a lady. They were excellent archers and hunted the swampy land around the island. They were also cannibals, especially eating children that they captured from other tribes. The Karankawa would not observe the Truce of the Tunas that was shared with other hostile Indian tribes in South Texas. When the sweet purple fruit of the prickly pear cactus, the 'tunas,' ripened each May, Indians from all along the coast would gather inland where they put away their tools and their weapons of war and migrated to the scrubby cactus and mesquite country. There they gorged themselves on the succulent fruit, danced, frolicked and generally conducted themselves like fools rather than warriors for as long as the fruit lasted. Then they returned to their own dwelling places and life returned to normal. But not the Karankawa. They were the meanest, greediest, laziest, most treacherous, lecherous, vicious, cowardly, insolent aborigines of the Southwest. But alas, the Karankawa are now almost all gone."

I asked him, "I can't say that I'm sorry they are extinct, but where did they go?"

"Between the French, the English, the Spanish and now the Texans, they were pushed farther south to Padre Island, or they have been massacred."

"But my dear, that was many years ago. More than 200 years ago, the explorer Cabeza de Vaca was shipwrecked on the island and lived among the Karankawa for several years as a medicine man and a slave. In about 1600, the French explorer Robert Cavelier La Salle claimed this area for King Louis and named it St. Louis."

He continued with his history lesson of Galveston. "Not so long ago, Galveston, or we should call it San Luis, was the base first for the pirate, Louis-Michel Aury. But one day when Aury returned from an unsuccessful raid against Spain, he found the island occupied by the cultured and debonair pirate, Jean Lafitte. Lafitte took up residence on the island because they had driven him from Barataria Bay off the coast of New Orleans. Lafitte organized the island into a pirate's kingdom he called 'Campeche' and made himself the head of government. Lafitte was quite a character. But his days were numbered. In about 1821, the United States Navy gave him an ultimatum: leave or be destroyed. Lafitte burned his settlement to the ground and sailed under cover of night for parts unknown."

I told him that I had no idea that pirates roamed Texas. He assured me that I had no reason to fear pirates in Texas, which relieved my anxiety tremendously.

I asked him about Galveston today. What should I expect?

He started another long narrative on the history of Galveston, "Galveston has been part of Spain, Mexico and now the Republic of Texas. And I think it will soon become a *part of the United States. You have heard that everything is bigger in Texas and everything in Texas is done first in Galveston. It has a custom house and a post office. It serves as the main port of the Texas Navy with a fort to protect it. But the thing that you might find the most disturbing is the slave trade. Galveston is the largest slave market west of New Orleans. When you see this, you should turn your head; it is not a sight for a lovely woman such as yourself."*

"Think of Galveston as a gateway to Texas. Many people from around the world come here – pirates, sailors, immigrants and visitors. There are craftsmen struggling to make their fortune. Anywhere you find sailors, you find women plying the oldest occupation in the world, prostitution. However, you will find a market house on twentieth street between Sound and Market Street. They have mercantile and food. It is a one-story structure with open windows to let the sea breeze blow through it. The island's breeze is full of dry, blowing sand highlighted by a hot sun. So, you should go there and purchase a bonnet for yourself. Also, purchase a dress that is loose fitting with long sleeves. You will find that the mosquitoes are numerous in Texas. They hum and annoy a person. No one can sleep with their incessant attacks on the skin. But long sleeves will help."

"I must tell you to be careful. There are sometimes alligators walking down the street, but the most dangerous creatures of all thrive in Galveston. That's the rattlesnake. The eastern tip of the island is called 'Point of the Snakes.' They can be small or even five foot long. Their bite is poisonous and deadly. I recommend that you always wear your boots and stay away from the sand dunes. This island is made up of sand, silt and clay brought in by the waves, so there are marshes all around the city where birds such as pelicans roost. Just don't go wandering out to see them. And stay out of the water. It is filled with purple Portuguese man-a-war

that have dangerous trailing tentacles that can inflict a chemical burn that is extremely painful."

My thoughts were swirling in my head – cannibalistic Indians, pirates, slave traders, mosquitos, alligators and snakes – I am more than a little apprehensive for what I will find in Galveston. But I graciously thanked Basile for his stories. He lifted my hand and gently kissed the top of my hand, saying, "The pleasure was all mine."

June 2, 1844 *We are headed into Galveston, a port city in Texas. Our ship could not dock at the harbor in Galveston because the water was too shallow. Sailors scampered around the ship, dropping the anchor. The big sails flapped in the wind until finally the sailors climbed the rigging and tied them down.*

I stood on the deck watching the seagulls swoop through the air. They were so graceful in their flight. I could hear the steady whiffle of wind blowing at a rate that could easily support a kite flown from the deck. But above the wind, we could hear a steady, low roar from the Gulf. I could hear individual waves as they run with a shhhh sound to the shore and then break with a ka-shhh on the sand. I listened carefully and counted. They arrived about every six seconds. The boat was rocking to and fro as we waited to see what action was next.

Suddenly I saw some flat barges rowing toward our ship. That's when I realized we would have to disembark off our ship onto these barges to be taken to the pier. Eventually all our trunks were loaded onto a barge; soon we were slowly moving toward the main pier.

Oh, the utter surprise of the land around this harbor. We have passed so many small inlets of water that the men on the ship call bayous. There are bays of stagnant water all along the coast surrounded by flat, sandy dunes with little or no vegetation. Coming into Galveston Bay, I could see the fort that Basile mentioned with cannons pointing out across the water.

At last, the barge docked at the wharves. There were huge steamers carrying cargo of every kind lined up along the port wall. Prince Carl told us, "There are shipments of cotton and cottonseed oil, hogsheads of sugar, barrels of molasses, animal hides and pecans." Over the shouting of the sailors, I could hear cattle and goats being shuttled onto ships. There were smaller boats at the dock with their fishing nets being cleaned and readied for the next day's fishing trip. Some boats obviously were for oyster gatherers who would go out to the shallow water where they would find oyster beds and use their four-foot rakes to scoop across the reef. The place smelled of fish rotting and drying on the deck where they had been dropped without care.

The streets were nothing but cleared paths of packed dirt, muddy from all the wagons traveling to the dock and back. I saw few children or women near the docks. Sailors leered at me with smirks and jeers. Jacob stared at their rowdiness with a look that said, 'Back off or I'll beat you senseless.' This must have worked since most of them turned back to their work.

To my horror, the most shocking thing I saw was the slave auction. There were black men and women and children bound by shackles sitting in the blazing sunshine waiting their turn to be put on the auction block. The auctioneers carried short whips which they used liberally to maneuver the slaves. Many of the women had been stripped down to their waists. I suppose that much of the lewdness was to entertain the men bidding on the property. Sometimes men were separated from their wives and children. The anguish and suffering of these people made me ill in my stomach.

Prince Carl led us from the ship and through the crowded streets to Hotel Meyer where we were provided a room. Our trunks were delivered by two black men whom I supposed were the slaves of one of the harbor masters.

Galveston could not be more disappointing. It was crowded and dirty and noisy. It was the most desolate place I have ever seen. Hell could not be worse! I just sat in our hot steamy room and cried.

Chapter 3

Sheriff Russell Lacy, several deputies and the county medical examiner, Lee Galvez, all stood around staring at the skeleton. The medical examiner had allowed Clint and Casey to continue removing the dirt around the bones very carefully. He had marked off the area with yellow crime scene tape, even though no one had a clue what or if there had actually been a crime.

Lee told the group that he would need to take the bones back to his lab and examine them to determine their age and how the person died. However, he could say without a doubt the remains were very old. Jessie and Kelly rolled their eyes at his remark, a statement of the obvious, since no one had been in this barn for at least twenty years.

Russell and Lee continued to examine the bones and Russell stated, "There's a few things remaining of the person's belongings. See these little bits of black cloth around the neck? Even though they are fragile and rotted away, it appears it may have been a priest collar. There is something metal that could confirm it – the cross on the chain around the person's neck."

Lee pointed out that next to the remains, there was a leather pouch. For its day, it had been excellent quality and still appeared sealed closed. Lee said he would take it back to his office, too. But Russell cut him off, "No, I'll take that and the cross necklace. Those could be evidence to a crime."

Kelly and Jessie were excited and eager to see inside the pouch. They had to conceal their enthusiasm so that Lee would not suspect their curiosity. However, they were sure that Russell would let them see what was inside the bag.

In two days, they had found three carousel horses signed by HHM and now a skeleton, maybe a priest, and a mysterious leather pouch. The unsolved puzzles left them giddy with excitement.

Finally, Lee Galvez left with the remains. He seemed somewhat relieved to turn over the cross necklace and the pouch to Russell. To him, it just meant he was not responsible for explaining their meaning or purpose.

As soon as Galvez was out of earshot, Jessie excitedly said, "Let's go look at the pouch. I want to see what's inside." Russell held up his hands, "Whoa, this is still a crime scene and evidence can't be played with, even if it is very, very old. You two will just have to wait. But I promise, as soon as we take an inventory and information about the pouch, I'll let you look at it."

After Russell and his deputies left, taking with them the cross necklace and the pouch, Kelly and Jessie finished clearing out the barn. Casey and Clint built the stack of wood to wait until a rainy day when they could safely burn it. Casey headed back home with the bobcat as quickly as possible, and Clint pulled the trailer to the salvage yard.

Kelly and Jessie stood in the dimming daylight staring at the old barn. The implications of their findings in the barn overpowered them. Oh, the baffling stories that barn could tell if it had a voice! Did this mean that Granny Franny knew secrets to their family tree that she had chosen never to reveal? Or were these things that even she was not privy to? The sisters sighed and vowed to find out what this all meant.

After cleaning up from their day of grungy work, Kelly and Jessie, along with their husbands, planned to meet at the Wildflower Café for dinner. Kelly's daughter, Carol, who was also Sheriff Russell Lacy's wife, owned the Wildflower

Café. Saturday nights the café became a community gathering place. They knew that by the time they arrived, the gossip on everyone's lips would be the horses and the skeleton, the new Gristmill hot topics of conversation.

Squeezing around a large table, Sister Elizabeth, a Catholic nun, joined Kelly, Jessie, and Diane Crowder, their friend from San Antonio. As was becoming a common routine, Diane drove to Gristmill each weekend to spend her days with Claude.

Diane was a prosecuting attorney in San Antonio. She had worked in the criminal court system for many years, often doing *pro bono* work. However, her work with the DVCC, the Domestic Violence Crisis Center, had brought her back to her hometown asking their help with the El Asilo Project, or the Sanctuary Project. About a year earlier, she instigated a program to help rescue girls who had been arrested for prostitution, and who in fact were often captives of sex traffickers. Several judges recognized that many of these girls had no other options in determining where their lives would turn. Diane worked with the San Antonio District Attorney, where these cases would come through the justice system. Sometimes, there were girls whom the judges thought could still be rescued from their situation. Diane would make arrangements to have the girls whisked away mysteriously in the middle of the night, leaving their pimps bewildered by their disappearance. For the past year, Diane had transferred several of these girls to El Asilo in Gristmill. El Asilo was an arrangement made with Tom and Jessie to build a dormitory type building on their property where the rescued girls could get a new start in life away from their pimps and drugs.

Diane had grown up with Kelly, Jessie and Kathy Morriston. Sister Elizabeth had moved to Gristmill as the head nun at the local Catholic Church much later, but she became an integral part of their friendship circle. The women were close, trusting and depending on each other. They were all excited that Diane, a widow for many years, was now dating their friend, Claude. Claude was a well-dressed modern Texas cowboy. To the uninformed eye, he didn't look any more dressed up on Saturday night than when he was out separating the weaning calves from their mother cows. He still had on jeans, boots, belt and a western straw hat. However, these boots were Lucchese black buffalo boots, not made from cowhide, and cost in the neighborhood of $500; his jeans were so starched they could have stood up on their own, and his belt was hand tooled, held in front by a two-tone oval silver buckle, not a gaudy rodeo type buckle. His pearl snap shirt was pressed and neat. Claude was always the gentleman. When not ranching, he played a mean guitar in the Tres Vaqueros Band and was often their lead singer. Clay sometimes joked that Claude's voice was as smooth as good whiskey could make it.

Claude and Diane had been dating for almost a year. They met during the historical marker celebration a year ago and, since then, Claude had played a major role in the El Asilo project. It thrilled the friends that the couple seemed to share more and more time together. They were speculating as to how soon they would tie the knot.

And to everyone's surprise, Kathy Morriston was back from Port Aransas. They each embraced Kathy knowing that she had escaped to the coast for two weeks after Christmas. Kathy's husband, Joe, had died unexpectedly a week before Christmas. Family and friends had surrounded her, giving her no time to mourn or just reflect on his death. Just after Christmas, she closed her antique shop and left to seek solace in quiet solitude, just sitting and staring at the ocean. The group of friends had all been heartbroken at Joe's death. Even now it was hard not to imagine him being with the Saturday evening dinner party. Through a melancholy smile, Kathy assured them she was better. She thanked them for their concern and suggested that time would help her heal. But they all knew that the huge hole left in Kathy's heart would never be completely mended.

Of course, the next big topic was the barn discoveries. Jessie and Kelly described what they knew; but in truth, they knew very little about the horses or the skeleton. Sheriff Russell came through the door and headed toward their table where he whispered. "I just heard from the medical examiner; the skeleton is of a man who probably died about 150 years ago! Because the dirt floor of the barn was relatively dry, and had not been disturbed for all these years, the skeleton was in fair shape with little disintegration. Lee Galvez said that there was a large indention in the back of the skull, which would show some heavy object had struck it. It's in the wrong place to be from a fall so we're thinking it was probably intentional, a murder." The table of friends quietly gasped. Not only did they find a skeleton, but it was of a murdered man. As the obvious questions began to pour out, "Who was he?" and "Why was he in their barn?" and "Who knows what he was doing here 150 years ago?" All were valid questions, but who could answer them? They decided that maybe they should go back to Kelly's home before discussing the mystery further. Too many listening ears filled the cafe to be comfortable with the expansion of the rumors that were already swirling.

As they finished their dinner, the Methodist minister, Reverend Brown, came in and moved toward their table. He greeted them all in his gentle demeanor, which often concealed his strong faith and determination to seek mercy for those betrayed with injustice. They had all appreciated his help with their mission, El Asilo, the Sanctuary. For the protection of the women, it was a well-kept secret that they were providing a home for several women who had been involved in sex trafficking. The previous autumn one of these liberations had led to a dangerously close call, so confidentiality was crucial. Reverend Brown had been part of El Asilo from the beginning, and true to his word he had been the quiet liaison between El Asilo and those in the community who needed to know its details.

They all warmly greeted Reverend Brown, and he asked, "Did you hear that we're moving the Tasting Luncheon to the bed-and-breakfast?"

"No, why are we changing it from the Methodist church?"

"Well this year, the funds from the event will provide some financial needs for El Asilo. Of course, I can't tell people the exact nature of that ministry so I'm just leaving it as a local charity. However, since the Texas Independence Day celebration is the first weekend in March, we thought we would get a better turn-out if we moved it from the church to the bed-and-breakfast. Then it becomes a goodwill for the whole community. And with all the tourists who come to Gristmill for the celebration, we should have a larger attendance. Also, it will help the local bed-and-breakfast get some attention. Overall, it should be a win-win event for everyone."

Before he left, he told them, "Another new part of the Tasting Luncheon will be a 'Nailed It' competition. I don't exactly understand what the idea means; but, according to Mrs. Gilbert and Mrs. Campbell, there are lots of people who find interesting cooking ideas on social media and then they try to duplicate the recipe. Actually, I thought that was what all cooking recipes involved, but they assure me that there is much more to this than just preparing a recipe. Supposedly, who 'Nailed It' should bring a lot of interest. I'm taking their word on this, and I hope you ladies understand it, because I certainly don't."

They all laughed as he left to join his wife at another table. With the close of their meal, they all left the café and headed to Kelly and Clay's home.

Kelly had prepared coffee for everyone and as they all settled into her comfortable overstuffed chairs in front of a roaring fire to enjoy the camaraderie, Kelly said, "Oh, I have a letter from Karen." Everyone perked up. Karen had been one of the girls at El Asilo, her arrival one they would never forget, because they had rescued her on a midnight run to the San Antonio jail. Karen had lived at El Asilo for several months. Eventually, Diane had found her grandparents and helped them file for full custody of her, since her mother was the one responsible for leading her into the sex trafficking business. Kelly read the letter aloud.

>Dear friends at El Asilo,
>
>I am so grateful to all of you for what you did for me. I had no hope of ever being free or safe and especially not happy again. But I have found all of that. You saved my life. My grandparents are wonderful people who love me very much. I have an aunt and uncle nearby who also care for me. I have returned to school and I'm making good grades.
>
>Please give Lupe and Gus a big hug for me.
>
>All my love, Karen

They all felt a tightening in their throats as they remembered Karen. She was their first rescue, and they had been more terrified than Karen. The midnight run to the San Antonio jail, the deserted dark streets, the quick pick-up, and the race back to Gristmill were terrifying. After finally hearing Karen's horrific story of her experience in the human slave trade, they realized how serious and dangerous their actions were. It had made them angry and determined that they could and would help these forgotten girls. A success story, Karen had survived and was now happy, safe, and loved.

Jessie asked if she could take the letter to share with Lupe and Gus. Gus had been a ranch hand on the Moniac ranch for many years, even before Jessie was born. Then, as he and his wife, Lupe, grew older, they helped with cooking, cleaning and general ranch repairs. When El Asilo was built, it included an apartment for Lupe and Gus at the front, with all the conveniences of a modern space. Gus and Lupe had never had children, so the Moniac children were like grandchildren to them. Now the girls at El Asilo also enjoyed grandchildren status. Lupe had a gift for listening and talking with the girls, reassuring them of their safety and their value as human beings. Gus and Lupe would be excited to hear about Karen.

As the evening progressed, the conversation drifted to what was at the top of each mind. Who was the skeleton? Kelly retrieved Granny Franny's ranch book. It contained pristine black and white photos taken by a family friend, Neil Simpson. Kelly began, "They published the book in 1932. And I've tried and tried to remember if Granny Franny ever mentioned a murder in our family history. I think I would remember a story like that. And I never heard her mention anything about carousel horses either."

The analytical mind of Diane kicked in with "Well, what do we know as facts?"

"First, we know 150 years ago would be long before Granny Franny. Even though she knew the family history, she probably didn't tell us everything she knew," said Jessie. "Kelly, do you still have that chart you printed out of the ancestry website with all the family tree?"

"Yes, let me get that off my desk." She returned with several pages printed from her computer. "We know that HHM, the initials on the horses, are probably Honey Hickson Moniac. She was the wife of Gebhardt Moniac. Gebhardt was born in 1851 here in Gristmill. He was the grandfather of Franny's husband, Adam Moniac. He married Honey in 1872. But when I search on Honey Hickson in the 1870 census, I don't find her. There are no records of her existence until the 1880 census when she is married to Gebhardt."

Claude interrupted, "I would bet my last dollar that the mysterious Honey Hickson and the skeleton have something to do with each other. To start with, 150 years ago would make his death around 1868 so the timeline fits. She may have been here in Gristmill at that time."

"Except that she's not on the 1870 census and they didn't marry until 1872. If she was here in 1868, then she would have been on the census because there was a real census taken in Gristmill in 1870. So there is no evidence that Honey Hickson had anything to do with the murdered man," stated Diane.

"Spoken like a true lawyer," joked Claude.

"Do we know anything else?" asked Tom. "Kelly, you said that the family portrait in your office was painted by HHM, and we can assume that was Honey Hickson Moniac. Is that correct?"

"Yeah, Clay reminded us of that yesterday when we were trying to figure out who HHM was. I'm sure HHM is Honey Hickson Moniac."

Kathy had been silent, but now pondered aloud, "You know, if someone was gifted and talented enough to paint that family portrait and to paint, and maybe carve, those carousel horses, then that person would have had to be trained as an artist. I have spent most of my life developing my skills as a painter, and I know that the person who painted your family portrait was an incredible artist."

"How does someone with that much talent end up in Gristmill only to be completely blotted out of all family records?" questioned Sister Elizabeth as they were all thinking the same thing. "Maybe the leather pouch will give us some clues. The sheriff seemed to think the dead man might have been a priest. Did Russell give you any idea when he would let you look at the pouch?"

"No, but I'm sure that he'll offer to let us look at it as soon as he completes his investigation of it. But for now, I suppose we're just left with a lot of questions."

"To change the subject, what did you think of Reverend Brown's idea to move the Tasting Luncheon to the bed-and-breakfast," asked Jessie. "I think the new location will attract more attendees than we've had at the church. And what a great idea to have it during Texas Independence Celebration Weekend."

The Tasting Luncheon was a tradition at the Gristmill Methodist church that helped them raise funds for various mission projects. It was always well attended by people from all denominations within the community. With this year's changes, maybe more people who were visiting Gristmill from out of town would also attend. The Tasting Luncheon was a giant buffet of many dishes prepared by members of the church. For the price of admission everyone attending would receive a cookbook containing all the recipes and a small plate. As they approached each dish, the cook for that particular dish would serve them one spoonful on their plate. They could then taste it and mark their cookbook as to whether they liked the dish or not, hopefully in anticipation of preparing it for themselves. People enjoyed the event because they got to taste the best that each cook had prepared. It was always a success and a fun time for everyone!

Sister Elizabeth shared her thoughts, "I really like moving it to the bed-and-breakfast. I think that will make it more open to the public. A lot of our parishioners at the Catholic Church would like to attend, but just don't feel comfortable going to the Methodist church. It just sort of feels like you're intruding on a family meal when you're not part of that family. I know that no one intends for it to be that way, but it just is. Also, by making it part of the Texas Independence Day Celebration, there may be more attendees and we'll make more money for El Asilo."

"Do you think people will object to the 'local charity' idea, not knowing exactly which charity is being supported?" asked Diane.

"I'm sure Reverend Brown will direct that attention away from El Asilo without raising flags. Diane, these extra funds will be such a help. Your financial supporters have been great in helping us build the building and taking care of the big stuff, but there are some things that the girls need that the supplemental funds could help pay for, like clothes, shoes and make-up," said Kelly.

'I love making 'Nailed It' part of the Tasting Luncheon. There are so many recipes on social media that I try to make, and then they don't turn out anything like the picture," expressed Jessie. "I tried to make this rainbow Jell-O salad. You were to make red Jell-O and put it in the bowl to congeal, then when it was firm you added lime Jell-O and let it congeal, and then you repeated this with grape, peach, lemon and orange to make rainbow layers. But my Jell-O salad turned out to be one big bowl of grayish mauve. I guess I didn't wait long enough between layers or the new layer was still too hot. Anyway, I didn't 'Nail it' at all!"

Kathy laughed, "Yeah, I tried making an Easter lamb cake last year. The picture on the internet was so cute. It was three dimensional with little ears and a bow around its neck all covered in coconut. My lamb looked more like a vampire wolf. Its eyes were crooked, and its head was cocked to one side. And it was sort of spread out all over." Everyone was now laughing so hard they were in tears. "Joe said the best thing we could do for it was to cut it up and put 'us' out of 'its' misery."

"Sounds like something to look forward to – disaster dishes," joked Claude.

"Hey guys, why don't you finish watching the basketball game while we walk Kathy home," said Kelly. The girls headed out the back door to accompany Kathy, which wasn't necessary since Kathy and Kelly had lived across the street from each other for most of their lives, but they all genuinely wanted and needed to hear for themselves how she was coping with widowhood: "How are you doing?"

Kathy replied, "I'm just trying to get through one day at a time. Sometimes I tell myself that I'm all cried out and I'm ready to move on, or at least I'm ready to stop crying. But then the smallest thing – a commercial on TV, or I open Joe's closet, or I smell his shaving lotion, and I'll just break down in tears."

"We're all so sorry, is there anything we can do?"

"No, just keep doing what you're doing. Be my friends and listen and understand that if I'm not excited about something, I'm just doing the best I can."

"Are your kids coming into town soon?"

"Yes, my son from Dallas is coming for a visit in a few weeks. You know, January is a busy time for CPAs, with W-2's and payroll reports to complete. But my daughter, Sherry, and her husband, Lance, are coming this weekend."

"Can we bring you some food for your company?" asked Jessie.

"Oh no, I still have several large casseroles left from the funeral. People were so generous and kind but, we just didn't eat all the food that was brought so I froze some of it. It will come in handy now."

Kelly responded, "Well, if there is anything we can do, please just ask."

"There is one thing, and you might think I'm crazy for asking, but I would like to give the carousel horses a try – you know, sand them down and repair them and repaint them. I promise to refurbish them exactly like they originally looked. I can do the work in Joe's woodworking shop. I think it would be good therapy for me."

"But what about your antique shop? Don't you need to reopen it."

"Not just yet. There're very few tourists this time of the year and my heart is just not into going back to work at the shop. It has so many memories of Joe and me running the store and planning for the future. It's just too hard for now."

"Well, I can't think of anyone more qualified to restore the horses. It would thrill us for you to work on them," responded Kelly.

"I'll get Clint and Casey to bring them over tomorrow. This is so exciting!" exclaimed Jessie.

When they had all given Kathy a big hug, they left her at her back door and returned to find the men watching the last few seconds of the basketball game. Jessie and Tom, Diane and Claude and Sister Elizabeth all gathered up their jackets and prepared to leave. Everyone promised that if they heard anything from Sheriff Lacy about the skeleton or the leather pouch, they would call each other. Kelly and Clay returned to the living room and sat on the couch in front of the fireplace holding hands. Despite Clay's dementia, they still enjoyed holding hands. She often wondered how much longer she would have this precious time with him. All she knew for certain was that for now, it was good.

Chapter 4

Diary of Suzanna Kosovitsky – 1844

June 2, 1844 *It has been a long day, and I wanted to go to bed but there was a pounding on our door. Prince Carl wished to discuss with Josef our plans to prepare for the German colonists. They sat at the table discussing the problems of getting the preparations made while I lay on the bed and pretended to sleep. It amazes me that Prince Carl seems to be a dreamer. He has visions but does not understand how to make them happen. Josef grew up with a father who was a banker, and then he worked with his brothers in construction. He seems to have a much better grasp of how to plan for the colonists.*

Josef explained to Prince Carl, "Holding the colonists in Galveston will be very difficult and very, very expensive. The Adelsverein simply does not have the money to do this. Also, Galveston is just a village. The arrival of several hundred families will cause all sorts of chaos here. I'm afraid trouble will follow."

Prince Carl simply replied, "So, we must find a better place to bring the colonists to shore. In the morning we will hire a coastal steamer and travel along the coastline until we find the right place where a ship can dock."

June 3, 1844 *While I waited on Josef and Prince Carl to commission a coastal steamer, I found Basile's mercantile store where I purchased more suitable clothing for myself. My dresses from home are tightly fitted and seem to be getting tighter through the waist. I found two cotton shifts that have long loose sleeves and an apron sash. I also purchased a cotton bonnet that will help to cover my face from the hot sun.*

We loaded our trunks onto the steamer and by noon we were on our way down the Texas coastline. Prince Carl and Josef were studying over the map. They first considered the little town of Port Lavaca as the arriving port, but then learned that the hazards of navigating through and over the sand and mud bars in Lavaca Bay dimmed its promise as a haven. It would have been promising with its high bluff and its freedom from swampy terrain and flooding by storms, but the dangers of vessels being grounded in Lavaca Bay forced that location to be abandoned.

They chose the second location from the map after two days of moving along the coastline. They chose the west bank of Matagorda and Lavaca Bay. From the shoreline, a direct route could be laid out to the lands of western Texas where it was anticipated that sites might be secured for the colony. This place was only a bulge in the shore and marked on the map as Indian Point or Indianola.

The small steamer brought us to shore. Indianola is really an island made of fine, white crushed shell that has been firmly packed by the waves pounding the shore. We met a man on Indianola named Samuel White. He said he owned Indianola. As far as I could tell, his house was the only shelter on the island. White was receptive to Prince Carl's suggestion that he allow the colonists to disembark on his property where they might stay for a few days and then journey on westward. I think he was envisioning development of his property and maybe some profits.

White was a storyteller, and he delighted us with tales about the Texas Revolution. He had taken part in drafting resolutions against the Mexican government. He told us about the Alamo and the Battle of Velasco, where he had been a captain in the Army of the Republic of Texas. He was not happy about the possibility of Texas joining the United States but seemed resigned to accepting it because he was uncertain Texas could defend itself again against the Mexicans if a war started.

White had more maps that Prince Carl and Josef studied. They were confident that this was the best location to land because it lies south of the Trinity, Brazos and Colorado rivers – which means there were no great streams to cross on the way inland. The settlers would travel along the more southern Guadalupe River, a crystal clear, spring-fed river with many fords upstream that make an easy passage possible. The problems posed by little firewood, and no safe drinking water seemed of little consequence to Prince Carl, since the colonists would only be here a few days.

June 6, 1844 White allowed us to spend the night at his home and then rented us three horses to ride on our trip inland to Nassau Farm. I was thankful that I had purchased the new shifts to wear. I would have been miserable in my German dresses.

We left Indianola traveling west across an unending prairie of flat, desolate, marshy land. I don't think I saw a single tree for miles. We finally came upon some small shrub trees and then more and more trees. We camped near a muddy creek called Chocolate Creek. The water was a quagmire of slushy mud that looked like chocolate milk. It was miserable sleeping on the ground; and I could not get to sleep with all the night noises. A cacophony of screeching owls, howling wolves, chirping crickets, and other unimaginable wild animal sounds made my blood run cold.

Basile was correct. The pestering, loud hum of mosquitos interrupts any thought of peaceful sleep. They bite your neck or legs, leaving you itching unbearably, scratching until your skin bleeds. I believe that everything in Texas either has thorns or bites!

June 7, 1844 *We arrived in Victoria. Since this is an older town in Texas, I thought it would be larger, but it only had a few houses. Up until this point, I had heard mostly German language, since Josef and Prince Carl surrounded me. I had heard many languages at the port in New York, but more and more, the common languages seem to be English and Spanish. It surprised me to discover how proficient my English had become from studying it in Mainz.*

Prince Carl and Josef heard that there might be land available near the Comal Springs or possibly land near Cyril Hill, which is close to the Nassau Farm property already owned by the Adelsverein.

June 9, 1844 *We traveled toward Nassau Farm. The riding was now much more pleasant. The road was rocky but had been cleared, since many of these roads were used during the Texas Revolution a few years earlier. There were little settlements all along the way. More and more, we saw rolling hills with oak trees and crossed small creeks along the road.*

The Adelsverein had developed Nassau Farm as a fully operational plantation using slave labor.

Upon arriving at Nassau Farm, Prince Carl inspected the acreage and was appalled that slaves were being used for labor. This directly opposed the purpose of the Adelsverein about protecting the colonists and freedom. One night as he talked, Josef said, "I can do nothing but recommend the Verein divest itself of the property, rather than associate with slavery. I will not have the colonists come here, even for a temporary layover, on their way to their new homes."

June 11, 1844 *We stopped at Cyril Hill. It was a tiny town that had been established two years earlier. I loved the people in Cyril Hill. They were Czech; and they spoke the Slavic language. Even though there were only a few people,* *they made me feel at home. However, Prince Carl did not want to start a new town with Czech roots for the arriving Germans. He thought there would be too many conflicts between the groups.*

So, we left Cyril Hill and traveled on to Comal Springs. Comal Springs is breathtaking. The springs are crystal clear and the land has low, rolling hills. The pastoral valleys are a little slice of heaven compared to the harsh, brutal terrain of the coast. Prince Solms purchased two leagues of land from Rafael Garza and Maria Antonio Veramendi Garza for $1,111. This would be the half-way stop for the German colonists on their way to the Fisher-Miller land grant farther northwest.

Prince Carl named this settlement Neu Braunfels after himself Prince Carl Solms-Braunfels.

June 12, 1844 *Prince Carl and Josef have had their heads buried in maps and drawings all day. When not studying their maps, they are out walking the property, deciding where things should be built. "We should build the Sophienburg on this spot. It will be a fort and center for the immigrant association. From here we will plot the land lots in Neu Braunfels and in the Fisher-Miller land grant."*

June 15, 1844 *Prince Carl, Josef and I traveled to San Antonio where Prince Carl set up a line of credit for the Adelsverein where drafts could be deducted for expenses. This evening, he said that he was leaving in the morning to return to Galveston to purchase supplies for the emigrating colonists and to prepare for their arrival. He planned to leave us in Neu Braunfels to build shelters for the emigrants. Josef is to paint landscapes of the new land, which we will take back to the Adelsverein when we return to Mainz after the first emigrants arrive in Neu Braunfels.*

We purchased a wagon and an ox to pull it. Then Josef and Prince Carl purchased supplies of lumber and hand saws and nails. I purchased food supplies: burlap bags of flour, beans, and corn, and cans of lard. We felt these would be all the materials we will need over the next few months.

June 16, 1844 *Prince Carl left early this morning. He left the two horses that he had rented from White saying that he would pay for them when he returned to Indianola. It is very quiet without Prince Carl's constant chatter about his plans. Josef is excited about starting to survey the land and to build us a shelter.*

I'm concerned about our safety. Are there Indians near here? Are there wild animals lurking in the woods? My thoughts turn to Basile's warnings about snakes and alligators. And even though he assured me that the Karankawa were no longer a threat, on our journey I heard about the Comanche Indians and they sounded just as ferocious. However, it is so peaceful and at night it is very dark. Sometimes the stars are so bright it seems you could just reach up and touch them. It soothes my fears of wild animals and Indians.

July 15, 1844 *Josef and I have finished a very rustic first shelter. It is not much, but it is a roof over our heads. We have been sleeping in the wagon. Josef erected an arch of wood over the top of the wagon and I hung some of our blankets over the structure. It all works fine unless it rains; but since it is July, that doesn't happen too often.*

Josef and I work hard every day in the July heat. I can feel the rivulets of sweat rolling down between my shoulder blades and between my breasts. At night my feet are so swollen that my boots restrict the flow of blood in my feet. The lifting of timbers and dragging of chopped down trees has made me much stronger. My arms have muscles that bulge much like a man's. Our friends and family back in

Prague and Mainz would not recognize me and Josef. We are tanned and much leaner; and we're always exhausted and bone-tired.

Our biggest relief comes from bathing in the springs. The water is ice cold. Jumping in, we shiver until our teeth chatter. The refreshing chill is offset by lying on the warm rocks and letting the sun dry our skin. We can lie there naked, because we're as alone as Adam and Eve. The dragonflies skip and swoop over our damp bodies and our muscles relax while we listen to the bubbling of the springs.

This evening, Josef rolled toward me and I could tell he wanted to make love to me. We did not have any privacy while traveling from Europe, and now we find ourselves completely alone. He reached out and ran his fingertips across my bosom and my stomach. Then he kissed me as if he were trying to find that fountain of cool water. We pleasured each other; and then giggled at the mockingbird whistling above us as if he were announcing our intimacy to the world.

Later tonight, Josef and I concluded that if we are going to get all this work finished in time for the emigrants, then we need help. We decided that Josef should go to San Antonio and hire several good men to work for him. The Adelsverein seems to have plenty of money and Prince Carl did say, "Whatever you need to get the settlement finished."

July 16, 1844 *Not long after Josef left, I heard a knocking on the door. Thinking it was Josef returning, having forgotten something, I rushed and opened the door only to see an old Indian man staring at me.*

Chapter 5

"Clay, you've got to take a bath!" exclaimed Kelly, exhausted and frustrated. She knew it was pointless to argue with someone with dementia, but it was just so hard when he refused something as straightforward as a bath.

Clay rejected the whole bath idea, "I just took a bath and I don't need another bath."

"No, Clay, you have not had a bath in three days. You really need a bath."

"You're wrong, you just didn't see me take my bath. I don't need another bath."

Finally, Kelly's exasperation had the best of her, and she reconsidered what she had learned about dementia. Redirect the conversation–don't contradict. So, she answered, "Clay, your friend Jeryl will be here soon. You enjoy his visits, don't you?"

Clay's attitude immediately changed; he looked perplexed but said, "Yeah, I guess so."

Jeryl was an extraordinary man. A home health aide who came twice a week, Jeryl could get Clay to do things that Kelly, more and more recently, could not convince him to do. Some people who knew Jeryl called him the "bath whisperer." He was wonderful with Clay. She witnessed his little bath trick last week. Clay, as usual, was refusing to take a bath, but Jeryl took a little packet of honey like from the fried chicken fast food place. He tore it open and put a few drops on his finger. Jeryl then slowly moved over close to Clay and touched his forearm and said, "Man, your arm is sticky. Touch it. I think we need to wash it off. Oh, man, that sticky stuff is on the back of your neck too. Maybe you just need a bath to get all the sticky off." Clay had agreed with him and off he went to take his shower. While he was bathing, Jeryl substituted clean clothes for the ones he had just removed. And just like that, Clay had taken a bath.

Kelly chastised herself for even confronting Clay with a bath. She needed to learn to let the professionals do their thing; and she needed to be the loving companion to Clay. Still, it was just so hard.

After Clay's bath, Jeryl brought out some dominoes and challenged Clay to a game of dominoes. Clay had always loved playing dominoes and was an excellent player. Clay seemed excited about the idea, so Kelly slipped out the back door, taking advantage of two hours away from Clay and his incessantly repeated questions.

She headed to the Wildflower Café to meet Jessie and their friends. Diane had called from San Antonio to say she had something to discuss with them. Kelly also had some interesting news to discuss. Kelly was the first to arrive and was enjoying the warm delight of a good cup of coffee when her sister came through the door.

Jessie inquired, "What's up. Did you learn anything about our mysteries?"

"No, well, it's a long story. Get you some coffee and I'll explain as soon as the others arrive."

When they all had arrived and gotten their morning java, Kelly began. "You know I've been playing with that ancestry website, mostly trying to find out about our mystery dead man and Honey Hickson. But even before then, I sent off my DNA sample. I didn't know what to expect, but just thought it might be fun. Well yesterday, I got a response from the ancestry website. It told me the obvious thing like my ethnicity was Native American, Mexican and a lot of

German, which we already knew. It also said I was 16% Eastern European – and that, I don't understand at all."

Jessie listened patiently. The whole ancestry hobby was not her thing, but she realized that Kelly enjoyed it, so she would be the happy sister coming along for the ride.

Kelly continued her story, "Along with the ethnicity comes all these connections, like cousins: First, second, third, even fourth and fifth cousins. Some I recognize, but most I do not. I guess we could contact some of them, but that's not the shocking news. Along with cousins is another relative. It says I have a half-sister, and it is 100% sure she is my half-sister. How can that be? Jessie and I know our parents and our grandparents. Neither of our parents were married and divorced before we were born. I just don't understand it."

"It must be a mistake," assured Diane. "Websites are notorious for misinformation."

"That's why I want Jessie to send in a DNA sample. Let's see if she comes back with the same half-sister. When hers comes back without the half-sister, then we'll know the whole thing is false."

Jessie interrupted. "Yeah, my guess is that they just got something mixed up. But have you heard anything further on the dead man?"

"Nothing, Russell hasn't called, and I didn't want to be the pushy mother-in-law so I've been waiting patiently. But the mystery is killing me," complained Kelly.

"Changing the subject," interjected, Diane, "I have something to discuss with all of you. I have a new client for El Asilo. We would not be rescuing her from jail. They assigned her to the Uvalde Rehab Facility for drug rehabilitation. The place is west of San Antonio. I'm not sure the county or state will pay for the time that she will need to completely rehab from her drug use. This may be a very difficult transition, but she has nowhere to go. If we release her back onto the streets, her pimps will find her and start trafficking her with drugs within a day. I really need to bring her to you for an extended rehab time," pleaded Diane.

They had never dealt with someone recovering from a drug problem, and they were not at all sure they were equipped for it. Diane saw their concern and added, "You will have some professional help. I will send a psychiatrist to consult with you prior to my bringing this girl. You will need to know what to watch for in her behavior to recognize problems."

Sister Elizabeth agreed, "I think we all need some training on drug addiction before we take on this situation."

They all nodded. Diane told them, "The girl's name is Melissa. She will be at the rehab for another two weeks, so I will get someone here in the next few days to consult with you. But I thank you so much for considering this. It may be a challenge, but one well worth it. Melissa is only 14, and we're hoping this intervention will save her life."

Toddling up to the table came Mrs. Gilbert and Mrs. Campbell. They obviously had an agenda to discuss with the group. Mrs. Gilbert questioned, "Have you ladies decided what you are bringing to the Tasting Luncheon? You know you're supposed to have your recipes in to Janelle by Thursday."

Jessie said, "I thought we were to give our recipes to Mrs. Tilley like last year."

"Umph,' said Mrs. Campbell, "that lady's cornbread is not done in the middle. If we left it up to her, we would never have a cookbook."

In a demanding voice, Mrs. Gilbert asked, "So, what are you planning to bring?"

Jessie answered first. "I plan to bring Granny Franny's Peach Cobbler. I have plenty of peaches left from last summer and it's a favorite for my family. I'm not entering anything in the Nailed It competition."

"I'm bringing Mushroom Chicken and Rice," announced Kelly. "And for the 'Nailed It' competition, I'm making a cake with a white layer, a strawberry layer and a red velvet layer with cream cheese icing. I saw a photo on the front of a Christmas magazine. The Christmas cake had snowflakes cut out of fondant icing with edible glitter on top, but I'm changing snowflakes to white stars with some red and blue fondant streamers for Texas Independence Day."

Kathy spoke up, "I'm making Shrimp Newburg. I had the dish while in Port Aransas and it was delicious. I'm having to make up my own recipe. I've been testing it to get the ingredients correct. But for my 'Nailed It' entry, I saw this thing online where they take melted chocolate and dip the bottom half of a small blown-up balloon in the chocolate. Then they take the balloon out and let the chocolate harden. Then very carefully, you pull the balloon out of the chocolate coating. This forms a chocolate shell. I'm putting a custard cream in it with a few raspberries on top."

"Wow!" Exclamations immediately erupted, and Kathy laughed and replied, "You can see that I have too much time on my hands."

Sister Elizabeth between laughs said, "I'm just the opposite. I have no time on my hands and I cook little, but I can make pimento cheese. I spice up my pimento cheese with some chopped green chiles. Everybody says they love it. I will make bite-sized pimento cheese sandwiches."

"I'm afraid I won't be entering the contest, but I'll be here to help," added Diane.

Mrs. Gilbert and Mrs. Campbell seemed satisfied with their responses and as they left, they both warned, "Don't forget the deadline, next Thursday." The five friends acknowledged, "Yes Ma'am." Together they chuckled and retorted, "I hope when we're their age, we're still that feisty and busy with life."

"I almost forgot," said Kathy, "Sherry and Lance want to move to Gristmill and manage the Antique Shop, if I will sell it to them. I'm seriously considering it. While working on the carousel horses, I realize how much I miss painting and I think I want to retire and spend more time with my art."

They were all thrilled that Kathy's daughter and son-in-law were stepping up and they agreed that, if this is what Kathy wanted, they would support her one-hundred-percent.

Just as they stood to leave, Sheriff Lacy came in the door and came straight to their table. He nodded, reacting to their questioning faces, "I checked with the San Antonio Catholic Diocese to see if they have any records of a missing priest near Gristmill or if they have a record of a priest dying in Gristmill. Since this happened about 150 years ago, they were not too confident that their records would reveal anything, but they said they would try. I explained the situation to them, and they said they would get back to me as soon as possible."

"On another subject, I finished inventorying the pouch. You are welcome to examine what's inside. I didn't bring it because I didn't want other people seeing me carrying evidence around. I'll bring it by Kathy's home tonight." He couldn't help but chuckle as he walked away and could hear the ladies excitedly discussing plans to get together tonight to examine the pouch.

The five friends left the café with a plan to meet at Kelly's to look inside the pouch. Diane agreed to stay over another night because she wanted to see what the pouch held.

That evening after dinner, they were all gathered in Kelly's den including Clay, Tom, and Claude. The excitement was electric! Kelly carefully opened the pouch. There inside was a leather-bound book. When she took it out of the pouch, they could all see it was etched with flowers and vines with the initials "RK" in the center.

Jessie said, "This is so exciting! What's inside the book?"

Kelly gently opened the book to some very brittle, yellow pages of paper. It appeared to be a sketchbook. The pages were filled with pencil drawings. Kelly observed, "The drawings look like religious-type drawings. I recognize several as scenes from the Bible."

"That one looks like a manger scene," offered Kathy.

"And that one looks like Jesus' baptism in the Jordan River."

"And that one looks like the crucifixion of Christ on the cross."

"And that one looks like the women at the tomb."

Sister Elizabeth recognized the pattern, "These sketches are the life of Christ. That would explain a priest having them in his possession."

Tom, examining the sketches said, "I understand all of them except this one. It looks really strange. Christ is standing on some broken doors with a monster under the doors, and there are all these saintly looking people standing around him. It's right between the crucifixion and the women at the empty tomb. What is Christ doing there? Also, there seems to be quite a few of this same sketch. What do you think Sister Elizabeth?"

Sister Elizabeth easily recognized the depiction, "This is how the Catholic tradition, especially the Eastern Catholic tradition, differs somewhat from what we currently observe in the Western Christian tradition. The Eastern Orthodox Church, and now the Eastern Catholic Church, observes Holy Saturday. As you know, we celebrate Good Friday and Easter, but we don't mention too often what happens on Holy Saturday, meaning what happened at the exact time of resurrection, not the resurrection seen as the open tomb."

They were all enthralled with her explanation, "As you know, in the Apostles' Creed it says in the ecumenical version, 'Christ was crucified, died, and was buried, He descended into the dead. On the third day He rose again, and you know the rest. Some older versions of this creed even says, 'He descended into hell.' This sketch is a drawing of Christ descended into the place of the dead. He has broken the chains of death; that's the broken doors with all the chains and the locks on the ground. The monster, as you called him, is Hades. He is the gatekeeper of the place of the dead. This sketch shows that Christ overcame death, and He is carrying his cross in His left hand."

Kelly, looking closely at the sketch, asked, "Who are all the surrounding people?"

"Well, He is reaching back with his right hand and grasping the wrist of Adam, and Eve is right behind Adam," Sister Elizabeth continued. "That might even be Abel behind Eve. They represent all of humankind. Christ is pulling them from Hades. Some other people are the Old Testament prophets. Then on Christ's left side, or over to the front of Him are two men with halos and crowns. The older one would be King David, and the younger one would be King Solomon. Behind them is a man with a ragged beard and dressed in animal skin; that would be John the Baptist. These are all saints who died before Christ was crucified, and now they are being brought from death to life everlasting. They are being raised with Christ. There are many verses in the Bible about being raised with Christ, like Colossians 3:1."

Jessie commented, "I never thought about it like that. But these people in the sketch were already dead when Christ was crucified. Where does the Bible talk about them rising with Christ?"

"You remember the scripture in Matthew 27:51-53 that says the curtain was torn in two from top to bottom? The earth shook and the rocks split."

"Yes," says Jessie, "but I don't remember dead people rising."

"We don't talk about that part very much but in verses 52 and 53, it says that the tombs broke open. The bodies of many holy people who had died were raised to life. They came out of the tombs after Jesus' resurrection and went into the holy city and appeared to many people."

"In the Eastern Orthodox Church, and the tradition follows Catholic churches that have Eastern roots, they call this 'resurrection,' or the Greek word for it, which is 'Anastasis,'" explained Sister Elizabeth.

"You're right," said Kelly. "I see now that there is a word at the bottom of this page that says 'Anastasis.' I thought it was someone's name, but it is really the title of this sketch, 'Resurrection.'"

Diane, thinking carefully, pulled all the facts together, "So, this tells us that a priest with a book of religious sketches, possibly with the initials 'RK,' somehow was killed in Gristmill and was buried in your barn about 150 years ago. And maybe there is absolutely no connection between this priest and Honey Hickson Moniac. It could just be a coincidence that you found items from them on the same day. Is that about correct?"

"I guess so," said Jessie. "It's just very strange."

"Maybe when we hear from the Catholic Diocese in San Antonio, if we hear anything, we'll be able to figure out more."

After sharing some cherry pie that Kelly had made earlier, the guests left. Kelly gazed wistfully at the pouch. It had been so promising, but ultimately offered only more mysteries with no answers.

Chapter 6

Diary of Suzanna Kosovitsky – 1844 - 1869

July 16, 1844 *The old Indian man just stood there staring at me. I was terrified, yet at the same time strangely calm, and not alarmed at him. He rubbed his belly and motioned with his hand toward his mouth. Obviously, he was hungry. I gestured with my hands he was to wait on the porch, and I shut the door. Searching through our food supplies, I found an empty burlap bag and put a few potatoes, onions, and some cornmeal inside. I did not know if these were suitable or not. When I returned, he was sitting on the porch. I gave him the bag, and he touched his forehead and turned to leave. It was a strange meeting.*

July 17, 1844 *I woke early to noise coming from outside. I could not imagine that Josef would already be back from San Antonio. I peeked out the door to see the old Indian man chopping logs at Josef's bench. Again, strange. I walked out to the wood stack and sort of gestured "What?" He motioned that he was working, so I supposed that he was trying to pay me back for the food. I gestured to him like he had gestured yesterday by touching my forehead. I returned to the cabin but kept a watchful eye on him.*

It was blazing hot being the middle of July, so at noon, I took my Indian acquaintance a glass of water and some biscuits I had made. He seemed immensely pleased and then he said, "Thank you." Clearly, he said "thank you"! I watched him carefully and then I said, "You are welcome." The old Indian nodded, and I asked, "Do you speak English?"

He quickly answered, "Yes, but you do not."

He had been watching us build our cabin and clearing some land. We speak our native Slavic to each other, so he thought we did not speak English. I convinced him that I did, indeed, speak English. Then we sat in the cool shade of a tree near the springs for a long time, discussing the situation of our lives.

His name is Hickory because he was born under a hickory tree. And in the Indian tradition, they name a child after something that happens at their birth. He has a wife and a grown, married son living near here. During the Texas Revolution, Hickory worked as a guide, but now that the war is over, there is no work for an old Indian.

I told him that when Josef gets back, he would hire him to help us build more cabins for the German colonists. He continued to work in the afternoon and then left.

July 18, 1844 *Josef returned today and brought with him four Mexican men to help build the additional houses and the Sophienburg. They will rest today and begin in the morning. I prepared a good meal for them tonight with some supplies that Josef brought from San Antonio. He brought fresh peaches, and I made a peach cobbler to go along with the dried venison and a big pot of beans.*

It looks like I will do a lot of cooking. To keep all these men working, they will need food.

The Mexican men are putting up tents for a place for them to sleep. And even as hot as it is, they have built a fire. They say it will keep wild animals from wandering into the camp. Plus, they like their coffee in the morning heated over the warm coals from the night before.

I told Josef about Hickory and he was skeptical of hiring an unknown Indian. But this evening, Hickory walked into the camp and I introduced him to Josef. He assured Josef that he would be the best worker of all the men and begged for a job. Josef felt better and welcomed any help he could get, so Hickory will start in the morning with all the men. However,

Hickory did not bring a tent; he chose to sleep with his blanket on the ground.

November 20, 1844 *It has been some time since I last wrote in my diary. I have been so weary and tired. I get up before the sunrise to cook. Josef now has eight men working for him. They are clearing land and surveying plots. But the surprising thing is that Hickory is now his foreman. He seems to know everything, such as where the best trees are located; and, when a man gets injured, he knows which berries or leaves to use to heal the injury. He says he was the Medicine Man for his village many years ago.*

Recently he brought his wife to the camp. They now sleep in the wagon and his wife, White Feather, helps me. And I need help. I am pregnant. Our baby is probably due in April. My morning sickness is sometimes so bad that I can hardly get out of bed. White Feather has been a tremendous help with the work, and she makes a special tea for me that helps to settle my stomach. The loose dress shifts I purchased in Galveston are now very convenient, since my middle is getting larger by the day.

We have heard nothing from Prince Carl. We keep building and clearing forest hoping that he will return soon. However, the bank in San Antonio keeps paying for our supplies and the wages of the men. Since Josef is working like the men, he pays himself a wage as well, because this is not what Prince Carl had promised. Josef has not painted in months, but at least our little savings account in the bank in San Antonio is growing.

December 25, 1844 *Christmas was very lonely. I miss my family. Christmas in Prague was always a time of the family being together and going to church and good food. This year it was just me and Josef. Josef gave me a new shift dress because my old one was getting very tight with the baby. The Mexican men brought tamales for us. They said it* *was a Christmas treat. Tamales are a small amount of stewed meat, probably venison or javelina, wrapped in masa, and the whole thing wrapped in a corn husk. They were tasty but not as good as our Czech pastries with fruit in the center. The Mexican men all went home to their families for a week, leaving the place just to me and Josef. Hickory and White Feather also left, but said they would return.*

Josef brought in a little cedar tree for us to use as a Christmas tree, and I hung some colored ribbon on it and a proper star on the top.

Merry Christmas to us. I feel like the little tree, so sad and gloomy, a scrawny sapling of what should have been a glorious, beautiful giant.

O Tannenbaum, O Tannenbaum

Wie true sind deine Blatter!

Du grunst nicht nur zur Sommerzeit,

Nein auch im Winter, wenn es schneit.

O Tannenbarm, O Tannenbaum

Wie true sind deine Blatter!

O Christmas tree, O Christmas Tree

How loyal are your leaves!

You're green not only in the summertime,

No, also in winter when it snows.

O Christmas tree, O Christmas tree

How loyal are your leaves!

December 30, 1844 Prince Carl arrived today with two wagons with families. He left the families with us and they moved into the temporary homes that Josef has built. Prince Carl left to go on to San Antonio to settle some accounts with the bank for the full purchase of this property.

The families told us horror stories of the conditions at Indianola. There is no shelter, no food, and no fresh water. Many of the families are living in dirt hovels. There has been a death in almost every family from pneumonia or some other malady. It thrilled them that they could leave. There is little hope of more wagons to help those remaining in Indianola to travel inland any time too soon because the wagons that were planned for these families' transportation have been conscripted for use by the military. It is a dire situation for those remaining at Indianola, and there are more and more families arriving every week.

January 15, 1844 Prince Carl returned from San Antonio and stopped for only two days before leaving to go to Indianola. He had found wagons to help transport the other families inland. His instructions to Josef and the rest of the men were to continue to build temporary housing for those who are coming.

March 15, 1845 What a glorious day! Wagon after wagon of German immigrants arrived from Indianola, exhausted and starving. We prepared a buffet of food: biscuits, roasted prairie chicken, venison, roasted corn, and tortillas. The Mexican men who worked with us taught me how to make tortillas and the German families loved them.

The immigrant families mostly built tents around the compound. That first night with all the tents and the small campfires and the voices of families with children sounded like a heavenly chorus to me. I realized that I missed people and family more than I thought.

A man named Nicolaus Zink arrived with the Germans. He is a German civil engineer sponsored by the Adelsverein to build a fort. He and Josef talked almost all night discussing where the fort should be built. They decided they would locate the fort on a steep rise on the east bank of the Comal Creek, near several of the newly constructed homes.

March 16, 1845 *This morning Prince Carl, Nicolaus Zink and Josef met with all the heads of the families and announced that they must move their tents to the bluff where the fort was to be constructed. Most of the people will continue to live in their tents until the wagons move on to the Fisher-Miller Land Grant farther into Texas.*

The fort will have two cannons for protecting the settlers from the danger of Indian attacks. Since we arrived, we have only met two Indians, Hickory and White Feather. Neither of them is likely to attack. However, I can see that a larger settlement of people may alarm the Indians in the area and result in them attacking the settlement. We have heard horror stories of the Comanche Indians farther west who attack settlers in their homes killing and scalping them.

Prince Carl spoke to the settlers saying, "This city shall be called New Braunfels to be named after the Solms ancestral castle on the Lahn River, southwest of Wetzlar, Germany. The fort will be called Fort Zinkenburg after our builder, Nicolaus Zink. And before long, we will begin work on another fort, Fort Sophienburg. Both forts will protect you from the Indians. Each day men will carry out target practice. This alone should deter any Indians considering attacking our settlers."

April 10, 1845 Our son was born yesterday! We named him Konrad. I think Konrad Kosovitsky is a wonderful sounding name. Konrad is healthy and strong, praise God. Josef just adores him and coos and tickles him. White Feather helped me tremendously with the birthing. The pain seemed unbearable but White Feather held my hand and talked to me and hummed songs; I didn't understand the words, but they were comforting. She was like my mother to me. Josef had purchased some little blankets in San Antonio; and we wrapped Konrad in them.

The German families brought food and congratulations to us. So many of them had lost family at Indianola, most of them children, and I think the birth of a new child brought hope to them in this new terrifying world called Texas.

I am surprised at the effort it takes to care for a baby. Konrad nurses and eats just fine. But he soils himself, and I must constantly wash his wraps. He wakes several times during the night so I must get up and nurse him each time. But for all the trouble, I just gaze at his precious face and little hands and feet, and I am amazed. My love for him just gushes over and consumes me.

The Lutheran minister accompanying the Germans wanted to baptize Konrad, but I just did not feel comfortable with that. Josef and I are not Lutheran, so we declined his offer and said that we wanted to wait for a Catholic priest. He seemed offended but accepted our decision.

May 14, 1845 The work is continuing. Fort Zinkenburg is almost complete and Fort Sophienburg is well on its way. Prince Carl came to our house tonight to tell us he is leaving tomorrow to go back to Indianola and then to Germany. He is very discouraged by the support that he is receiving from the Adelsverein. Their financial backing is disappearing, yet they keep sending more families. He feels *that he must return to them and negotiate more funds for the settlement of New Braunfels, but even more for the Fisher-Miller Land Grant.*

Josef questioned him at length about our situation. Our agreement was for Josef to paint pictures of the land and then we were to return to Mainz. So far, Josef has done only a little painting and his time has been consumed mostly in the construction. Prince Carl assured us that when he returns, there would be time for painting for the promotion of the Fisher-Miller Land Grant. He urged us to continue work on the forts.

May 20, 1845 *It is only a few days since Prince Carl left, but a new man and his entourage arrived. His name is Baron Otfried Hans Freiherr von Meusebach, but he calls himself John O. Meusebach. He told us upon his arrival that he is now the commissioner general of the Texas Adelsverein. Apparently, Prince Carl has made some very poor decisions financially, and the Adelsverein has called him back to Germany and relieved him of his position.*

What a shock this is to us. But the worst part is that Meusebach met with Josef this morning and informed him that his service was no longer needed. He thanked him and told him he was being relieved of his position. According to Meusebach, the Adelsverein can no longer pay for a "painter." Josef tried to explain that he has been working diligently to build temporary homes for the past nine months so that the immigrants would have a home when they arrived, but Meusebach turned a deaf and unthankful ear to Josef's plea.

What are we going to do? We did not receive the acres granted to the new settlers because Josef was to be paid a salary and then our passage back to Mainz was to be paid by the Adelsverein. Now we are stranded in Texas with only the little money that Josef paid himself for his work. Meusebach even informed us we were to vacate the home Josef built for us. Fortunately, he told us we could have the wagon because it is in pitiful shape and not worth fixing. I am angry and hurt. Meusebach does not appreciate the effort and struggle it has been for us. He has decided to just kick us out. When I hear the Germans speaking German and talking about their plans, it just makes me sick. I know it is not the settlers that made this decision, but I can't help but hate them along with Meusebach. They do not appreciate how much work we did to prepare for them. They just take it for granted. I do not think I can stay here in New Braunfels.

As cold-hearted as Meusebach treats us, he is even more uncharitable and cruel to the Mexican men who have worked here for weeks. He has sent them away without even a "thank you." Josef shook the hand of each of the Mexican men and wished them well as he bid them goodbye.

I would not wish ill on anyone, but Meusebach is ruthless and unkind and will someday get what's coming to him.

May 21, 1845 Last night, Josef and I decided that we must move. We do not wish to remain in New Braunfels. We remembered Cyril Hill where we stayed on our journey from Indianola. It now seems a lifetime ago, but we remember the Czech people who lived there. They were friendly, and we enjoyed the comforting Slavic language they spoke. Their community is more settled; also, it is more likely that they need someone who can build permanent homes with architectural skills. We will leave today to move to Cyril Hill.

Hickory and White Feather came this morning to see us. They do not wish to stay here any longer, since Hickory's services are no longer needed. So, we decided we will all travel to Cyril Hill to find a new home.

We've gathered a few belongings and stacked them in the wagon. Josef will drive the oxen to pull the wagon while White Feather, Konrad and I sit in the back. Hickory will ride Josef's horse along-side the wagon and accompany us. Little Konrad sleeps most of the time, unless he is nursing, so he will be well.

May 24, 1845 *We arrived in Cyril Hill. I had forgotten how much I loved this little town. It has grown since we were here a year earlier. There are more houses. The people welcomed us and shared a meal with us. One family even offered to let us sleep on their porch, an offer that we graciously accepted.*

After dinner, a man named Simon Moravec joined us. He is the mayor of Cyril Hill. Simon said that the Catholic Church had been meeting in his home, and they would like to build a church like their church back in Prague. He also told us that Cyril Hill has a one-room schoolhouse, but no teacher. The man offered us the supply room at the back of the schoolhouse for a temporary home if I would teach the children to read and write. Josef could begin work on the church construction, which would pay him a small salary.

God has blessed us. We feel we can build our own home here in Cyril Hill and be a part of a Czech community. I am excited about teaching. And it delights Josef that he will build something other than dog-trot temporary houses. Hickory will again work with Josef and White Feather will help me with Konrad. Hickory and White Feather plan to make their home in the wagon just outside the back of the schoolhouse. God is good!

June 1, 1845 *Simon Moravec came to visit tonight. He is a nice man, very intelligent and quiet spoken. Simon left Prague when he was 17 years old; being the eleventh child in his family, there was no future in his homeland. After stowing away on a ship to America and landing in North*

Carolina, where he was forced to become an indentured laborer, he was finally able to pay off his debt for the ship travel. As soon as his contract was complete, he left for Texas and in 1836 he fought in the Texas Revolution. He then married a Mexican woman named Yolanda. I think he made his wealth by herding wild horses and trading them to the United States government. In 1843 he purchased 100 acres of land along Yaupon Creek and moved his family here.

Simon told us, "At first, the area was called Yaupon, but the area attracted other Czech immigrants and as the little town grew, we changed its name to Cyril Hill. The citizens of Cyril Hill are all Catholic but from the Eastern Orthodox roots. They consider Saint Cyril and Saint Methodius as Apostles to the Slavs. Do you remember their stories from your childhood?"

I answered him, "I remember that Saint Cyril and Saint Methodius were two brothers born about 827 AD in Thessalonica. They were Byzantine Christian theologians and Christian missionaries. Through their work, they influenced the cultural development of all Slavs. They translated the Bible into our Slavic language and they continued to work with the Slavs until their deaths."

"Yes, both brothers are venerated in the Orthodox Church and Catholic Church as saints with the title of 'equal-to-apostles,'" said Josef.

Simon continued, "The people of Cyril Hill do not discredit the Roman Catholic saints of Peter and Paul, but we honored our Czech legacy by naming our town after Saint Cyril."

My spirits leaped to hear this! At last, a place that feels like home.

"We celebrate mass at my home for the community, but we're eager to build a church. Everyone believes that once we have a church, then the mother church in Prague will send us a priest. A priest is needed to baptize our children and to marry our young people," said Simon.

Josef agreed, "Yes, our son, Konrad, needs to be baptized as soon as we have a priest!"

Simon and Josef discussed ideas about the church and how it should be built. Simon was knowledgeable about Eastern Orthodox Catholic cathedrals and had as many ideas as Josef.

The conversation was exhilarating! Simon said enthusiastically, "I think we should build the church in a crucifix shape with the three parts of the cathedral that matched the great Temple in Jerusalem. First, there would be a narthex or the entrance court. Then the largest part of the cathedral, the nave, where the congregants would stand to hear the liturgy, would be two aisles with columns supporting the domed arches."

Before he could continue Josef interrupted, "Yes, and at the front would be the altar, the holiest place, similar to the inner-most part of the great temple where the Ark of the Covenant was kept." Both agreed that an iconostasis, a wall of icons or religious paintings should adorn the altar.

Both men were intensely sketching out the layout for the iconostasis.

Josef proposed, "I believe that the bottom row of iconic paintings of the Sovereign would have an icon of Christ symbolizing his Second Coming and on the left side would be an icon of the Theotokos, or Virgin Mary, symbolizing Christ's incarnation. To either side of these two icons would be the icons of Saint Cyril and Saint Methodious. Then on the *second tier of the iconostasis would be a large icon of Christ Enthroned, with John the Baptist to the left and the Virgin Mary to the right, both in attitudes of supplication."*

Simon picked up the idea without missing a breath, "Icons of the Archangels Michael and Gabriel would then flank them, with Saint Peter and Saint Paul included on the outside of the wall. Then on the top tier we would have paintings of the twelve Old Testament prophets and the twelve apostles."

Both men agreed, but then Simon ventured, "The problem is that I can't paint and there are no artists in Cyril Hill. By any chance, Josef, can you paint?"

Josef laughed uproariously, "Oh yes, I can paint! I love to paint! The altar will be glorious with all the icons of Christ and the Saints!"

I thought the two men would join hands and dance around the room. They were smiling and their excitement was infectious. Actually, I was amazed at the information that Josef remembered from his studies back in Prague.

Josef and Simon continued their plans. "The apse or the vaulted dome above the altar is my biggest concern. This will be an architectural nightmare," worried Simon.

Josef responded, "Don't worry, it will be fine. It will just take time. I have seen the inside of the domes in many cathedrals with a painting of Christ in His Glory surrounded by angels. If we carry the domed arches out over the nave, we could paint the nave blue with stars and angels holding harps. We need to have a simple wooden barrier to separate the apse from the nave. This barrier would represent the meeting of the earthly, the nave, and the heavenly, the altar."

"Do you think we can build this?" asked Simon.

"It may take us years to accomplish, but I believe it will be worthwhile."

Simon confided, "If we are dreaming, then at some point in the future, I would like to see sculptures of Christ, Saint Mary, Saint Paul, Saint Peter, Saint Cyril and Saint Methodius." He laughed, "You are correct. This may take years, and probably our lifetimes, to build such a place, but it is a holy and sacred dream to bring the Slavic Catholic Church to Texas."

Josef, in agreement, said, "Building will take years, but our more immediate problem will be finding the material to build our church. Around Cyril Hill there is no stone to be quarried for the walls. We will have to settle for lumber, because trees we have in an abundance."

Simon expressed with concern, "Materials are limited, and finances may be a problem. However, I am determined to persevere until we have our church."

September 1, 1845 *So much has happened since I last wrote in my diary. Josef is building homes for many of the families and at night he works on designing the plans for the church. The people who want homes prefer the Fachwerk style that Josef built with his brothers back in Prague. In Texas, fachwerk is the perfect way to build. The builders work directly from logs and trees rather than pre-cut lumber. They hew it with broadaxes, adzers and draw knives and using hand-powered braces and augers. The heavy timbers are carefully fitted and joined with large wooden pegs. The structural frame of load-bearing timbers is left exposed on the exterior of the building. Then the area between the timbers is filled with plaster and straw. Inside the home, the walls are plastered completely.*

Josef's skills at directing the cutting and placement of the large timbers is astonishing. The homes are sturdy and stunningly magnificent. His work is in high demand. Every new family wants a splendidly crafted home by Josef.

I have been busy getting ready to teach classes. I will have children of all ages in my one-room school. Reading, math and writing will consume my teaching time.

Little Konrad is growing and is now making baby sounds. He is adorable. White Feather helped me make a sack wrap so I can carry Konrad on my back when I am washing clothes and working in our garden. She calls it a papoose.

September 1, 1846 *A whole year has gone by since I last wrote in my diary. I have been so busy with the school and our new baby girl, Hanka. She has dark hair like her brother. Josef and Simon have finally begun construction of the church building. They must get volunteers to help cut the timbers and then plane the logs into smooth lumber. It is very time consuming, and the building seems to progress slowly. However, Simon and Josef are still both excited about its future.*

May 15, 1852 *Josef has started creating arches for the church. They must cut each timber with slices to bend the curves into the wood. They put the wood into vices to hold it to just the right curve and then place it in the creek to let it soak for several days. Josef and his men pull it out and bend it more and again place the vices along the curve. They repeat this process over and over to get the correct curve for the arches. I do not understand how they will get the arches on top of the columns inside the church, but I am sure they will find a way.*

Konrad and Hanka are now 7 and 6. They both attend my school. We live in a nice home that Josef built. It has a large room in the front with a table and chairs and shelves for books. The kitchen is right behind the large room. The kitchen has a large fireplace where I can cook and heat the house in the winter. To one side of the large room is the bedroom for Josef and me, and then behind our bedroom is a room where Konrad and Hanka sleep.

Josef has even built a home for Hickory and White Feather behind our home. Still, I often see them sleeping outside on warm nights. They say that they feel smothered inside the house. Hickory is strong as ever and he continues to work with Josef, but I worry about White Feather. She seems frailer, and she tires easily.

December 25, 1854 The church is complete. Well, the walls and the roof are complete. We will hold mass in the church tonight. I am pregnant again. The baby is due any time. I hope it will be soon. My back is very painful.

December 28, 1854 After Christmas Mass we came home and, a few hours later, I delivered our baby just before midnight! Her name is Ruzi! Ruzi means rose. I was reading my Bible from the Song of Solomon at chapter 2:1. It reads, "I am the rose of Sharon, and the lily of the valleys.....He brought me to the banqueting house, and his banner over me was love." I think often how God's love provided for us after Prince Carl stranded us and Meusebach kicked us out. I now can look back and see how God uses even the terrible things in our lives for good. In Cyril Hill I have a home among friends and neighbors who love me. I have a husband that loves me and now three beautiful children. I spend my days teaching and doing what I love to do. I am so blessed. I look down at this little girl and know that she is my rose, my Ruzi.

But she is not like Konrad and Hanka. They have a dark complexion with dark hair and small, brown eyes. This little girl has blond, almost white, hair that is curly and freckles on her nose and big brown eyes. White Feather looks at her and says that she is a spirit child. I don't know what that means, but she says it is good and terrible at the same time.

December 25, 1861 For a few years, I lost my diary and only found it a few days ago. It seems appropriate to be writing again at Christmas. Ruzi is now seven years old and Konrad is sixteen and Hanka is fifteen. Our house is lively with music and a large Christmas tree. I remember the tiny cedar sapling that Josef and I celebrated with seventeen years ago.

Last year, Josef purchased an accordion for me. It came with a simple manual and was easy to learn to play. The accordion is a new instrument that was only invented about 30 years ago. My children and my students at school enjoy the music. Music has opened up a whole new setting for my classes, because the children can learn to sing.

This Christmas, we've invited several families to join us for lunch and we will have music and dancing for entertainment. Many of the families have heard little music since they left their homeland. With the dreary news of war and the constant discussion about slavery, we need a time for happiness.

White Feather can barely walk but Hickory plans to help her to our house for the festivities. Ruzi especially loves White Feather. She is the grandmother that Ruzi adores. Hickory delights in Ruzi. Early on she could not pronounce his name, Hickory, but she called him, Hick Man. Now that is what she calls them. They are her White Feather and Hick Man.

May 12, 1863 Ruzi refuses to go to school. Some people in the town have even started talking about her as if she is a little rebellious heathen. She wants to wear pants, not a dress, and she would rather be at the church working on the building and the painting than learning to read and write. Josef does not help the situation because he lets her *do whatever she chooses. It so devastated her when White Feather died and maybe that is why we let her get by with her antics. Now there seems no way to rein her in. She is happiest when she is dirty and helping the workmen on the building.*

We gave her a sketch book for her birthday. It has a leather cover and lots of blank pages. He etched her initials "RK" on the front of the book. Josef has shown her his drawings and sketches for the iconostasis paintings. We both agree that her drawing skills are amazing. She has an eye for details.

Konrad and Hanka are excellent students. They love school and reading. I have been able to get books from Schulenburg for them to read.

We finally have a priest, Father Jonathon. He is a kind man, and he loves his parishioners. He and Simon and Josef seem to agree on most things about the church. However, he would really like to see Josef begin the sculptures of Christ and the saints. That is a big project when the iconostasis paintings are not yet complete around the altar.

June 15, 1865 *Sitting here listening to Josef explain to Ruzi about his latest painting is fascinating. She's only ten-and-a-half, but she fixates on his every word. He is showing her a sketch of the Anastasis. He explains to her that Christians often remember what happened to Christ on Friday when he was crucified, and then we remember what happened to Christ on Sunday when he arose, but we overlook what happened on Saturday. Josef describes that in the Apostles Creed we say "was crucified, dead and buried. He descended into Hell. The third day He rose again from the dead. He ascended into heaven." Josef then questions, "So, Ruzi, what happened on Saturday?"*

Ruzi looked at him and answered, "Christ descended into Hell."

"Yes, that's right and we know from other parts of the Bible, that Christ tramples on the doors of Hades and grabs Adam's and Eve's wrists to pull them from their graves, while an angel carries his cross."

Ruzi questioned him, "What does your sketch mean?"

Josef explained, "The drawing is the best that I can remember from years ago in Prague where I saw the painting of Anastasis. Christ is the central and tallest figure in the sketch. You can tell that it is Jesus Christ because of his cruciform halo and above his head is the traditional two-letter Greek abbreviations IC XC, and he is holding a long ceremonial cross in his left hand. He is striding forcefully to the right but looks backwards as his right hand firmly grasps the right wrist of a white-haired, white-bearded man. That man is Adam and behind Adam is a woman, who is Eve."

"But Papa, why is he pulling Adam and Eve?"

"Adam and Eve represent the universal human race. He is liberating them from the prison of death."

"I don't understand. Do we go to prison when we die? Did White Feather go to prison when she died?" asked a frightened Ruzi.

"No, Ruzi Honey, of course not, White Feather did not go to prison when she died. But the Bible tells us that the wages of sin is death and that means we could go to the prison of death. But the good news is that when Christ died for our sins, we no longer go to prison or hell when we die. Let's look at the rest of the sketch and I think you will understand. Look behind Adam and Eve, and you will see

some other figures. They are the prophets. Also, there is Adam and Eve's son, a young Abel. Then on the left side of Christ are two figures, both crowned, one older and one younger. That is King David and King Solomon. Then behind them is John the Baptist. All of these figures have halos."

"Yes, I see them."

"Now look below Christ's feet. See the ugly figure on the ground. That is Hades. He is the custodian of the dead and the gatekeeper of the Kingdom of the Dead. He does not have a halo. Scattered around Hades are locks and chains and bolts, but they are all broken and loose. There are also two doors that have been broken away and are lying in a cross pattern. Those are the gates of Hell."

"Oh, I see."

"Look closely, there are three sets of crosses in the sketch. In Christ's halo, there is a cross. Christ is carrying a cross on a long staff and the doors that Christ is standing on are in a cross. These represent a connection between Christ's crucifixion and the Anastasis."

"Papa, what does that word mean you keep saying 'Anastasis'?"

"Anastasis means the resurrection of Christ. It is the moment of resurrection and what happened at the moment of resurrection, not the next day when the women find the empty tomb but what happened when Christ was resurrected. We, as Christians, believe that this vision is of Christ breaking forcibly into the place Hades, scattering its bolts and locks all around, forming its gates into a cross, chaining the Hades persona, and liberating from the prison of death the whole human race, personified by Adam and Eve. This is Anastasis! This is the Good News that Father

Jonathon spoke about. If we believe in Christ crucified for each of us, then death no longer has a power over us."

Ruzi comments, "I like the angels!"

"Yes, the angels are there with Christ. I like them, too."

"I think I understand. Can I copy your sketch?"

"Yes, my little Ruzi Honey, you copy all you want. This is part of the series of paintings in the church that will tell the life of Christ. First are the Annunciation, the Journey to Bethlehem, the Nativity, and the Adoration of the Magi."

"I like those sketches the best. Jesus is the baby in the manger and the shepherds all around him with Mary and Joseph. I like the songs we sing at Christmas," interrupts Ruzi.

"Ruzi Honey, do you see that by following these sketches when they are paintings, that the parishioners can see the life of Christ. It is like a liturgy for us. Next is the Baptism, the Raising of Lazarus, the Transfiguration, the Entry into Jerusalem, the Last Supper, the Betrayal of Judas, the Crucifixion, Anastasis, the Women at the Tomb, the Blessing and Mission of the Apostles and the Ascension. Wow, I have to finish a lot of paintings for the church!"

"Can I help? I've been working very hard on my drawings, and I've helped with painting the icons at the front of the church. Please, please Papa, can I help?"

Josef finally agreed. "Ruzi Honey, you can work on the sketch for the Anastasis and when it is just right, then I will let you paint it. We can't waste the paint because it is so difficult to get more paint from Europe, but I think you can try to paint this painting."

"Thank you. I will try really, really hard."

July 2, 1867 Josef says that Ruzi is almost as accomplished in her sculpting as he is. She often sees small changes that improve the sculptures that even he doesn't see. Now she plans to prove herself as accomplished in painting as Josef. She is our gifted little Ruzi Honey.

Josef has been very discouraged lately. Father Jonathon was called back to Prague. Father Anton Bithowski replaced him. He is much younger, but a larger man with mean eyes and a critical attitude. Nothing is ever good enough for him. He has a bitter, harsh tongue. He also complains that there is something that doesn't feel right with wooden walls, not stone walls. I think he is dreaming if he thinks we can find large masonry in central Texas.

September 9, 1867 Ruzi finished the painting of the Anastasis. It is so beautiful that Josef says he will use it in the iconography of the Life of Christ. We are so proud of Ruzi. I think it thrills her that her art will be a part of the church. She has sketched every painting that Josef has finished, but the Anastasis is her best work.

April 1, 1868 Father Bithowski has complained so much about the wooden walls in the church that Josef and Hickory have finally decided that the only way to solve the problem is to convert the wooden walls to fake stone walls. Josef remembers from architectural classes they talked about a process called Trompe-l'ceil where an art technique that uses realistic imagery to create the optical illusion that the depicted objects exist in three dimensions. Josef thinks they can paint the wooden walls to look like stone and maybe Father Bithowski will be satisfied. He thinks the plastered dome ceiling can also be painted to look like stone. I am not sure this will work.

The problem is that will take an enormous amount of paint to transform the walls and ceilings into a faux stone imitation, and we do not have the paint.

Hickory suggested they use some old Indian methods to create the paint that is needed. He says there are many plants and soil that can be mixed to create the pigments for our paint. Hickory and Ruzi will go into the forest and fields tomorrow to look for plants with good pigment qualities. It thrills Ruzi that she gets to spend the whole day with her Hick Man.

April 2, 1868 *Hickory and Ruzi have found piles of bluebonnets and they are now pulling the petals from the plants to dry them and then crush them for their blue pigment. They also brought in buckets of wild blackberries to cook down to form a dark blue pigment base. And finally, they brought back a wagon full of reddish clay that they were mixing with turpentine and other compounds. They even found some sunflowers with bright yellow petals and their brown center seeds.*

I never saw two chemists back at the university who were as excited about a discovery as Hickory and Ruzi. They are mixing and testing and cooking their concoctions.

June 3, 1868 *Hickory and Ruzi have found a combination of compounds to create the paint needed to transform the wooden church structure into the looks of a stone cathedral. First, they made an undercoat of cream-colored plaster from crushed limestone and shells. Then, by using a daub and smear method, they will paint a light coat of the brown paint, then cover the walls with stenciling to exact the shape of large stones. Then, shading with a darker brown that comes from boiling peach skins will complete the stone appearance. Josef believes they have captured the essence of large, stone blocks. The problem is they need huge* amounts of clay, flower petals and dried fruit skins to make enough pigment for the painting.

The people in Cyril Hill have complained about the wagon loads of plants and dirt and the smell of their concoctions but I think, when they see the effect, they will be pleased. I hope so.

The blue pigment for the ceiling has been much more difficult. Just collecting enough bluebonnets and berries to make the pigment needed has been challenging. In addition, Hickory is not sure the pigment is strong enough to hold to the plaster. Everyone is worried about the sky-blue ceiling.

September 15, 1868 Konrad married a girl from Cyril Hill named Becca. Their marriage was at the church and afterwards we had a feast of food. She is a sweet girl and was one of my best students. I played my accordion and everyone at the party danced. It was quite a celebration. Konrad and Becca will live in the little house that Josef built for them, which is next door to our home. Josef has been busy building the home for Konrad, so he has not been working on the church as much as usual. Father Bitkowski is always angry that progress is not moving faster. However, Hickory and Ruzi are working as hard as they can on the paint.

September 20, 1868 Today, Josef, Simon and many of the parishioners have begun to plaster the walls of the church. It is a very time-consuming project. The plaster must be mixed to just the right consistency, which it seems only Ruzi and Hickory know how to judge. Then the plaster must be smeared smoothly on the wooden walls. Sometimes it falls off and sometimes it cakes up. It is a very frustrating process.

Becca and I drove the wagon to Galveston for a load of books for the school. The books are old, but still useable. When we returned, we started unboxing them into the classroom. I'm excited about the new reading material, because many of the students have read every book we have in the school. Becca will assist me as a teacher.

November 20, 1868 Josef is furious with Father Bithowski! The walls are only about half complete. Father Bithowski wants it finished by Christmas Mass and Josef says that there is no way it will be ready. Simon is trying to negotiate between them, but I'm not sure it is helping.

December 25, 1868 A compromise was reached between Josef and Father Bithowski. Josef finished the walls and columns and arches of the church. They look just like large stones. Before Christmas Mass I saw people running their hands over the walls to see if they were really stone or wood. I think it amazed them. Even Father Bithowski seemed pleased.

February 23, 1869 Josef and Simon and Hickory are working on plastering the church ceiling domes with the undercoating. They have built scaffolding throughout the building. I fear for Ruzi's safety. She is on top of the scaffolding; lying on her back and painting the sky using the two shades of blue from the berries and the flowers along with some gray from ashes from the fire. Josef decided that he would order paint from Europe for the painting of the angels on the ceilings and domes. We are waiting for it to arrive in Galveston.

It has been raining and raining. It seems there are ponds of water everywhere. Josef, Hickory and Ruzi constantly complain that the plaster and the paint will never dry with all this rain. And, of course, in Texas when it rains, then comes the mosquitos. The children in my classes have mosquito bites all over their legs and arms. It brings back terrible memories of our first days in Texas when we were camping by Chocolate Creek and the mosquitos almost ate us alive.

April 1, 1869 The paint has arrived in Galveston. Josef and Simon will go there and pick it up, along with other supplies. The ceiling domes look amazing.

April 3, 1869 Josef said that there are many people sick with yellow fever in Galveston. He says they do not know what is causing it. He said that everyone is terrified. One person told him about a 25-year-old man who was healthy one day and dead three days later. They said he went from a state of debility, fever and pains in his legs and arms, to vomiting blood clots, to jaundice and death. They call it black vomit. The doctors do not know how it is being spread. The city is trying to clean up the garbage heaps. Some people say that the stagnant ponds are causing particles in the air that are carrying the disease.

Yellow fever is very scary. I hope it does not come to Cyril Hill.

May 13, 1869 It continues to rain and rain. The mosquitos are so thick that you can see black clouds. We have been wearing long sleeve shirts and trousers to keep them from biting us, but they still bite. At night they are in the house and they bite on any skin that is available.

Ruzi and Josef are busy painting the angels on the ceiling domes in the church. I overheard Josef tell her, "Ruzi Honey, just remember that one angel must have a harp that has no strings in the harp."

"Why, Papa?"

"It is believed that God's house on earth should never be finished until we go to heaven to His house in heaven. So, *we should always leave one little thing that needs to be finished."*

Ruzi laughed, "I bet Father Bithowski does not believe that. He always complains that we will never get finished."

When we went to bed tonight, Josef said his legs and arms were sore. He thought he had painted too much holding his arms above his head.

May 15, 1869 *Josef is very ill. The doctor believes he has yellow fever. He just lies in bed with a high fever. He is sweating so much that the linens are soaking wet. I fear that he indeed has this terrible illness. I have prayed to God that He does not let him die.*

May 22, 1869 *Yesterday we buried Josef. I cannot think what my life will be like without him. I feel like someone has hit me in my stomach. I cannot stop my tears. I miss him terribly; I just want to hold his hand one more time. I know that Konrad, Hanka and Ruzi are hurting as much as I am. I worry now because Konrad and Becca are both ill. It seems like everyone in Cyril Hill is sick with the yellow fever. I know it is yellow fever because they are already vomiting black blood. The doctor says there is not much we can do for them but keep them comfortable.*

June 10, 1869 *How can God let this happen? I want to scream at God. I have always tried to live as a good person. I have prayed and I have followed His ten commandments. Why is He doing this to me? I have buried my husband and now two of my children. First, Konrad and Becca and then Hanka. Konrad and Becca were so ill for days on days, but Hanka got sick and died quickly. All I have left is Ruzi. Please God, I beg you, don't take her from me.*

June 18, 1869 *I am afraid that I have yellow fever, too. My arms and legs ache. And I have a fever. I went to see Father Bithowski and asked him to pray for me, but I do not think that will do any good. I have talked to Hickory and asked him to watch after Ruzi, but that is no job for an old Indian man. I went to see Mrs. Svobodova. She is a neighbor with five children of her own. She has been lucky; none of her family have died of yellow fever. Mrs. Svobodova is a stern woman, but I think she is a compassionate woman who will take care of Ruzi if I die.*

I have loved my family with my whole heart. I am not sure I want to live any longer without them. I cannot understand why God is doing this to me. I see clearly that my grave awaits me.

Chapter 7

They were all gathered at Jessie's home, waiting for Diane and the psychiatrist to arrive. Everyone had found comfortable seats on the leather, ranch-style furniture. The room was large and open windows displayed breathtaking views of pastures and cattle. Overhead, a king-sized fan turned slowly with a soft creak as its blades circulated the cool air. Jessie had served sweet iced tea to her guests. Tom and Claude, Gus and Lupe, as well as Reverend Brown, were included in the group, knowing that they would all need to interact with this new girl, Melissa. Kelly had left Clay at home with Mrs. Brauder. More and more Clay was becoming confused, and Kelly certainly didn't want him thinking about sex trafficking and drug addiction.

While they were waiting, Jessie brought out her DNA report from the ancestry website. It matched identically to Kelly's ethnicity. It also showed that she had a half-sister, the same half-sister as Kelly. Jessie commented, "Maybe we should just ignore this and assume it's a mistake."

But Kelly replied, "No, I think we should pursue it just to see why this happened. Do you think our father or mother could have had a child out of wedlock before they married each other?"

"I don't think they could have kept that a secret all the years we were growing up. But, on the other hand, we're finding that family secrets are not as uncommon as we thought. If Gebhardt and Honey kept secrets from the family, even from Granny Franny, then I guess it's possible," mused Jessie.

"I'll email the person listed as our half-sister. If she responds, then we'll decide what to do next," said Kelly.

In the lull in conversation, Kathy spoke up, "Well, I've decided to officially retire from the Antique Shop. The papers are being drawn up for me to sell the shop to Sherry. She and Lance will be here next week. They hope to get it ready to re-open on the weekend of Texas Independence Day."

They all congratulated Kathy and wished her well in this transition.

It seemed that everyone had an announcement to make. Reverend Brown, reminded them, "According to Mrs. Campbell and Mrs. Gilbert, the cookbooks are being printed. Could I get two you to go to the bed-and-breakfast to plan for setting up the Tasting Luncheon? Lila, the lady that owns the bed-and-breakfast, is a little concerned about how it will work and how the attendees will circulate through the line. I think she's very excited about it, but just needs some help in organizing the setup." Jessie and Kathy agreed to go that afternoon to visit Lila.

After a quick tap on the front door, Diane came in, along with a tall, thin woman sporting wire-rim glasses and a short, neat hairstyle and looking somewhat professional, with a warm smile. Diane introduced her as Stacy Neidemeyer. Diane said she had worked with Stacy through the district attorney's office for many years, but said she would allow Dr. Neidemeyer to explain to them what she does.

Stacy began by thanking them for what they were doing. She explained, "I am by education a psychiatrist, but by profession I am also an addictionologist. I work with people who are addicted to drugs, help them to enter a rehab program, and then help them to stay sober from drugs. Also, I spend much of my time working with the re-entry of sex-trafficking survivors back into society. These two interests go hand-in-hand. Most people, and in particular, women who have been forced into the sex-trafficking business, are addicted to drugs. The pimps, or the more current name, 'kings,' use drugs to control their victims."

They all listened intently as she continued, "When the new girl arrives, you'll notice that she has a tattoo low on her neckline, almost at the top of her left breast. It's a tattoo of a crown. This means a 'king' owns her. The crown has two initials inserted between the points of the crown; that identifies her original owner. You'll also see several other tattoos on her neck. I believe Melissa has a bow and a money bag tattoo. Each tattoo reveals a time when she was traded. This is how controllers brand their slaves."

"We are seeing more and more very young girls who have been kidnapped into the sex trade. With social media, the controllers constantly troll teenage websites for teens who are talking about loneliness or unfair parents or whatever. Sometimes the parents are completely unaware that their teenager is talking about such things. And many times, the teenager is just ranting with no real justification for their complaints. But the exploiters are watching. They target these kids and reach out to them at malls and after school hangouts. They often begin by giving them expensive gifts and gift cards. Over time, they pull them in by providing them with drugs. Once the hook is set and they addict the young girl to the drugs, they can easily manipulate her to do whatever the captors please. And very often this means they kidnap the girl from her home and her community. This is what we think happened to Melissa."

Tom asked, "Do you know where Melissa's parents are?"

"No, Melissa doesn't talk very much. She's only fourteen, which is very young for the number of years she has been working. We think she may have had a botched abortion and her king wanted to get rid of her, so he gave her an overdose and left her in an alley behind a building in San Antonio. When the police found her and took her to the hospital, she was almost comatose."

"If we find Melissa's parents and they have a home where she can safely return, the road to reunification is still a long process. We are certain she suffers from emotional exploitation and commercial sexual exploitation."

"So, is it true she hasn't been arrested and has not been sent to the rehab by a judge? Is that what you're saying?" questioned Jessie.

"That's correct, she falls into the category of a victim and the State of Texas will pay for certain expenses for rehab of a homeless person or a victim. However, Melissa may not be able to completely rehab in the short period of rehab paid for by the state. She has not spoken about how she got into this predicament or about her parents. She can physically speak but refuses to. We're not sure if this is from her experience being held captive or if she's afraid to speak, not knowing what will happen to her; we just don't know."

Kelly asked, "What behavior should we expect from her? How will we know if something is wrong?"

"When she comes to El Asilo, she will no longer be taking heroine or any other opioid drug. I expect she will be withdrawn, anxious, and nervous. She will probably avoid eye contact with you."

"I have prescribed for her a drug called buprenorphine in the brand name drug Suboxone. Buprenorphine was originally used as a pain reliever. Even though I think Melissa has some fairly severe pain coming from the botched abortion, the prescription is for drug rehab. You may have heard of methadone. I no longer prescribe methadone. Instead, I use buprenorphine which is a safer opiate treatment than methadone. Suboxone, Melissa's prescription, is a combination of buprenorphine and naloxone. The naloxone prevents someone from injecting the medication to get a high. The Suboxone reduces and eliminates cravings for heroin and other opiates. It also helps prevent the person from experiencing withdrawal symptoms. Hopefully, this drug will help her remain safe and comfortable during her detox."

Lupe raised her hand to ask her question, "Will she be giving the medicine to herself or will one of us dispense her medication?"

Stacy responded, "That's a good question. She absolutely should not be in possession of her medications. We will give someone the responsibility to give her the medication. And they must give it on an exact schedule, which must be adhered to strictly. And, on that subject, it's essential that everyone else who is around her to keep their medications in a locked place."

"Let me back up a moment and explain some things about being addicted to drugs. We all have receptors in our brain. When we take a drink of alcohol, one of these receptors will become active and respond, 'that was nice.' When we take a second drink, the receptor will again become active and it will open up a little more, responding 'that was nice again.' You may notice that your words are becoming a bit slurred, so you tell yourself, 'I should stop drinking, I've had enough.' Then the receptor in your brain will close and your brain allows you to stop drinking. But if you are addicted to alcohol, the receptor will not close and you can't help yourself from drinking another drink. Basically, the receptor never closes, so you constantly want another drink. This works in the same way for a drug abuser. Their receptor that measures their desire for opioid drugs, whether for a high or for pain relief, is open and wants more and more."

"While buprenorphine isn't a full opioid, it acts much like one, causing moderate receptor site activity. It allows the normal body pain relief mechanism to act. It does not create a euphoric state, when taken like it is prescribed. So, it is very important that Melissa take her medication on time and at the prescribed interval."

Diane interrupted. "Stacy, could you tell them what they should watch for?"

"Yes, we're very concerned that Melissa may relapse. Even if she is not getting opioid drugs, her body may not be completely detoxed. If this happens, she will become very agitated; she may describe feeling that she has spiders and bugs running up and down her arms and legs. Or she may have hallucinations and see things that are not there. If any of these things happen, you will need to call me immediately. Also, you will need to keep a very close eye on her, because she may decide that she needs to leave this property in search of more drugs. If she runs away, please call me and call your local law enforcement."

"Do you have any more questions for me?"

Sister Elizabeth inquired, "What can we do for her, or how can we best help her?"

"The best thing that you folks can give her is a safe place to recover, time to recover and a listening, loving, compassionate ear if and when she begins to talk. If she tells you anything about her family, please pass that information on to Diane so we can determine if it might be possible to reunite her with them, or if we will eventually need to find another long-term solution for her."

Diane told the group, "I will bring Melissa in about two days, if they release her from the rehab center as planned. I'll call before I come. Again, thank you all for what you're doing."

Diane and Stacy left to return to San Antonio.

The group sat in stunned silence until Jessie said, "When we started El Asilo, I was all rainbows and butterflies about it. I thought we could just swoop in and miraculously make things perfect for these young women. After what we've seen with the mid-night runs to the San Antonio jails and the near disaster of the pimps attacking our home, I've sobered up to the realization that this is dangerous work!"

Sister Elizabeth reflected, "But the blessing is that if we do our work, then someone's life can be changed. We can help these women survive this terrible ordeal. We helped Karen and the other women. This is just going to be a new challenge. But it's our calling to help them survive."

About that time, the back door opened, and in burst Sheriff Russell. "I'm glad I got here while you are all still here. I have news about our murdered man!"

The excitement in the room exploded as they all wanted to hear. "The Catholic Diocese in San Antonio thinks the man was named Father Anton Bithowski. He attended a dinner party at the orphanage in Gristmill in 1871 and then disappeared never to be heard from again. They said there was an investigation by the church, but they found no clues; no one in Gristmill or at the orphanage knew what happened to him. The case was never closed."

"This is exciting," exclaimed Kelly. "We can now look up Anton Bithowski in the ancestry website. Maybe we can find out something about him that will help us put this puzzle together. It's too bad we can't get some DNA from the bones, so we could find out more. But the medical examiner told Russell that the DNA was too deteriorated to provide much help."

Claude said somberly, "The only problem is that AB are not the initials on the sketch book, so I'm not sure this will clear things up."

Chapter 8

1869

"The child is wild. She's always inside the church mixing up stinking, rotten-smelling concoctions," whispered Mrs. Svobodova. She was a buxom woman with a sagging second chin and a large bosom matched only by her round belly, almost hidden by a flower print apron. Mrs. Novakova shushed her and, looking somewhat embarrassed for her friend, she said, "Now's not the time for speaking and spreading rumors."

"Well, it's true. They should never have named her Ruzika. Who would ever call her a rose; they even call her Ruzi for a little rose? She's not a little rose; she's more a kocourek, a little tomcat. She never attends classes at school. She just hangs around her father's workshop with that old Indian man and claims she's helping him paint the church," hissed Mrs. Svobodova. "With that flaxen hair and those big brown eyes, she could just as well be the spawn of the devil."

Mrs. Svobodova stared at her friend with a warning glare. "Father Bithowski is coming to the door, so hold your tongue."

Ruzi could hear every word they said, but none of it mattered. Her grief overwhelmed her and was so great that it made her whole-body ache. She thought nothing could hurt as much as her father dying just two weeks ago and watching as they lowered his casket into the ground. But then her brother and sister died; and now, holding her mother's hand, feeling the fragile bones held together by hot and clammy skin as thin as parchment paper, she wept. Hearing the gurgling in her mother's throat as her breathing became more and more labored, she knew the end was near.

Father Bithowski greeted the women in the parlor and then turned toward the bedroom. Ruzi could see his large frame in the doorway. Ruzi never considered the Father mean, but he wasn't like her Papa who was always smiling and laughing and talking to her as if she were an adult. Father Bithowski spoke softly to Ruzi. "How is your mother doing?" Ruzi just shrugged. What was she to say? My Mama looks just like my Papa just before he died?

Father Bithowski leaned over the other side of the bed. He removed his stole and kissed the upper edge to offer last rites for Ruzi's Mama, Suzanna. He told Ruzi, "She has received the penance and viaticum of our Lord so you can be assured that she will be in heaven with your Papa." Ruzi looked at the Father; and she hated him for saying such a thing. Mama was not dead, so don't go saying those things! Not yet.

Ruzi studied the filtered sunlight shining through the window. Funny how you could see little flecks of dust in the sunlight and on the glass pane that you'd never noticed before. Ruzi was praying so hard, "Please God, don't take my Mama. Not now, she's all I have. I love her so much and I don't think I can live without her. Please, God, if I've been a tomcat like the church lady says, I'll change. I'll go to school every day. I'll do whatever you want me to do, but let my Mama live."

But that prayer was not to be answered as Ruzi wished. Just as the sun was setting, Suzanna breathed her last breath and passed from this world to the next. Ruzi hugged her mother's still body and sobbed uncontrollably. Father Bithowski lifted Ruzi from her chair and guided her to the parlor where Mrs. Svobodova announced that she would take the girl home with her for the night. Ruzi was numb as they led her away from her home and down the street to the Svobodova house. As she left her home, she saw Hick Man standing off to the side of the house with his head bowed. He looked up just in time to catch her glance and his eyes said everything to her. He felt the same pain that was a dagger through her chest, keeping her from breathing.

With five children of her own, Mrs. Svobodova didn't think one more would matter. She fed them the venison stew that she had left simmering on her stove earlier in the day. They gave Ruzi a hard pallet to sleep on the floor, but all night she lay there awake, listening, thinking, crying.

At the following mid-day, Mrs. Svobodova walked with Ruzi to the little cemetery behind the church. Fresh soil formed a little mound over the place where her Papa had been buried just two weeks ago. Three other mounds were just past her Papa's grave. Now there was a new dirt cavern dug beside Papa's grave. Encircling the hole was a simple wooden casket on one side and a few somber-looking townspeople on the other side. Simon and Hick Man were there, both with somber faces, both lacking words for Ruzi. Father Bithowski started talking or preaching, but she really didn't hear a word he was saying. They lowered her Mama into the ground and people came by and said they were sorry for her loss. Some patted her on the top of her head and others squeezed her hand. Her throat hurt so much she thought she couldn't breathe. Maybe she could simply be the next to die.

Then Mrs. Svobodova moved in like a hawk ready to snatch up her prey. She told Father Bithowski, "I'll take Ruzi back to her home to pick up her clothes and some of her belongings. She can stay at my home for a few days, but you know I've already got five children of my own, so I can't keep her for more than a short time. You also know she's a troublesome child. I don't want her teaching my children how to misbehave."

Looking down at Ruzi with icy indifference, Father Bithowski responded, "I'll figure something out for Ruzi's care. I'll come for her tomorrow." Ruzi did not understand what they were talking about. She had never considered that she couldn't go back and live in her own home. When everything looked terrible, and she thought things could not get worse, she realized how dreadfully wrong she had been.

As Ruzi walked up to her beloved home, she looked up at the beautiful fachwerk with the large wooden beams crisscrossing the sides of walls. Between the beams a stucco of sticks and limestone clay made the house sturdy. The roof had a steep pitch, made of shingles that she had helped her father create. There were shuttered windows that adorned no other houses in the town. But what she loved the most were the baskets of flowers under each window. The flowers reminded her she needed to water them because they were looking droopy. She knew her home was special. Her Papa was an architect and he had designed the home especially for her Mama. It had a large parlor just inside the front door with a large table desk that her parents used for reading and drawing. Off to one side was their bedroom with the large bed that her Papa had built, covered with her Mama's quilt. She remembered all the times that they had cuddled up together on the bed and her Papa would start tickling her, her brother, her sister, and her Mama. They would giggle and Mama would laugh. Just the thought made her smile.

Her Mama's kitchen was behind the parlor. Just recalling the aromas from the pies, bread, and roasted meat made her stomach growl as she realized she had not eaten today.

After her brother was born, her Papa had added a new bedroom behind the front bedroom. It was this room that she had shared with Konrad and Hanka. This is where they had talked and played, where Konrad had told ghost stories scaring Hanka. The room had a window with shutters, and she often looked out at the tall pine trees surrounding their home. At night, a cool breeze often blew across her bed.

When she entered the front door, she saw all her Mama's books on the side shelves and the big fireplace on the outside wall. The floors were dark wood, which her Mama kept polished and clean. But what almost brought her to her knees was the smell of her Papa's pipe. For a moment, she started to call out to him; then she remembered he wasn't there. They were all gone, gone forever.

Mrs. Svobodova hurried her to her room. She collected her clothes, her childhood doll, and her sketchbook. She clutched the sketchbook to her chest, remembering how Papa was so proud of her drawings. She rubbed her fingers across her initials, RK, etched on the cover. Papa had made her a leather pouch to carry the sketch pad and her pencils. She had carried the pouch with her when she and Hick Man had searched the woods for flowers and berries for pigments that they used for paint. Papa had told her to write down all the formulas for the paint that they used.
 As she worked with him, he showed her how to record details for the painting of the angels on the ceiling domes. Each sketch had details of the exact paint that they used. She held the leather sketchbook and pouch close to her heart as Mrs. Svobodova grumbled at her, "Hurry up child, I don't have all day. Get your belongings and let's go." Having no box or suitcase, or even a rucksack, she put her things in the middle of her parent's quilt and tied the corners together. This would give her something to sleep on tonight, softer than the hard pallet from last night. Besides, the quilt held the lingering scent of her parents, and she could dream they were still with her.

Arriving at Mrs. Svobodova's home, Ruzi saw the two boys and three girls, ranging from two to fourteen years old, staring at her. Ruzi had refused to attend regular school, even though her Mama was the teacher. Her Mama taught her in the evenings, and during the day she would go with her Papa to wherever he was working. Papa said a child could learn more from working than just sitting and reading. The school was normally chaos with 25 students of varying ages and different knowledge levels. All Mrs. Svobodova's children attended school, and they were all dark-haired, so they regarded Ruzi with her flaxen hair as peculiar. The other children made fun of her accent, which was unlike their heavy Czech accent. After a while they shunned and ignored her, which was fine with Ruzi. She didn't want to befriend them or have anything to do with them.

That evening, when she settled down on her pallet hugging her quilt around her body, she relaxed to the sweet smell of her Mama's perfume. She still had trouble sleeping, wondering what tomorrow would bring. When would they let her go back home to live? As she finally drifted off to a restless sleep from pure exhaustion, she remembered the stories that her Papa and Mama had told her about where they grew up in Prague and how they had traveled to America with Prince Carl. Papa had told her about the princes and princesses in the old country. She dreamed of being a beautiful princess and that a handsome young prince would come and take her away from all of this.

The next morning, Mrs. Svobodova woke the children early. She made a breakfast of mush. The other children ate ravenously. They were excited about their day. The older children would help their father in the garden, leaving the little ones to help their mother. Ruzi felt completely at a loss. She wasn't eager to help in the garden but was probably expected to do so. Suddenly, there was a knock on the door and Mrs. Svobodova invited the guest, Father

Bithowski, into the kitchen. He completely ignored Ruzi and directed his conversation with Mrs. Svobodova.

The Father said, "I have converted the storage room at the back side of the narthex into a bedroom. It should be sufficient for Ruzi to live in. There are women in the town who can bring her food. However, she will have to work for her keep. The church domes must be completed. Her painting skills are as good as Josef's. She is the only one who can finish the painting and I believe God has allowed her to live so that she can complete His house of worship. Therefore, I will oversee her care until that work is complete. Then I can decide where she should live after that."

"That's an excellent idea, Father. I will see that she gathers her belongings and brings them to the church this morning," said Mrs. Svobodova, obviously relieved that she was no longer responsible for this rebellious tomcat.

Ruzi listened quietly, not believing her ears. They wanted *her* to finish painting the church's ceiling domes! How could she do this by herself? How could she do it without Papa?

Later that morning, Mrs. Svobodova took Ruzi and her few belongings to the church. When Ruzi walked into the small storage room, she saw the tiny wooden bed with the thin corn husk mattress, bare without a linen sheet, that would be her bed. The room had no window and was stuffy and hot in the late June heat. Mrs. Svobodova told her the room would be fine and that she should be happy that the Father had provided her a place to live. With that parting statement, Mrs. Svobodova shut the door and left Ruzi by herself.

Shortly after that, Father Bithowski opened Ruzi's door and stood in the entry and began to speak to Ruzi, "You are now a ward of the church. You are an orphan, and I have not found a family in Cyril Hill that wishes to take you into their family. So, out of the mercy of this church, I am providing you with a room in which you can live. Each morning, one of the women from the church will bring you some biscuits and milk for breakfast and each night you will be provided with a meal that you will eat in your room. In order to pay for your keep, you will work to finish the painting of the domes that your father never completed. Each day you will attend Mass. I shall have no shenanigans from you. Do you understand?"

"Yes sir," whispered Ruzi.

"I expect the dome and the rest of the church to be completed before Christmas Mass. With that deadline being only six months away, you should plan your work to be concluded prior to that time. Besides the domes to be finalized, there are several paintings that your father promised that are not yet finished. Your father also had drawings for a lectern or pulpit that he was to build. I expect that you should be able to accomplish this, too, since you did much of the work in sculpting the statues of the saints."

Ruzi wanted to cry and run away but there was nowhere to run. Her family was gone; she was all alone. She was terrified that if Father Bithowski became dissatisfied with her work, he would force her to leave the church. She should be grateful for his generosity, but she didn't feel that way. Again, she answered him, "Yes Sir."

As Father Bithowski turned to leave, he sneered at Ruzi and muttered under his breath, "You ungrateful little ruffian."

The next morning, she received a biscuit and a glass of milk from a nice lady she did not recognize. She quickly went to the interior of the church and returned to gather the paint, brushes and rags from the storage room, her bedroom. As she climbed the scaffolding, she saw her only friend, Hick Man, coming to help her. He smiled at her but said nothing.

She worked all day doing the tedious painting of tiny stars and angels on the dome while laying on her back and reaching upward. By the end of the day, her back and her arms were aching. She hoped she had the yellow fever like her Papa and Mama so she could leave this place, even if it meant she was dead.

For weeks she worked on the ceiling domes, painting every day. August was extremely hot; and since the heat rises, the dome area was even hotter. She always saw Father Bithowski staring up at her. His eyes seemed riveted to watching her every move. Didn't he know that she was working as hard as she could?

In the evenings, she would sit outside under one of the oak trees and work on the columns of the lectern. Hick Man had found four oak branches that were straight and about four feet long. She was sitting with her Papa's knife and carving them into a spiral. She planned to construct the lectern with the four columns on the corners, then paint the lectern to look like stone. She enjoyed working in the evening because it was cool and quiet. This also delayed the inevitable time when she had to go to her little room to toss and turn and try to sleep. Each night she took the columns into her room where she kept them until the next evening. When she looked at them, they made her feel close to her Papa, as if he were looking down from heaven on her.

One evening early in September, as she was climbing down from the scaffolding, the Father smiled at her and asked if he could massage her shoulders, knowing that she was achy from all the painting. His smile made Ruzi's skin crawl, and she answered, "No thank you." But the Father just grasped both of her shoulders and insisted on rubbing them. Then it turned more into caressing her shoulders. It alarmed Ruzi so much that she jerked away and ran to her room.

When the lady brought Ruzi her dinner, she told Ruzi that Father Bithowski wished to see her in his chamber office immediately. Ruzi was apprehensive to go to Father Bithowski alone, but she slipped out the front door of the church and walked to the parsonage next door. She was afraid of the Father and worried sick that he would tell her that her work did not satisfy him. When she knocked on his door, she was jittery, and her hands were sweaty.

Father Bithowski called out, "Come in, child." When she came into the dark room, it took her eyes a moment to adjust but she could see the Father sitting in an armchair with only a robe covering his portly body. His appearance alarmed her. She was sure from his leery scowl that he intended to harm her. He continued speaking, "Do you like your job here at the church?"

How could she answer, except to say, "Yes, sir."

He looked at her with those mean eyes and threatened, "You need to be more willing to take on challenges. Your work is exceptional; I can make you very successful. There are many churches in Texas that would welcome your talent if I just make it known that you are available to share your gifts. You are alone in this world and you will have to earn your keep until you can get some man to marry you. But for now, I can do things for you; in return, you can do things for me."

He terrified Ruzi. Now, she completely understood what the Father was saying and what he meant. She ran back across the grassy yard to her little room and shut the door. She took one of the lectern columns and propped it against the door. In her haste, she knocked over her dinner plate but no matter; she didn't feel hungry. What was she going to do? No one would believe her, and she had nowhere to go. She lay down on her bed and sobbed.

Finally, she must have gone to sleep, but was awakened by a pushing sound on her door. The column that she had used to prop against her door fell to the floor with a bang. Then she could see the large silhouette coming toward her. She crouched against the wall at the back of her bed, but she couldn't escape. Suddenly his hands were all over her, pulling at her clothes and squeezing her breasts. His words were slurred, but she could make out words she knew were sinful to say. A scream came up from her throat but was halted by his wine-tasting mouth covering hers. He smelled of tobacco and beef stew. She tried to scramble away from him, but he held her down. He ripped her trousers from her legs and slid his hands upward to her private parts. At that moment, she knew she could not escape and decided to endure the pain and the humiliation in order to live. She knew that if she fought him, he would kill her. As he was finishing his deed, she dropped her arm down beside the bed and she felt the wooden column. She grasped it tightly and, with all her might, she swung it as hard as she could, hitting him on the head. His eyes popped open as he stared at her and she swung the column a second time, again hitting him on his head. This time she heard a crack and knew she had broken his skull. He fell flat on top of her, dead. She broke loose from his weight and pushed him off, then grabbed her trousers and ran.

She raced out of the church, not knowing where she was headed, only that she had to escape. She darted between the trees in the churchyard and headed toward the forest. At first she ran, but then had to slow down to keep from falling. In the dark, she fell over and over. Each time scratching and bruising her hands and her knees. Finally, deep in the woods, she collapsed amid a flood of tears.

In desperation, gasping for breath and trying to halt the tears, she realized she must stop and determine what to do. She listened quietly to see if anyone had heard the scuffle. Were they looking for her even now? She had killed Father Bithowski! Would they find her and hang her? She was guilty of murder. Not knowing where she was or how far she had run, she could hear the hum of mosquitos and the croaking of frogs. In a tree somewhere close, she could hear a dove cooing. The forest noises were comforting. She realized that when morning came, she could recognize her location from the times that she and Hick Man had looked for plants for pigments. She found a flat area that had some cool grass and she lay down, falling asleep almost immediately. But her sleep was not peaceful; in her dreams, mad crowds of people, shouting, "Murderer, Murderer!" chased her.

Sunlight sprinkling through branches of oak trees awakened her fitful sleep. Sitting up, she realized she had not eaten since yesterday's breakfast. Her stomach was growling. Then, looking down at her arms and legs, she saw she was dirty with sticky, dried blood between her legs and her clothes were ripped. She could not go into any town nearby without someone knowing right away that she was guilty of something or that she was a runaway. As she sat listening, she could hear the babble of a little creek nearby, and she knew that the forest was full of berries that she could find to eat. Hick Man had shown her which berries were safe to eat and which ones were poisonous. Slowly, she made her way toward the creek.

The water in the creek was clear and cool, even though it would be a searing hot day. She drank water until she was no longer thirsty. Then she took off her blouse and trousers and washed herself in the creek. The trousers were torn in a few places but by brushing them off, she could probably pass without someone suspecting foul play. The blouse was a different story. It was torn down the front. She contemplated how to fix it and decided that she could rip her bloomers into strips of cloth and use those strips to lace up the front of the blouse. It did not look elegant, but it would have to do.

Now she had to find something to eat. Most of the berries that were available in the spring were now gone, but as she walked, she found a pecan tree. This year's pecans were not yet ready to drop, but there were plenty of last year's crop on the ground. She gathered a pile of pecans and sat down with a small rock to crack them open. Some had gone bad over the year, but most still had their meat inside the shells. The pecans satisfied her hunger. With all the emergencies out of the way, she had to decide what to do next about her predicament.

Questions swirled through her mind. Have they found his body? Would the nice lady who brought her a biscuit every morning find him? How soon would a sheriff be coming to arrest her for murder? Could she change her name and escape like an outlaw? She had heard of the notorious gang called Hottentot who roamed these woods. Maybe she could join them, since she was now an outlaw, too. Or maybe there were Indians, like Hick Man, and she could join their tribe. Probably not, because they would not trust someone with her blond hair. Whatever she would do, she had to decide soon.

Suddenly, she heard a rustle in the underbrush nearby. Wow, the sheriff and the posse are here much quicker than she thought possible. She hid behind the pecan tree and held her breath. Out of the grove of trees, stepped Hick Man. What a beautiful sight. He grinned at her and for the first time ever, he hugged her. She felt safe in his arms. Did he know what she had done?

Ruzi looked at Hick Man and said, "Have they found Father Bithowski's body? Do they know that I killed him?"

"No child, you did not kill him. I think he has a bad headache this morning, but he is not dead."

Feeling relieved that she was not a killer, she responded, "What did he say happened?"

"The Father is telling everyone that you are a thief. He is saying that he discovered you stealing the gold chalice used in the sacraments. And that when he surprised you, you hit him on the head with a wooden column."

"But that's not true."

"I know. I saw your room and I know what happened. I've been watching him for weeks. I knew he was up to no good."

"Oh, Hick Man, what am I going to do? No one will believe me. They will think I am a lying thief."

"I brought you some clothes from your room, but you will need to disappear. I'm afraid the sheriff will believe the Father, and he will put a bounty on your head. I have Indian friends who will care for you for a short time. Then we'll find a way for you to move away from here. It's the only way for you to be safe."

Chapter 9

As Kelly and Jessie pored over Kelly's computer searching references to Anton Bithowski in the ancestry website, Clay sat in his recliner watching the TV Land channel. They could hear the "Andy Griffith" show beginning. Clay was at peace watching these old TV shows. The more current shows seemed to disturb him, with all the violence and fast action.

There was very little about Anton Bithowski. It listed him on the 1870 census as living in a town called Cyril Hill, Texas. His occupation noted he was a priest and his age as 37. It listed his birthplace as Prague in the Kingdom of Bohemia. It did not list his parents' names or places of birth. However, in 1880, Anton Bithowski was nowhere listed in the census.

Jessie, looking up from her pad of paper stated the obvious, "If our dead man is Anton Bithowski, then he must have been murdered between 1870 and 1880. That fits the medical examiner's timeline. Do you know where Cyril Hill is?"

Kelly was already googling Cyril Hill, Texas and replied, "It's near Schulenburg and it's still an active town. Let's see if they've got a Catholic church in Cyril Hill."

With an instant answer, Google told them that, yes, Cyril Hill has a Catholic church.

"Maybe sometime, we should go on a road trip to Cyril Hill and see what we can find out about Anton Bithowski," said Jessie.

"I agree, maybe 'sometime' we should do that, just not today." And they both laughed.

Jessie stood up and stretched, yawning, "It's late, and I need to head home. Before I leave, do we want to email our new half-sister?"

"I guess so. What do you think we should say?"

"Just tell her we're very surprised about this report, and we would like a time to meet her in person to discuss the situation. Be sure you tell her we were not aware that either our mother or father had a child out of wedlock," Jessie said thoughtfully.

"OK," replied Kelly. "I'll send it right away. Be safe traveling home tonight."

When Kelly followed Jessie out, she came back by Clay's recliner. He was drowsy but was still watching TV Land. Now, "Bonanza" was playing, and it was probably Clay's favorite. Kelly told him she would write one email and then she would fix them some dinner. Clay looked at her as if he didn't know her but nodded his head in acknowledgement.

Kelly quickly finished and emailed the half-sister. She then sautéed some chicken and heated some green beans. Clay used to love green beans, though now he claims they taste like cardboard. So, she sprinkled a dab of sugar over the beans like the support people had suggested. Kelly thought he might be losing some of his taste buds, and the little bit of sweet might make them taste better.

In the middle of the night, the overhead light in their bedroom suddenly turned on. Kelly sat straight up in bed completely bewildered and alarmed. She looked toward the light switch and found Clay standing there. He was dressed in a pair of slacks that were buttoned but not zipped, wearing a different shoe on each foot and three shirts. She stared at him and asked, "What are you doing? It's the middle of the night."

Clay agitatedly said, "I've got to go to work. Where is my gun and my badge?"

Without thinking she responded, "No, it's the middle of the night. You need to come back to bed."

Clay became more agitated beginning to get angry at her. Realizing she needed to diffuse the situation, she softly said, "Clay, you worked all day yesterday, and you said that your deputies could handle it for the night. You need to get some rest before you have to go back to work tomorrow. Why don't you come back to bed and in the morning, you can go back to the sheriff's office?" As she was talking, she was moving toward Clay offering to help him put his pajamas back on.

Fortunately, he accepted her offer and was almost in bed when he said, "Lady, you need to leave in the morning before my wife gets home and finds you in our bed." Then he climbed in bed and went to sleep.

Kelly was distraught. Clay had never confused her for someone else. He sometimes got the names of the grandkids wrong or he didn't recognize someone from the town. This was different; he didn't recognize her as his wife. She lay there on her side of the bed and silently sobbed. She was losing him. Worse, there was nothing she could do about it.

The next morning, Jessie and Kathy came by to see if Kelly wanted to go with them to the bed-and-breakfast to meet with Lila about the layout for the Tasting Luncheon. They both looked at Kelly and said, "You look tired. What's wrong?"

"I just didn't sleep well last night." She wasn't ready yet to share Clay's situation with anyone. Kelly decided it was best if she stayed at home with Clay. When he woke up, he had absolutely no recall of the previous night's hullabaloo. He greeted Kelly with his normal kiss on the cheek and a smile.

They sat together and watched "I Love Lucy" and then the weather channel. Clay enjoyed the weather channel. It just repeated over and over the same stuff, which seemed just fine to Clay. He would comment that it looked like they would have rain. She would agree. Then as the station again ran the segment on the chance of rain. Clay would repeat his comment that it looked like they would have rain. Kelly sat quietly thinking, Alzheimer's is a cruel disease. You see your loved one's memory fading away, and there is absolutely nothing you can do about it. But then she thought, yes, there is something I can do! I can love him and make sure he knows he is loved and safe.

Carol brought them some of today's special from the Wildflower Café for lunch, King Ranch Casserole and Strawberry Cake. She knew it was her father's favorite. Clay's face always lit up when Carol came by. He enjoyed listening to her talk about her children. Turner, the oldest, was now playing baseball and Kenzie, her daughter, had taken ballet lessons. She showed Clay some photos of the grandchildren on her phone and he looked at them and smiled.

After lunch, Clay took a nap and Kelly checked her emails. There was an email from Brenda Hall, the half-sister. She told Kelly a little about herself, that she lived in Austin, Texas, and her parents adopted her as a baby. She would really like to meet Kelly and Jessie and invited them to come to lunch at her home soon.

A few moments later, Kelly heard a car pull up in her driveway. It was Jessie. She was coming back by to just check on her sister. It worried her that Kelly looked tired lately. She wasn't sure what was going on, but suspected it had to do with Clay's behavior because of his Alzheimer's.

Jessie came in to find Kelly pondering over the email from Brenda Hall. Kelly allowed Jessie to read the email. "So, let's take her up on this lunch. I want to see for myself if she's authentic or if this is some kind scam," Suggested Jessie.

Together they called Brenda Hall. A pleasant voice answered and seemed thrilled by their call. She again invited them to lunch, and they accepted. She told them she lived on Wathen Avenue, just west of the University of Texas campus. Kelly told her she was familiar with Austin, since she lived there at one time, although that was nearly fifty years ago.

As the luncheon day approached, Jessie coaxed Tom into staying with Clay, so that Kelly would not be concerned about him. Tom was more than happy to do it but did not intend to sit all day and watch TV. He started planning things that he and Clay could do together.

The morning of the trip to Austin, Tom came early with Jessie. He brought apple fritters for him and Clay to have with their coffee. After breakfast, they headed to the ranch to ride the four-wheeler and look for mama cows that had recently calved. Tom knew exactly where they were; but since he needed to check on them anyway, he made the trip fun for Clay pretending to search for the cows. Clay was as excited as a little boy going on his first camping trip.

Jessie and Kelly left for Austin, not knowing what to expect. They headed up interstate 35 through New Braunfels and San Marcos. Coming into Austin from the south, they crossed the bridge over the Colorado River. It had been many years since Kelly had been to Austin, but she gazed out at the river remembering times that she and Clay had shared at Zilker Park, along the south side of the river. They turned onto 19th street, now renamed Martin Luther King Boulevard. Heading west along the south side of the University of Texas, they passed the Bob Bullock Texas Historical Museum on the left, then she unexpectedly asked Jessie to pull over in front of the AT&T Hotel Center. They parked and got out of the car. Kelly had attended four years at the university, but Jessie had never gone. She tried to imagine what her sister was thinking.

As Kelly gazed back at the Texas State Capitol to the south and then turned toward the University Tower, she was reminded of her summer of 1966. She spoke to no one in particular, "I remember that August day in 1966 as if it were yesterday. It was one of the worst days of my life. I was here for band orientation before fall classes started. I was walking across the south mall in front of the tower when suddenly the sniper started shooting from the tower. There was nowhere to go and nowhere to hide. He hit me in the shoulder, and it left me lying in the open, waiting to be shot again. Then a handsome young UT football player risked his life to run out into the open and pull me behind a stone column. I don't remember too much more except that when the shooting stopped, he carried me from the tower plaza down to the next street where ambulances were picking up the wounded. Later that night, I found out his name was Clay. That night they decided they had to operate on my shoulder, which destroyed my scholarship as the feature baton twirler for the UT band. I was heartbroken. It shattered my dreams. But I fell in love with Clay that day and I've loved him ever since."

Tears were streaming down Kelly's face. Jessie wrapped her arm around her shoulders and whispered, "He's always been that hero you fell in love with and he always will be." Knowing no mere words could suffice, she urged a diversion. "Let's go on to Brenda's house." Kelly nodded, and they got back in the car.

Their GPS took them across Guadalupe Street, "the drag" as Kelly remembered it, down to Shoal Creek and then wound through west campus to Wathem Avenue. Brenda's home was beautiful. It was an older two-story, red brick home with vines growing up one side. The lawn was immaculately manicured with small groups of roses and azaleas clustered under very old, tall, gnarly, spreading oak trees.

When Brenda opened the door, it left them almost speechless. She looked exactly like their mother, Wendy Burnett Moniac. Kelly and Jessie both resembled their father. Their father Hayden's ethic mixture of Native American, Mexican, and German had given him a dark complexion and dark hair. But their mother had been tall and slim with long, beautiful blond hair. She had often reminded them she held a former Miss Dallas County, Miss Fort Worth Stockyards, and other beauty pageant titles.

The lady in front of them was a mirror image of their mother as she had grown older. The blond hair, now more a soft gray, was pulled back at the nape of her neck, and was cascading down her back in a single plait. Her face was a chiseled beauty with high cheekbones and narrow nose. She greeted them graciously, but her smile betrayed some misgivings about their meeting.

They joined her in her very formal living room, which was absolutely covered in photos, presumably of family, but which actually looked more like a collage of children from the United Nations. She saw their curious stares and laughed, "Yes, they are all our children. Quite a mix don't you think?"

Her husband joined them and introduced himself as Kenneth Hall. He was a neatly dressed man of about 75 or 80. It was difficult to determine because he was tan and slim, like he played tennis or golf every day.

Brenda offered them iced tea and then jumped right to the topic of the day – how were they kin to each other? Kelly approached the subject. "If I had to guess and if the DNA is correct, then I would say that we share the same mother. You look almost exactly like our mother when she was older."

Brenda told them, "All I know of my birth mother is what little information they gave to my adopted mother when I was adopted from the Buckner Baptist Children's Home, which is east of Dallas. They told her I was the daughter of a young girl from the Dallas area, but nothing more than that. I was born in 1939."

Jessie replied, "That all makes sense because our mother was born and grew up in Dallas. We know she was born in 1926. But that would have made her only thirteen years old when she gave birth to you. She was from a very prominent family is Dallas and I can't see her getting pregnant at thirteen."

"But there is another possibility! Our mother was a very vain person in some ways, and she may have lied about her age. Really, none of us ever saw her birth certificate! Our father was born in 1917. She may have wanted to appear younger than she really was, or maybe she wanted to avoid explaining some extra years in her life. If she was actually born in 1917 to 1922, then a birth in 1939 could easily have happened," considered Kelly aloud.

Jessie responded, "I think it is easy to conclude, that you are our half-sister and that our mother for whatever reason gave up her baby, you, when you were born."

"Can you tell me something about your mother, my birth mother?" urged Brenda. "You can't believe how much I've waited for this moment in my life. My adoptive parents were the best parents a person could have, but I've always wondered about my birth parents."

Kelly spoke first. "Our Mother's name was Wendy Burnett. She was the daughter of Jackson and Deloris Burnett of Dallas. Our grandfather, Jackson, was an oilman. He was a bigger-than-life Texas guy. He was more on the financial and banking side of oil. I guess you'd call him an oil and gas speculator. Deloris was a socialite, but she died before Wendy married our father, Hayden Moniac, so we never met her."

"Wendy married Hayden on December 6, 1941 in Dallas. Before that, we know she graduated from SMU and she was the President of her sorority Delta, Delta, Delta. She often told us about her many beauty pageants where she won the titles of Miss Dallas County, Miss Fort Worth Stockyards, and Miss Parker County Peach Blossom Queen. Her father, Jackson Burnett, called her his little peach blossom as long as I can remember," continued Kelly.

"We brought a photo of her and thought you might like to see it," said Jessie.

"Was she a happy person? Did she have any medical problems?" inquired Brenda.

"Our father was from several generations of a family who ranched. Wendy never liked the ranching life. After they married and moved to Gristmill, which at that time was a small ranching and oil town, they built a beautiful home that our mother designed and decorated. As a matter of fact, we grew up in that house and I still live there. We now realize that our mother was bi-polar. In that day, it was just called depression. There were days that she was euphoric and excited about everything, and then the next day she would become sullen and would hide in her room. Our grandmother probably did more to raise us than our mother. We remember our grandmother taking our mother to San Antonio to the doctor for her 'sadness,' but we were not old enough at the time to understand. Our mother was always withdrawn. She didn't take part in many family events and seldom supported either of us in what we did at school or college. During her later years, she mostly spent her days in solitary. Even when our children, her grandchildren, were born, she showed very little interest in them."

Kelly continued, "I hate to speak ill of our mother, but you asked, and I feel that I should be honest with you."

Brenda nodded. "That explains a few things. I was never diagnosed as bi-polar, but I've suffered from depression all my life. I take medication for it, and it makes life much better. Sounds like it is probably hereditary."

"On a happier note, tell me about yourselves," Brenda inquired.

Jessie and Kelly told her about life in Gristmill and about their children and grandchildren.

Brenda then shared a little about her life. "As I said, my parents adopted me when I was a baby. They were Baptist missionaries, and I grew up mostly in Taiwan where they were stationed. I returned home to attend the University of Texas in 1957, where I met Kenneth as a freshman. I was studying education, and he was studying electrical engineering. When we graduated, Kenneth went to work for Texas Instruments. I taught English at Austin High School. Then Kenneth went back to UT to get his graduate degree in 1968 in Computer Science. He and a friend started a company called Austin Business Data."

"That's fascinating," said Kelly. "Do you still own that company?"

Kenneth, Brenda's husband, who had been listening to the conversation, then continued the story, "We became the local distributor of Data General Computers. This was in 1970, long before PCs were available. We started by selling DG Nova minicomputers. The software that Data General offered was very expensive, so we started writing business software for our customers. The State of Texas was in a frenzy to become computerized, so we were putting computers in almost every department. However, we had one small client called Scandinavian Imports. They purchased a DG computer, and we provided their custom software. But then they decided they needed to have a way to easily convert US currency to Scandinavian currency and vice versa. It was no problem to write a program to do this calculation. Then it occurred to us that other businesses might have the same problem and need this same calculation. We expanded the program and provided it to many different companies for their currency exchange for whatever currency they did business. We were growing and sending off the daily currency rates by wire, which was transcribed to paper tape to upload on our customers' computers. It was a huge hassle. Compared to the way we do things now with the Internet, it was a nightmare. Then one day a huge company that managed all the airline reservations in almost the entire world showed up at our door. They needed our currency conversion software, and they were willing to pay well for it. We gladly sold them the software and our copyrights and suddenly we were wealthy. It was a heady time in Austin in the 1970s, lots of people were doing things on the cutting edge of technology. It was exciting."

Brenda interrupted Kenneth, "All during that time, we were trying to get pregnant. And after four miscarriages, we gave up, but we still desperately wanted children. My parents pushed us to adopt, since they had adopted me. We adopted our first son, Marcos, through the Texas Baptist Children's Home in Round Rock. He was this perfect little boy."

Jessie spoke up, "OK, but who are all these other children?"

Brenda winked at Kenneth who smiled back at her as she started to explain, "One day my father called and said there was a pastor in Taiwan who was a friend of his. Someone had left a little girl at his church. She had severe eye problems and, if they turned her over to the Taiwanese state children's department, she would probably be euthanized or live a terrible life where no one wanted her. My parents were sick about this, and they begged us to consider adopting this little girl. The Texas Baptist Children's Home handled all the legal entanglements for the adoption, and that's when Lin Li came to live with us."

"We began to research orphaned children in the United States and around the world. Our hearts were just torn by the number of neglected children. But at the same time, the world was jumping on the abortion band wagon. We were against abortion, but we felt that we couldn't be pro life without doing our part to offer a home to some of the children whose mothers chose life over abortion."

"At about this time when Kenneth sold his business and our lifestyle changed, we no longer needed to work. So, we've dedicated our life to doing what we can to help orphaned children. We're now on the board at the Texas Baptist Children's Home. A few years later, we adopted Denise. Her mother was a drug addict, and she was born as a baby addicted to heroin. Her mother was in prison when she was born, and the State of Texas removed her from her mother's custody. Then we adopted Hector, a little Hispanic boy, who was born with all sorts of physical special needs."

"Then in 1994, when we were both fifty-five, we adopted our twin sons, Douglas and Daniel. They were both born with Down syndrome. Their single mother had no way of providing the care they needed. She left the hospital without them and had given a false name when she had arrived, so the hospital had no way to find her. Normally, a couple aged 55 would not have been allowed to adopt any child, much less twins, but the children's home knew us and they knew that they would not be able to care for these boys and that no one would come knocking at their door asking to adopt two Downs children."

Kenneth chimed in, "Doug and Danny are now 25 and they are the sweetest two boys you've ever met. They and Hector live in our guest house behind our home which provides the three of them some independence, but still a space close to mom and dad. So, that's the way we came about our mixed family."

Brenda and Kenneth laughed as she commented, "We love to take family photos because people always look in amazement at our mixed group. But, enough talk, let's eat lunch and I want to know so much more about your families and what you do."

Brenda had prepared a nice lunch of shrimp salad and avocados followed by a lemon sorbet. Brenda and Kenneth asked lots of questions about the ranching operation and seemed genuinely interested in their lives. One thing was clear: they were passionate about their stances on pro-life, adoption, and foster care.

Brenda hopped onto her soap box with, "We, as Christians, cannot ask women to not seek abortions if we don't accompany them along their journey making sure they have access to health care, vocational opportunities, consistent housing, family planning resources and counseling. We cannot in good conscience shout pro life and then ignore the crisis of the children who are not aborted."

"I'm sorry for going on and on. This situation just disturbs me greatly as I see churches insisting on promoting pro life and then ignoring the women who don't get abortions and ignoring the children in orphanages."

About that time, the back door swung open and banged closed. Three young men traipsed in, bumping and shuffling each other. They each had a backpack that they carelessly dropped on the sofa as Brenda jokingly scolded them not to leave their stuff sitting around. Obviously from the photos, this was Hector, Doug and Danny. Brenda made introductions around the room and the young men headed to the kitchen to find more to eat than a shrimp salad. Kelly and Jessie could hear them joking and clowning around. The boys gathered their food and sodas and were gone out the back door.

Brenda said, "It must be after 3, they ride the bus home from their jobs when they get off work. We try to give them some freedom and independence. But it is very hard. I fear for their safety all the time."

Jessie and Kelly could not believe how the time had flown by. They expressed to Brenda and Kenneth that they had thoroughly enjoyed the visit and then insisted that Brenda and Kenneth and their children and grandchildren should come for Easter weekend to visit them. They explained that the Saturday afternoon before Easter was their traditional family picnic, and they wanted to introduce Brenda's family to their extended family.

Brenda hugged them goodbye and said she was so glad to finally meet her birth family.

As Jessie and Kelly headed back to Gristmill, they felt a warm glow replacing the apprehension that this may have been a scam. Kelly said, "Brenda is truly a kind person. I wish our mother had gotten the chance to know her. I wonder if Mother's depression somehow stemmed from the guilt of giving her up at birth. But Brenda is a survivor, and she has taken something that was tragic and sad, and turned it into something wonderful by giving life to others."

Jessie said, "Yeah, I hope they come for Easter."

When they pulled into the drive at Kelly's home, Tom and Clay were just getting home. They had been to Turner's little league baseball game. Clay looked happy and tired, so Kelly hoped they would both have a good night's sleep.

The next day Diane called and told Jessie that she and Stacy were bringing Melissa from the rehab facility to El Asilo. Jessie called Kelly, Kathy, and Sister Elizabeth. Kelly decided that Clay could go with her since he was comfortable at Jessie's home, and he could sit on the patio and enjoy some sunshine. They all arrived and were waiting on Diane.

When she arrived, she introduced them to Melissa. The girl looked too young to have been involved in trafficking and to have had a pregnancy. She was sullen and gloomy. Her eyes seemed to be riveted to the ground showing no interest in the conversations going on around her. She carried herself shoulders bent over, looking scared, lost and intimidated. Lupe directed her to one of the apartment rooms, which was decorated pleasantly with spring flowers. Melissa's only belongings fit into her small backpack. She set it on the floor, then lay down on the bed turning away from Lupe to face the wall. She pulled her legs up toward her chest.

Lupe chatted, expressing how happy she was that Melissa had arrived, describing the dinner that she was preparing, and asking her what she liked to eat, but Melissa responded with a shrug.

Finally, Lupe left her alone to nap.

Jessie had made sandwiches for the women and Clay. They all sat on the patio eating lunch as Stacy went into her psychiatric evaluation. "Melissa is no longer taking illegal drugs, but she has not responded very well to counseling. Her mind has shut out the world as a mechanism to protect itself. She doesn't want to feel anything, because it may cause her more pain. It is much like the battered-wife syndrome, where a woman has been told over and over that she is not worth anything until she finally believes it. They have destroyed Melissa's self-image. We know nothing about her past, so we don't know if this started when she was kidnapped by the traffickers or if someone abused her as a young child. If you can get her to talk to you, make a note of anything about her past, it will help us figure out what her future will look like."

"That poor child," said Lupe. "She needs a lot of love and the time to heal."

Diane added, "It's important that she feels safe. The traffickers abandoned her after they tried to overdose her. But she could still feel some bond with them. We just don't know."

"Well, she's definitely safe here; and we can give her love and time," responded Jessie.

"And we all know Lupe's cooking can help heal anyone," complimented Diane.

Stacy reminded them of the signs they should watch for if Melissa were relapsing. Then, leaving Jessie, Lupe and Sister Elizabeth to sit watch over Melissa on her first evening at El Asilo, the rest left, knowing that the girl didn't need to be overwhelmed with too many people.

Time would tell.

Chapter 10

October 1869 to 1870

True to his word, Hick Man took Ruzi to his tribe's camp. His son and daughter-in-law agreed to take care of Ruzi for a while.

Hick Man left Ruzi saying, "Stay here, child. My son and his wife will care for you. When I find a place for you to go, then I'll come back for you. For now, just rest and be patient."

Ruzi was content with Hick Man's family. She helped wherever she could, and she helped to care for the children in the camp. She didn't understand their language and only a few spoke broken English, but she felt that she was in no danger and that she was safe, especially from the law. Days and then weeks went by. Ruzi was learning the Indian language, and she had converted to wearing Indian attire. The only thing that gave away her ethnicity was her blond hair and big brown eyes. She often took some red brown clay and mixed it with water to wash into her hair so that the blond hair was not so obvious. One old Indian woman came to her with an animal skin cap and gave it to her, motioning that she could use it to cover her hair.

Ruzi still missed her family desperately, but she was determined to survive. She was lonely because no one in the tribe would befriend her – yet being alone was a small price to pay for her safety.

At night, she often wondered what became of Father Bithowski. Was he still the priest at Cyril Hill? Did he take the golden chalice?

She wished she had been able to bring her mother's quilt and her doll, but most of all she wished she had her sketchbook. There was nothing like it available in the Indian camp.

Finally, after a year, Hick Man came back to the camp riding a large horse. He was dressed as a cattle herder and the sun had tanned his skin to a dark leather. Ruzi did not understand where Hick Man had been or what he had been doing. She had almost given up hope and thought he had forgotten her. He told Ruzi, "I have found a wagon train headed west. They plan to travel south of San Antonio and then turn north on the west side of San Antonio to go to a small town called Castell. The immigrants are German and one family, the Groesbeck family, have agreed to take you with them in their wagon." Ruzi thought, "This must cost money!" She realized the only explanation was that Hick Man had been working at hard labor for this past year to raise the money to pay for her escape; his sacrifice overwhelmed her. She owed him a great debt of gratitude.

"You can go all the way to Castell with them, or you can stop at a town on the way called Gristmill. I have learned that Gristmill has a place called an 'orphanage.' I do not know what an orphanage means, but they have told me that children with no parents can go there to live. It is owned by the Catholic church. I think this would be the best place for you. I do not know what would happen to you in Castell. There may be people there who would harm you, but I think in this place called orphanage, you will be safe."

Ruzi listened intently and then replied, "You're right, Hick Man. I must find my destiny now that my parents are dead. And I realize that I will always be vulnerable to evil people. I don't know if I trust the Catholic Church after Father Bithowski, but I'm probably safer there than anywhere else. By now, maybe everyone has forgotten about what they say I did."

Hick Man squatted down to the ground and with a stick he drew a map of Cyril Hill, the Indian camp, the place called Schulenburg, and the place called Gristmill. He said that he and Ruzi would leave early the next morning and he would take her to Schulenburg, where she would join the Groesbeck family in their wagon.

Hick Man told Ruzi, "The wagon train will certainly stop at Gristmill, because there is a general store there where wagon trains can get supplies and there is an area where they can camp. Once they make camp and everyone is asleep, slip out during the night and make your way into the town and hide. The next day you can find your way to this place 'orphanage.'"

They discussed that Ruzi should tell no one her real name, but they should make up a name that she would use. Ruzi had no idea what her new name should be. Hick Man said, "Ruzi, your Papa always called you Ruzi Honey. Maybe Honey could be your name. Honey is good like you, the sweet from a bee."

Ruzi liked that because it would always remind her of her Papa. But she had no suggestions for a last name. Then she said, "My last name can be Hick Man, but in one word, Hickman."

Hick Man laughed but said that someone could recognize that she had always called him Hick Man. Not a big risk, but she couldn't take any chances. Together they decided that her last name would be Hickson, close to Hick Man, but just a little different.

Ruzi said it several times, "Honey Hickson, Honey Hickson." She liked the way it sounded, and it would always remind her of her Papa and her Hick Man.

They left the Indian camp just as the sun was rising, heading toward Schulenburg. Ruzi rode behind Hick Man on the back of his horse. Ruzi had been to Schulenburg several times with her Papa so she was familiar with many of the buildings. On the outskirts of the town they found the Groesbecks and the wagon train. Mr. and Mrs. Groesbeck were pleasant people. Ruzi could tell they had lived through hard times and were looking for a new life in Texas. She could hear the hope in their voices. They greeted Hick Man with smiles and shaking of the hands. Hick Man introduced Ruzi as Honey Hickson. They confirmed her suspicions that Hick Man had paid them money for her travel passage. The Groesbecks had two small children, and Ruzi agreed to help take care of them on the journey. Soon after releasing Ruzi to the Groesbecks, Hick Man gave Ruzi a quick hug. Hugging him back as tightly as she could, she heard him whisper, "Remember you are now Honey Hickson and you will define your destiny."

Traveling with the Groesbecks was pleasant enough. Mrs. Groesbeck chatted constantly about her children, their home left behind in Germany, her cooking and her ailments. Mr. Groesbeck whistled while he drove the wagon and, in the evenings, he talked with the other men as they made plans for the next day's journey. Mrs. Groesbeck gave Honey a bonnet saying that women should keep their heads covered but not with an animal skin cap. Honey didn't agree with that, but the bonnet would better cover her blond hair in case some sheriff was looking for her, so she happily accepted it.

When they stopped in New Braunfels, Honey looked around the town. She had heard stories from her Mama and her Papa and how they started the town along with Prince Carl before the man, Meusebach, fired her Papa and left them stranded. She resented the whole town, although she knew that most of the people in New Braunfels didn't even know her parents.

While she was waiting to draw water from the springs to carry back to the wagon, she overheard some young women gossiping. One of them told a story of a 14-year-old girl in Cyril Hill who had beaten up the priest and stolen a golden chalice. They all agreed that she must be a hellion because even a rowdy child would never beat up a priest. As the women walked away, one of them commented that she hoped the sheriff would find the girl and put her in prison. Even after a year, her story was still being talked about as scandalous news! From that point forward, Honey was extremely careful to wear the bonnet, and she even put some reddish-brown dirt in her hair so it would not be blond. She must be careful!

After a week of bouncing along in the wagon, they reached the town of Gristmill. It was a nice town located near the river. The cypress trees hung out over the water, providing a nice shade, and the river was clear. The Groesbecks made camp near the river's edge where the water was cool and their horses could drink. Mr. and Mrs. Groesbeck walked into the center of town to the general store for supplies, leaving their children with Honey. When they returned, Mrs. Groesbeck was excited about the things she found to purchase, such as the sausage, bags of ground corn, and buckets of honey. That night for dinner, Mrs. Groesbeck made corn cakes and sausage. They all poured some honey over the corncakes. Honey was so full that when they went to bed, she almost fell asleep. But she had a mission to accomplish.

When everyone was sound asleep, Honey very carefully eased out of her pallet and rolled it up. She tiptoed out of the campsite and followed the path she had seen the Groesbecks take into the town. Fortunately, there was a full moon and she could see where she was walking, but she had no clue where she should hide out.

On the north end of town, she saw a barn. That seemed like a good choice for a hiding place.

The barn was bigger than she realized from first glance. Inside there were cow stalls and horse stalls. At the end of the barn was a haystack. Perfect! I can sleep there until morning. She put her pallet down on the back side of the haystack so that, in case someone came into the barn, they would not see her immediately. No sooner had she laid her head down than she was asleep.

Early the next morning, she heard the wagon train scrambling to get organized and to get on its way. She waited, thinking one of the Groesbecks would come looking for her, but they never did. They were probably glad to be gone without her. They had their money from Hick Man and now they were released from caring for her.

Peeking out from the side of the barn, she could see the wagon train rolling out of town. She was now completely alone. No family, no Hick Man, no Indian tribe and no Groesbecks. She thought, it is now all up to me!

No sooner than that thought crossed through her mind, then the big barn doors swung open. A big man stood in the doorway looking around. Could he tell that someone was in the barn? She didn't think so; she had not moved a thing. But he stood there looking around. With a few big strides he moved across the barn past the cows and past the horses to the haystack where he shouted, "Whoever is in here, show yourself."

He terrified Honey. What if this man was like the Father? What if he was a mean evil person? What if he would turn her in to the sheriff? However, she had no choice but to step into the light with her hands held up.

The man eyed her up and down. He looked a lot like Hick Man. He looked like an Indian, but he dressed like a white man and he spoke like a white man. Finally, he said, "Who are you?"

In a whisper, almost too quiet to hear, she almost said Ruzi but then remembered and said, "I'm Honey Hickson."

"And why are you in my barn?"

Honey had not expected that question. How should she answer? "Uh, I needed a place to sleep."

"Well, I think I need a little more of an answer than that. Do you have parents?"

"No sir, they died of the yellow fever."

"Okay, how did you get here?"

"I traveled with the wagon train that arrived yesterday. But someone told me that Gristmill has an orphanage for people like me that do not have parents or a home."

The man chuckled. "Well, this is a new one for the books. I don't think we've ever had a child come to join the orphanage. Usually it is the church or the sheriff bringing the children here."

"To answer your question, yes we have an orphanage. As a matter of fact, my niece is Sister Carlita, and she manages the orphanage. But first, let's take you to my home and my wife can get you some food and some clean clothes."

The man motioned for her to come on out from behind the haystack. He continued talking, "You are obviously not Indian yet you're wearing Indian clothes."

Honey laughed at him and said, "You are obviously Indian, and yet you're not wearing Indian clothes."

"You got me there. My name is Caleb Moniac. Maybe you have a story that you can tell us about where you are from. So, come with me and let's go find you some food and clean clothes."

As Honey got into the man's farm wagon, she thought, "The food and clothes sound fine, but I will not be telling you my story. I will never tell anyone my story!"

When they reached the log house next to the gristmill, Caleb Moniac helped her down from the wagon and then opened the front door of the house for her. He was very friendly and seemed to be nice. Inside, he introduced Honey to his wife, Elsa.

Elsa was making bread. In many ways, she reminded Honey of her mother. A pang of sadness washed over Honey as Elsa greeted her. Elsa told Honey to sit down at the table and she would get some breakfast rolls and some milk for her to eat. After eating the Indian food for a year and then the wagon train food, this was a meal made in heaven!

When Honey had finished eating, Elsa asked her lots of questions about her family. Honey was as vague as possible, only explaining that her parents and whole family died of yellow fever about a year earlier and that some Indians took her in where she had lived until a week ago when she joined the wagon train. Elsa could tell that was not the whole story, but decided it was best not to press for more at this time.

Elsa asked, "How did you find out about the orphanage?"

Again, Honey was ambiguous with her answer saying only that a friend had told her about it.

"After you have time to bathe and clean up, I will take you to the orphanage to see if you might want to live there," Elsa stated, assuring Honey everything would be all right.

Elsa heated water to go in the large tub which was off to the side of the kitchen. Then she brought a bar of sweet-smelling soap and a towel for Honey. It had been over a year since Honey had had a real bath. She sank down in the tub, putting her whole head under the water. She scrubbed her skin so hard that it left red marks. She just wanted to be clean.

When she got out, she dried off and wrapped the towel around herself. Elsa then brought in a blue dress. Honey had almost never worn dresses. Elsa had also brought bloomers for her. Honey had not worn bloomers in over a year. She had worn trousers when she worked with her Papa and then she wore a leather shift that the Indians gave her. The dress felt different, but she felt elegant in it. Elsa handed her a hairbrush to use on her hair. The tangles in her hair were unmanageable. It had probably been a year since she had brushed her hair, but Elsa helped her and finally the tangles loosened.

Elsa stepped back and said, "You need some shoes and stockings to complete your dress." Elsa produced a pair of black lace-up boots and a pair of wool stockings. At last, they were finished, and Elsa took her hand and brought her in front of a mirror. Honey had not seen herself in a mirror since her mother died more than a year ago. She had grown from a fourteen-and-a half-year-old girl to a sixteen-year-old young woman with hips and small breasts. Honey's gasp was audible. Elsa admired her. "You look beautiful!"

Suddenly, the front door swung open and a young man walked in. He was handsome and smiling at her. His smile looked almost like he was teasing but his eyes carried a sincerity that was compassionate and kind. He looked at Honey and agreed with his mother. "Yes, you do look beautiful, whoever you are!" Then he laughed and asked, "And who are you?"

Elsa shushed him and said, "Gebhardt, don't be rude. This is our guest. Her name is Honey Hickson. She will live at the orphanage."

"Well, Honey Hickson, welcome to Gristmill! I look forward to getting to know you."

Honey thought, "If this is Gristmill, then I think I'm going to love it here." Caleb, Elsa and Gebhardt escorted Honey to the orphanage. Gebhardt couldn't take his eyes off Honey. He was gallant and shy at the same time. He would rush to open the door for her, and then when she would thank him, he would blush. She thought he was adorable.

When they reached the orphanage, Sister Carlita met them. Almost immediately Honey liked Sister Carlita. They talked again about her family and what happened. Honey again explained that they died of the yellow fever, but she never told them they lived in Cyril Hill. She told them they had come from Kentucky, but then made their home in Schulenburg. Honey thought she could fake answers about Schulenburg, because she had been there several times. She prayed that God would forgive her for lying. And she had to remember her story, so she would not get it mixed up if she ever had to repeat it later.

Sister Carlita explained that she could live at the orphanage, but that everyone in the home had to help with the garden, the cleaning, and she would need to attend school. The orphanage was self-sufficient, meaning that they either raised or hunted for their own food. They made their clothes, and they all helped with the chores. Sister Carlita expressed some concern that Honey was older than most of the children, but she thought it would be manageable.

They assigned Honey to a room with two fourteen-year-old girls. She was delighted with her room. It had a nice bed and windows that faced out over the garden. A cool fall breeze blew through the window as Honey sat on the edge of the bed. And for the first time in over a year, Honey felt safe and at home.

Chapter 11

"I think our mother was born in 1922, not 1926. I looked on the ancestry website and I found her birth certificate that has 1922 as the year, not 1926. When I created our family tree, I used the date on her tombstone, which is 1926. Her death certificate says 1926, but I'm guessing that's wrong. She always wrote 1926, not 1922, so no one ever questioned it," informed Kelly to Jessie and Clay. They were all sitting around the kitchen table talking about their recent trip to Austin.

"Why do you think she would do that?" asked Jessie.

"Maybe because she didn't want anyone asking what she did for a couple of those years, because she would have to explain that she left to have a baby. And since she competed in all those beauty pageants, she may have wanted to appear younger than she really was. But for whatever reason, she was very successful at keeping the secret. With her mother already dead and her father too busy to care about such things, my guess is that once she fabricated the lie, it was easy to continue with it."

Clay mumbled, "Or maybe she was just vain."

They all laughed. Clay was probably closer to the truth than the logical conclusions.

Jessie mused, "I can't imagine how hard it must have been for Brenda to go her whole life not knowing who her real mother was."

"Wait, her real mother was her adopted mother. Wendy, our mother, was only her birth mother," interrupted Kelly.

"I know, but how hard to accept that your birth mother gave you up for adoption. It seems that would leave a hole in your heart, making you wonder why you were not good enough for her to love," said Jessie sadly.

"Fortunately, wonderful people who loved her and gave her a good home adopted Brenda. I agree there was probably always that nagging question at the back of her mind: who am I?"

Kelly's cell phone rang. "Can you come over for a few minutes?" asked Kathy. "I want to show you the carousel horses."

They all grabbed their sweaters and headed across the street to Kathy's house. Clay appeared to be happy to be included in the adventure. Kathy met them at the door of the workshop. Inside, she had lined up the horses along the wall. She had finished sanding and re-painting them. Kelly exclaimed, "They are absolutely magnificent!"

Jessie, rubbing her hand over the smooth finish and peering into the eyes of the black horse, exclaimed, "They look almost real, especially their eyes!"

Kathy responded, "I continue to be amazed that the original work was so good. Assuming that your great-great grandmother, Honey Moniac, carved and painted these in about 1880, she was remarkable because the paints were not as good as now and the carving and sanding tools were no comparison to the ones I use today."

They all just stood there, admiring the beautiful horses.

Kathy asked, "What do you plan to do with them, now that I've refurbished them?"

Kelly and Jessie just looked at each other. "We don't know. Actually, we haven't given it much thought. I don't think either of us has a house large enough to display them. But we can't leave them out in the weather."

"May I offer a solution? You know that Sherry and Lance have bought the Antique Shop, and they are busy getting ready for their Grand Re-opening this weekend at the Texas Independence Day Celebration. There's plenty of room to display them in the shop. With the tall ceilings, the horses will fit in without overpowering everything else. They would not be for sale, but people could enjoy them while visiting the shop. They might also attract attention if people see them through the windows. Of course, this would only be temporary until you decide what you wish to do with them."

Kelly exclaimed, "That's a great idea!" She couldn't imagine trying to bring the horses back to her house. They had built her home in the fifties, with low ceilings and only moderate size rooms. Each horse was larger than any piece of furniture she owned. What a disaster that would be.

Thinking along the same line, Jessie said, "Oh Kathy, that would be great. I'll get Clint and Casey to come by after school tomorrow, and they can haul them to the Antique Shop for Sherry."

"Have you been downtown?" asked Kathy. "The Texas Independence Day committee has really gone over the top to convince all the merchants to decorate with Texas red, white and blue fabric draped across the fronts of the stores. They are also placing Texas flags on every corner. Someone told me they have restored the old cannon in front of the General Store and it is ready to fire on Saturday morning."

"From what I hear through Clint and Casey, there will be a big parade on Saturday. They'll ride their horses, along with Tom, Claude, and Russell. The high school band will march in the parade, and there'll be some floats. But the big event is the re-enactment of the Alamo in front of the General Store. The industrial arts class at school has built a wooden replica of the Alamo and lots of the kids are having costumes made to be Texans like William Travis and Davy Crockett, and others are dressing like Santa Anna's army," explained Jessie.

"It's a shame that we won't get to see any of it, since we will be working at the Tasting Luncheon. That reminds me, I need to go to the supermarket and purchase all my supplies to make my dishes," declared Jessie.

"If I plan to make the Texas Independence Day cake, then I better get started cutting out the fondant stars, so they'll have time to dry," voiced Kelly.

Then as they turned to leave, Clay asked, "Where's Joe?"

It embarrassed Kelly and Jessie that Clay asked where Kathy's deceased husband was. But Kathy quickly answered him, "Oh, he's not here right now." Thankfully, Clay accepted her answer with no more questions.

They waved goodbye to Kathy. As they reached Kelly's driveway, they said their good-byes and Jessie got into her car to head home.

Back in the kitchen, Kelly asked Clay, "Do you want to help me make the stars for my cake? They need to be glittered after I cut them out." Clay seemed eager to help. Then he again asked, "Where is Joe?" Kelly couldn't tell him that Joe had died, so she used Kathy's answer, "He's not home right now." Clay seemed troubled by that answer but said no more.

Kelly kept an old jam box in the kitchen that played CDs. She put on an album by Willie Nelson. The first song was Waltz Across Texas. It had always been one of Clay's favorite melodies, and it seemed to soothe his anxieties. When they finished the stars, Clay headed for his recliner and Kelly turned on the TV to watch another re-run of "Bonanza." She was sure Clay would be asleep in a few minutes.

Kelly prepared the three cake layers for her Texas Independence Day Cake and after they cooled, she wrapped them in plastic wrap and put them in the refrigerator. She wouldn't be icing them until early Saturday morning. Then she chopped all the green onions and mushrooms for her Chicken Mushroom dish. Finally, when all the prep was finished, she decided to take a nap.

She began waking from her nap after an hour. It was dusk and she was being pulled from the middle of a dream by loud yelling and shouting. Jumping up, she ran to the living room. Clay was not in his chair. She could hear him from the back porch that overlooked the river down below. He was hollering threats at something. She ran to the porch. There she found Clay, glaring down toward the river. He was screaming, "Get off my property. How dare you come up here with your wolves and your guns. Get the hell out of here."

Seeing no one, she asked, "Who are you yelling at?"

He stared at her blankly and barked, "I'm trying to scare the Indians and the wolves away from here. My daddy told me that the Indians were bringing in wolves to our land. I need my gun so I can shoot them. Woman, go get my gun!"

Kelly tried to calmly respond saying, "Clay, there are no Indians and wolves down by the river."

Clay screamed at her, "You don't know! Get the hell out of here!"

Ignoring her, he turned back to the imaginary Indians and wolves and fiercely shook his fist at them. "You better not come any closer."

Kelly replied gently, "Let's call Tom to help you scare them away."

Fortunately, Clay shook his head in agreement, and Kelly led him back into the kitchen. She pretended to call Tom, then reporting to Clay that Tom was on his way. She then suggested that she make them a cup of coffee while they wait. She quickly heated some cold coffee in the microwave and set it front of Clay. As he sipped his coffee, she turned the Willie Nelson CD back on. The music again soothed Clay's thoughts.

After a while, she asked Clay if he would like a ham or a turkey sandwich for dinner. Clay said, "Turkey would be great." She thought about asking if the Indians and wolves were gone, but decided it was best not to mention them again.

After dinner, they returned to the living room to watch "I Dream of Jeannie" and "Petticoat Junction." When "Gunsmoke" began, Kelly proposed that they were tired and should go to bed, because the last thing she needed was to have a western with cowboys and Indians.

What a relief it was for Kelly, as they slept through the night with no interruptions. Since they had gone to bed very early, she woke up feeling refreshed. She remembered that today Jeryl, the bath whisperer, was coming. She was ready for a few hours away from Clay.

When she told Clay that Jeryl was coming, he looked pleased. Clay probably couldn't tell her who Jeryl was, but he remembered that when Jeryl came to the house, he enjoyed the visit. She was eternally grateful that Jeryl had been so successful working with Clay.

Shortly after Jeryl arrived, Kelly received a call from Jessie. "We have a problem with Melissa. Lupe said that she was up all night talking about ants crawling up her legs and arms. She was sweating and tossing and turning. Lupe called me out to the apartments. We think Melissa is having withdrawal symptoms or a relapse. We know she's not taking more drugs, but we're not sure if her system is clear of the drugs. The psychiatrist called in a prescription for a heavy sedative to the pharmacy here in Gristmill. Diane and Stacy are on their way from San Antonio. Could you pick up the prescription and bring it here?"

Kelly quickly replied, "Sure. I need to get out of this house for a little while. So, I'll be there as soon as I can."

Kelly told Jeryl that she was leaving and would be back in a few hours. He quietly waved goodbye, not wanting to disturb Clay's attention. Kelly picked up the prescription and headed to the ranch and El Asilo. When she arrived, Jessie and Lupe were at the apartments watching Melissa who was agitated and twisting on the bed, all the while scratching her arms, legs and neck.

Lupe sat on the side of the bed beside Melissa and whispered, "Melissa dear, you need to take this pill. It will make you feel much better." Melissa complied and downed the pill with some water. She continued her struggling for a short while and then drifted off to sleep.

They sat in the kitchen waiting for Diane and Stacy. Kelly wanted to reach out to them and tell them about Clay's hallucinations, but she just couldn't betray his trust. Or at least it felt to her like she would be betraying his trust. She wasn't ready to let anyone in on these new problems just yet. Kelly was afraid that once the family knew how bad Clay's dementia was getting, they would want her to put him in a memory care facility. That day was coming, but not today.

A car crunched the gravel as Diane parked her car. Diane and Stacy entered the room, concern showing clearly on their faces. Stacy asked lots of questions of Lupe and Jessie. She told them she was quite certain that this was residual results of Melissa's withdrawal from the opioids and they would keep her sedated and let her sleep for several days. Hopefully after that, she would be able to completely rehab.

Lupe's concern for Melissa was heart wrenching, "She seems so blah, like she's not sad but not happy. She says almost nothing, and she doesn't want to eat."

"One thing that you need to understand about opioid addiction is that it affects receptors in your brain. When these opioid receptors are being supplied, the drug's reaction in a person's body produces a euphoric effect, one that fills them with a bliss bordering on ecstasy, besides relieving pain. In addition, the drug seems to completely obliterate any anxiety or emotional discomfort. People in this state do not even experience a sensation of being separated from their family or loved ones. They just don't emotionally feel anything. They have a sense of being deeply nourished and satisfied, as if there is not a thing in the world that they want, not even food."

Jessie said, "It's easy to understand how someone can become addicted to drugs."

Stacy continued, "The problem is that once the opioid receptors are empty, the body demands more drugs to refill the opioid receptors. Many people who have rehabbed from drugs often tell us that while they were on the drugs, they felt like they were living their lives in a cave. They could look out the opening of the cave and see the world going by. They knew what was going on in the world, but they just were not a part of it. They felt like they were just observers of events around them. They had no emotions like fear, hate, anger and sadness, but also no emotions like joy, contentment, courage, spiritual inspiration and love. They also experienced little or no drive status, such as hunger, thirst and pain. They were just in this state of bliss, letting the world go by with no conscious desire to be a part of anything."

Diane interjected, "You can see why someone who is being trafficked and forced to perform sexual acts over and over without their consent, needs this state of bliss that drugs provide."

"Now I understand why Melissa is so blah. The drugs have taken away all her emotions and feelings," said Lupe sympathetically. "I hope this new drug will help her find her way back to the living."

Stacy confirmed, "Yes, that's what we are hoping, too."

Diane and Stacy stayed with Jessie and Lupe, but Kelly returned home to check on Clay and Jeryl. Kelly took home some barbecue sandwiches for Clay and Jeryl for lunch. After lunch, Clay went to take his nap. Jeryl came back in the kitchen and asked, "Kelly, have you seen any changes in Clay's behavior? He seems more confused than normal. He can still play dominoes with the best of them, but several times he became quite aggressive with me when he disagreed with something."

Kelly almost broke down in tears at the affirmation of her fears. Jeryl had seen the changes that she knew were there. Clay's behavior was becoming much more challenging and soon she would have to admit it. Their lives would have to change, and she wasn't ready for it.

Saturday morning was hectic. Clay sensed the chaos and his anxiety level had him on edge. Kelly tried talking softly with him while she was busy preparing her chicken and mushroom dish for the Tasting Luncheon. Preparation was extra trouble because she had to cut the chicken into bite-size pieces rather than her normal serving method of a whole chicken breast. She could tell that Clay's uneasiness was speeding up, and then she remembered about the music. She turned on the jam box and again played the Willie Nelson CD. He immediately calmed down and sat at the table drinking his coffee. As she put the icing on her cake, she pointed out that he had made the stars for the top. She told him that if she won the 'Nailed It' competition, it would be because of his good-looking glittery stars. He seemed assured by her words that everything was all right.

As Kelly boxed everything up to take to the Tasting Luncheon, Mrs. Brauder arrived to sit with Clay. Kelly explained to Mrs. Brauder that she would be gone for about five hours, but Tom and Claude were coming by after the parade to check on Clay. However, if she needed anything, she should call her on her cell phone immediately.

Mrs. Brauder felt confident that she could manage and that she and Clay would watch TV Land. On Saturday they have marathon shows. Today, it would be "Green Acres" and then "Gunsmoke."

Kelly drove down Main Street on her way to the bed-and-breakfast. The town was decorated with red, white and blue, with single white stars everywhere. Every shop in town was offering sales and deals and other attractions. Visitors to the town were already arriving, trying to find the perfect parking place. When she passed the front of the General Store, she saw the big replica of the Alamo. It would be an exciting day for Gristmill.

Jessie, Kathy, Sister Elizabeth, and Diane were already at the bed-and-breakfast. Lila had done a magnificent job of decorating the big house with Texas flags and memorabilia. Inside, the long tables were set up with blue tablecloths for the tastings and the 'Nailed It" competition tables had red tablecloths. Kelly found her designated spot for her chicken dish and her cake.

She saw some bizarre dishes at the 'Nailed It' table, such as Pumpkin Spice Pizza, Quesadogas (quesadillas made with wieners instead of chicken), Cumin-glazed Ribs with Avocado-Pineapple Salsa, Kale and Apple Potato Salad, and Pickle Cheesecake. Who dreamed up these recipes? Are they crazy? Kelly was glad she wasn't a judge and had to taste all these dishes. A few things were not weird, and actually looked delicious, such as multi-flavored French macaroons, a snickers cheeseball, cannoli pancakes, cheesy ham omelet muffin cups, French Onion Meatloaf, and Shrimp Curry. Her Texas Independence Day Cake seemed rather simple and unpretentious compared to the others. She recognized Kathy's Chocolate Cups with Bavarian Cream and Raspberries. They looked especially fantastic and whimsical. From looking over the table with everyone's photo of what their dish "should" look like compared to what it actually looks like, she thought Kathy's Chocolate Cups or the French macaroons were the probable winners.

The hall was filling up with people bringing in their tasting recipes. Kelly set up her Chicken and Mushroom dish. Her place was next to Kathy's Shrimp Newburg. She told Kathy, "I think you have a good chance of winning the 'Nailed It' competition. Your Chocolate Cups are very fanciful and dainty. I think the judges will like them."

Kathy laughed. "You wouldn't believe how many broken chocolate cups I have at home. When I would try to separate the balloons from the hardened chocolate, the cup would break or crack. It was a disaster. What you see on the red table is one of the few cups that came out perfect. No one should try making those for a dinner party."

"Can you imagine attending a dinner party and the host serving Pickled Cheesecake for dessert?" laughed Kelly.

"No, but it would thrill me to have some of Jessie's Peach Cobbler. I hope she has enough left over so I can have a big bowl of it with some home-made vanilla ice cream," confided Kathy.

Sister Elizabeth had brought her little Southwest Pimento Cheese sandwiches. Her job of handing out small bites was greatly simplified by serving tiny sandwiches. She waved at Kathy and Kelly across the room as visitors started to pour through the front door. For a while, it was a scramble of chaotic fun. Everyone was having a good time sampling and marking their cookbooks. Reverend Brown came by their table and said the turn-out was excellent, so he was hoping they would raise significant money for El Asilo.

Finally, the judges came to the front to announce the winner of the 'Nailed It' competition. First place went to Kathy Morriston. Her award was a plaque with a huge gold painted nail. Kathy was thrilled and everyone clapped and cheered. Kathy told no one else about the disaster the dish had been to make.

As they were cleaning up, Sister Elizabeth came rushing across the room. She pulled Kelly, Jessie, Kathy and Diane together. She whispered urgently, "You've got to come and see this. You won't believe it." She headed off down a side hall and they followed her. She led them to an alcove with a large red, round couch in the center of the bay. They stared at her with the question on their faces–what????

She pointed to a grouping of paintings around the alcove. Before them were finished paintings from the sketchbook. Some of them could have been mistaken as similar paintings of the life of Christ that they had all seen, but there was one that was undeniably exactly from the sketch. The Anastasis, the resurrection sketch, was painted precisely as the sketch was drawn. The initials on each of the paintings was HH, not HHM. They all remembered the sketch in the pouch found with the body of Anton Bithowski had the initials RK.

They gasped as they stared in shock. Here was the connection. Honey Hickson had been at the orphanage before she was married and her initials at that time were HH before she became HHM. The sketches from the priest's pouch were obviously drawn by HH, but in the sketchbook, she had signed those sketches as RK. Some dots were connecting, but there were still so many questions.

Lila, the owner of the bed-and-breakfast, walked into the alcove and asked, "Can I help you?"

All at once they started asking her, "What can you tell us about these paintings?"

She explained, "Not much, they were here when we purchased the orphanage. This little room had a baptismal font, but it was broken so we threw it away and put the couch in here so our guests would have a place to rest when they first arrive at the bed-and-breakfast. The paintings were so quaint and yet excellent in quality that we left them as the décor."

They were giddy with excitement. Thanking Lila, they didn't try to explain anything to her. They just left her wondering why these five women were so excited about her tiny alcove.

As they returned to the hall, they were busy discussing what this could mean. Kelly's phone rang and when she answered it, she heard Tom speak. "Kelly, you need to come home now."

Kelly turned pale and told the others to please gather up her dishes, she needed to rush home. Kelly hurried as quickly as she could, wondering what had happened. The other four women rushed out behind her and headed to her house, too.

When Kelly got home and rushed into the house, Tom began telling her what had happened. "We came to check on Clay and Mrs. Brauder. When we got here, Mrs. Brauder was hiding in the pantry. Clay had a broomstick that he was swinging and shouting that he would knock out that woman in his house because she was trying to steal his money. Mrs. Brauder is all right, and we settled Clay in his recliner. Mrs. Brauder was upset, so we sent her home. Clay seems calm now, completely unruffled by the whole thing."

Kelly in tears said, "I'm so sorry. I know Clay is getting worse, but I kept telling myself that it wasn't too bad. Usually I can just redirect him to something else, and he is fine in a few minutes."

By this time, the friends were all in her kitchen. They were shocked by what Tom was telling them. Someone had called Carol and now she was there, too. Kelly told them some of the events that had taken place recently. They had no idea that Clay's dementia had deteriorated this much.

Carol insisted, "I'll call Russell and let him know that I'm staying here tonight and tomorrow night. On Monday morning, we're taking Daddy to the neurologist, and you're telling him what's going on."

Jessie sat down by Kelly and Carol. "You've got to start thinking about where you will put Clay in a memory care facility. I know you don't want to do it, but you're no longer safe living with him at home."

Kelly was so exhausted from holding all this inside that she burst into tears as Jessie and Carol held her. She knew that what they were saying was true, but she didn't want to face it. In her heart, she felt like she was letting Clay down. Everyone else knew she had done everything she could!

Chapter 12

1870 to 1871

Time at the orphanage was good. Every day Honey would spot Gebhardt coming up the road. He was always bringing firewood or homemade bread or fabric that had come from the general store. Sometimes he brought honey that his mother and aunt made from the beehives in the caves.

Recently, Gebhardt had started to visit in the evenings. On these occasions, he was there to visit Honey. They would sit on the front porch on the swing. Gebhardt told Honey all the stories about his family. He told her how his father and his uncle were left as orphans in Alabama when their parents died in an Indian massacre. He told her how they had come to Texas to find a new life, how they had both fought at the Alamo, and had only survived because they were couriers and were away at the battle's end. After the Alamo, they served as guides to the Texas army. Later they received a tract of land for their services. That tract of land is now Gristmill, Texas.

He told her about his mother, Elsa. She was from Fredericksburg where she was a German immigrant. He told her how Elsa plays the guitar and the piano. His father purchased Elsa a piano from New York, and it took more than a year to arrive. He also told her about his uncle Jacob who married Josefina. Josefina is from a Mexican family that lived in Texas long before the revolution. He told her, "Josefina's family taught her to make the most amazing tamales."

Honey asked, "What's a tamale?"

Gebhardt looked stunned. "You've never had a tamale! You don't know what you are missing. And my mother's kolaches are great, too."

"I know what kolaches are and I agree, they are delicious!"

Gebhardt told her the tragic story of how Sister Carlita had been attacked by Indians, later joined the convent in San Antonio, and now manages the orphanage. Carlita has a brother, and you've met him. He laughed and said, "Jacob, Josefina, Caleb and Elsa treat all the children at the orphanage like their own grandchildren."

Honey delighted in hearing Gebhardt's family stories and she found immense pleasure in his company. But she would divulge nothing about her family, dodging his questions with vague answers.

Christmas was coming and the whole orphanage was excited. They strung cedar greens on the staircase and stood a huge tree in the parlor. Gebhardt and his father and uncle had brought a giant yule log for the fireplace. Sister Carlita prepared hot cocoa and cookies for all the children. Elsa brought her guitar, and everyone sang old Christmas carols that Honey remembered from her parents.

In the hallway over one door hung a sprig of mistletoe. As Honey came down the hallway headed to the parlor, Gebhardt stepped out from behind a door, grabbed her by the waist, and quickly kissed her on the cheek. Honey giggled and pulled away. Gebhardt looked hurt and asked if it was wrong for him to kiss her. She laughed and timidly said no, "It was just right."

After the Christmas Eve festivities and the children were all put to bed, Honey and Gebhardt, his parents and extended family, sat by the big fire. Gebhardt pulled a package from his coat pocket and handed it to Honey. Her sweet look of surprise amused the group. She opened the package to find a dainty gold locket – a small heart surrounded by filigree. Blushing, she hugged Gerhardt and brought out a larger gift for him. Unwrapping it, he found a pencil drawing of himself. The detail was so exquisite and the likeness perfect. His eyes showed the mischievous twinkle and his mouth the always-present subtle merriment. Everyone stared at the drawing in wonder. They never suspected that Honey had such talent. Gebhardt reached out for Honey and kissed her on the mouth. It embarrassed Honey, but Gebhardt laughed, enchanted by her shyness.

The winter months were harsh at the orphanage. Keeping the big house warm and the children entertained when they couldn't go outside tried everyone's nerves. Honey was now helping to teach and care for the children. Sister Carlita had found paper and pencil supplies, so that Honey could teach drawing as well as reading. Honey often drew funny pictures for the children, and then they would wait for Gebhardt to arrive. He delighted in weaving intricate stories to fit the drawings and entertain the children. Sometimes the stories were funny, and the children would laugh so hard they would cry. Other times the tales were scary, and Honey would have to soothe a little one at bedtime. She would always teasingly scold Gebhardt about telling scary stories, but the children would beg him for more and more of them. Honey and Gebhardt became the evening entertainment for the orphanage and their help thrilled Sister Carlita.

At last spring arrived. The youngsters were restless to be outside. Honey looked forward to days of fresh air. She and Gebhardt were now established as a couple and could be found almost every day sitting and talking on the porch swing. The little children in the orphanage had a gay time teasing them. For the first time in a long time, Honey was happy.

One evening, Sister Carlita approached them with a proposal. "The Diocese would like for the orphanage to convert the south parlor room into a baptismal chapel. This is a small room that we almost never use, so it won't eliminate our living space. The priests who come by to visit would like a place to baptize the children who arrive to live here."

Capturing their attention, she continued, "In this baptismal chapel, we would like mural paintings of the life of Christ. Maybe not a full twelve paintings but at least a few. If I purchase the supplies, Honey, would you consider painting the murals? I have several old Bibles that you could use for ideas."

Honey was ecstatic! She could not believe her ears! Someone wanted her to paint! The very thing she loved to do. She exclaimed, "I'd love to do it! Excuse me, I would be honored to do the paintings!"

Over the next few weeks, Honey studied the six wall panels around the bay area at one end of the room. Maybe the builder had intended to have bay windows in this room, then changed his mind and just built the hexagonal-shaped half-room. It was perfect for murals with a baptismal in the center of the bay.

Honey sketched six drawings: the birth of Christ in the manger, the baptism of Christ by John the Baptist, the crucifixion of Christ, the Anastasis (resurrection), the women at the empty tomb, and the ascension of Christ. When she showed the drawings to Sister Carlita, she was astounded. How did this 16-year-old girl, who just showed up at the orphanage with little family or educational history, know so much about theology? Even without looking at the pictures in the old Bible, she knew just what to draw. The drawings were not only excellent artistically, but they were accurate theologically.

Then to Sister Carlita's bewilderment, Honey gave her a list of exactly the paint supplies that she would require along with a request for the six wall panels to be primed with an undercoat. When Sister Carlita asked Honey how she knew all this, Honey shrugged, offering no answer.

The paint was ordered, and the carpenters finished out the bay room just as Honey had requested. Honey was there at dawn each morning to watch their progress. As soon as they were finished, she began sketching her drawings on the wall.

At last the paint arrived, along with the special brushes that Honey had called for. She was in paradise. She was painting, and in a place that was not difficult to paint. She had Sister Carlita and Gebhardt there every day to praise her work. Some days she brought a lamp into the room late in the evening and painted through much of the night. She couldn't be happier.

Finally, in October, the diocese from San Antonio was coming to the orphanage and would consecrate the new baptismal chapel. A big reception was planned, and they had invited many of the people of Gristmill to attend. Although, everyone had heard about the murals, only Honey, Gebhardt and Sister Carlita had seen them.

On the night of the dedication service, everyone gathered in the foyer to the orphanage and the Bishop from San Antonio, along with the priests, led the way to the baptismal chapel; the community of Gristmill followed them. They asked Sister Carlita to speak, and she brought Honey to the front to recognize her for her diligent work. Shyly, Honey moved to the front with a timid, nervous smile on her face.

As Honey looked up through the crowd, she spotted a face. There was no mistaking the bulky body and the evil eyes staring right at her. She looked away quickly, hoping that he did not recognize her. Certain that he had discovered her and that God would punish her, Honey darted from the front and out a side door, sliding back into the rear of the home, struggling to lose herself in the crowd.

But there was no escape from the attention. The dedication ceremony dragged on as accolades were passed on to Honey. Eyes remained on her as the Bishop couldn't stop complimenting her for the magnificent murals. Dinner was served and Honey was led to the head table with all the dignitaries. Her level of anxiety climbed as Honey saw the pride on Gebhardt's face but realizing her hidden past was going to ruin everything.

Halfway through the meal, Father Bithowski moved to Honey's side and hissed, "Meet me outside the back of the orphanage after everyone is in bed. I have something to tell you." Horrified and desperate, Honey nodded in agreement. He would destroy her; her life here would be over. Her dreams of a life with Gebhardt would be over.

When the meal concluded, the officiates retired to their rooms and the community people of Gristmill left for home. Honey urged a quick exit for Gebhardt. The children who were helping clean up after the meal were finally finished and had departed to their beds. Honey reluctantly slipped out the back door.

As she stepped out into the moonlight, she could see that Father Bithowski was already waiting for her. Feigning courage, she turned her chin up and waited for him to speak the lies she had heard he was spreading. Then she saw under his arm the pouch with her sketchbook!

He sneered at her. "You didn't think you would get away with it, did you? You thought you killed me, but you didn't. I told everyone you were a thief and now the law wants you for theft of the golden chalice. When I heard about beautiful murals being painted at this orphanage, I suspected that it might be you. And I was right!"

She just glared at him.

"When I show them your sketches and compare them to your murals, you will be exposed. They will believe you are a thief, and you'll go to prison."

Honey was terrified at the prospect of prison. She begged him, "What do you want? You know I didn't steal the chalice. Please don't do this to me."

"I'm still offering the same arrangement to you as before. You can do things for me and I can do things for you. I can bring you back to San Antonio where you can paint when a church needs artwork; and you can be nice to me."

She was shaking with fear. She would have to go with him. She had no choice.

He knew he had her. He scowled, "I think I need a little taste of your appreciation right now. This is a nice moonlit night. Let's stroll down through the garden toward the tree grove in the back, so you can show me a little gratitude."

He grabbed her arm and dragged the sobbing girl toward the garden, then shoved her ahead of him. She couldn't escape this time. She would be his slave for the rest of his life. Every few steps he pushed her again and again.

Reaching the grove of trees, he forced her to the ground and threw the pouch with the sketches beside her. He pulled up his garments and his intent showed clearly in his eyes as he plunged to the ground over her. Honey's mind returned to the previous attack as her blouse was pulled back to expose her breasts. She felt his hands fumbling and gripping her body. She fought to push him away, scratching his face and kicking, struggling to avoid another rape.

Suddenly, she heard a swoosh and a violent thud. The Father fell face down into the dirt. Standing over Honey stood Gebhardt holding a large tree branch. This time there was no doubt Father Bithowski was dead. Blood was running from his head onto the ground. So much blood. Honey was in shock. No, no, no! Now Gebhardt was a murderer. He had saved her, but they would both go to prison or the gallows. Her past had destroyed the one person in her life who truly cared about her.

Gebhardt helped Honey up off the ground, saying in a steady but authoritative voice, "Go back to the orphanage and get a shovel. Don't let anyone see you. Then come back here and wait for me. If anyone comes, hide and do not come out." Gebhardt was so forceful with his instructions that Honey ran back without questioning him.

Gebhardt left the priest on the ground and ran toward his home. He found their hay wagon and brought it to the back to the garden. When he returned, Honey was already waiting with the shovel. It took them both to haul the priest's heavy body into the wagon. They used the shovel to clean up the blood and spread the dirt around where it had been disturbed. When Bithowski was securely in the back, Gebhardt kissed Honey and held her tenderly as he explained his plan, "Go back to the orphanage and do not tell a soul where you have been. Just go to your room and pretend that you are tired, and go to bed."

Honey had the pouch with the sketches clutched under her arm. Gebhardt looked at her sadly and said, "I'm sorry, but you can't keep that. It would just incriminate you if anyone starts searching. I'm so sorry, I know it must mean a lot to you."

Honey nodded and tossed the pouch into the back of the wagon. She scrambled back to the orphanage as Gebhardt slapped the flanks of the horses pulling the hay wagon. Within a few minutes, Gebhardt was north of Gristmill, far from the orphanage, driving the wagon into his father's field. He pulled the wagon up to the barn doors, unlatched them and drove the wagon inside. As quickly as he could, he took the shovel and dug a shallow grave in the back center of the barn.

The body seemed to be getting heavier as Gebhardt pulled it from the wagon and into the grave. He dropped the pouch with the sketches beside the priest. Sweating profusely, he was nervous that someone might have seen him, or have become suspicious at his driving the wagon through town so late at night. He worked furiously to cover the body and the pouch with dirt. Then he packed it down as much as possible. Finally, he gathered all the old lumber and farming implements and parts that were stacked around the barn and piled them on top of the gravesite. Hopefully, no one would ever find the body.

He then quietly drove the wagon out of the barn, latched the doors closed, and slowly walked the wagon back home. He tiptoed into his home and climbed in bed. No one ever asked him about that evening. He didn't know exactly what he had just pulled off, but he had saved the mysterious girl he loved.

The next morning at the orphanage, the officials from San Antonio gathered in the front room to say their farewells. Honey stood off to the side expecting someone to accuse her of her treachery. But no one came forward. No one said a word except to continue congratulating her on her artwork.

Soon the officials began to look around for Father Bithowski. They sent someone to call him from his room, but he obviously was not there and had not slept in his bed last night. The Bishop and the entourage were extremely concerned. They searched the house and the grounds, but they could not find him. After several hours of searching, they concluded that he must have left the night before to return home. The officials left, never suspecting they were leaving a dead Father behind.

Gebhardt waited a couple of days before he returned to the orphanage. He and Honey sat on the porch swing as usual. Only when they were completely alone did Gebhardt ask Honey about the Father. He said he had a good idea about what had happened, but he needed her to feel she could be honest with him. Honey, recognizing she could trust Gebhardt with her life story, suggested that they go for a walk away from prying or listening ears. They walked north toward the river and sat on the banks watching the flow of the water and a gaggle of geese that had stopped for a drink. Honey told Gebhardt her whole story – about her parents and family, where she had lived in Cyril Hill, how she had helped her Papa build the church and how she had learned to paint. She told him all about the yellow fever and the terrible days when first her father died, then her brother and sister, and finally, her mother. She told him about the excruciating loneliness and grief that was too much to bear. Then she told him how Father Bithowski took her from her home and declared she was an orphan of the church, demanding that she complete the painting at the church.

It embarrassed her to describe her feelings of helplessness against Father Bithowski's attack, but she did her best. Then she explained how she had hit him with the wooden pole and thought he was dead. Trembling as if it were happening again, she described running away through the woods to escape. Only when the Indian Hick Man came did she know that she had not killed him.

Later, when she heard about the lies the Father told everyone accusing her of being a thief, she felt hopelessly betrayed, and she was consumed with hating the Father, the Church and even God for letting her family die. But while she was living with Hick Man's family and the Indians, she had time to think and she realized she didn't hate the Church and God, but she still hated the Father.

With a sigh, she said she felt relieved knowing Father Bithowski was really dead, and he could never hurt her again. She expressed her thankfulness to Gebhardt, that he, knowing so little of her background, had killed a man to save her. The killing would haunt them both now. She wanted to say she loved him but could not bring herself to say the words out loud. What if he didn't feel the same way? He deserved to know her true story, including her real name. "I am Ruzika Kosovitsky."

Gebhardt took her in his arms and softly vowed, "I love you, Ruzika Kosovitsky. And Honey Hickson will you marry me?"

"Even after I've told you about my awful past, you want to marry me?"

"More now than ever. We'll never mention what happened again. Our secret is our secret. You will be forever, Honey Hickson Moniac."

He embraced her and passionately kissed her. She felt his strong arms encircle her and at last she felt safe and loved!

Chapter 13

Early Monday morning, Kelly called Clay's neurologist. Carol had spent the night at her parents' home. She listened as her mother explained Clay's aggressive behavior and hallucinations. The doctor insisted that Kelly and Clay come in as soon as possible.

Riding to the appointment, Clay's whistling was in a direct contrast to Kelly's impending sense of doom. Carol parked the car and helped her father from the vehicle. They settled into the doctor's reception area and were finally called back.

The neurologist talked to Clay first, asking him how he felt. He asked some of his diagnostic questions, such as what year is it, what season is it and who is the president? Clay answered all three questions incorrectly, as he had done at every visit for the past several years. Kelly was feeling frustrated with the neurologist when he eventually asked his assistant to accompany Clay to another room. He then turned to Kelly and Carol and asked, "Tell me what's going on. You've never mentioned that Clay's behavior was aggressive to you or anyone. We've discussed his sundowning and, I believe he even wandered away at one time. But hallucinations are also something new. Did these things just happen recently?"

Kelly bit her bottom lip to keep her emotions intact. She told the neurologist that Clay was becoming more forgetful and confrontational about the everyday things, like taking a bath and the food that he would eat. She told him about the incident in the middle of the night when he got up and dressed and was searching for his guns and badge to go to his old sheriff's office. She told him she was sure Clay sometimes did not recognize her as his wife.

The neurologist responded, "Have you taken all of his guns out of your home?"

"Of course," answered Kelly.

She continued explaining about Clay's seeing the Indians and wolves at the back of their home and the attack on Mrs. Brauder.

"I'm sorry, but it sounds like Clay's dementia has advanced to the next stage. I think we can help him with some anti-anxiety medication to reduce these types of incidents. But if his behavior becomes more challenging, which I suspect it will, then you need to plan for Clay to be admitted to a memory care facility. Without intending to hurt you, he might do so. You have worked hard to keep him safe. Now you must be just as diligent about keeping yourself safe."

Kelly wasn't shocked, but facing the reality was harsh and she was without words. Carol asked the doctor, "What will the memory care facility ask as a medical requirement?"

"I'll prepare a letter of authorization for you to take with you when you register with them. You should probably visit several facilities. This letter will introduce Clay and his situation to their admissions staff. They will most likely put Clay's name on a waiting list so that when you need to move him, you'll already be set up for his admission."

He continued, "I'm sure you are aware there is only one memory care facility in Gristmill. There are several in the southern part of San Antonio, but I realize that's a long trip for regular visits."

Upon hearing this, Kelly could feel the warm tears rolling down her cheeks. She could not fathom "visiting" Clay. No, she wasn't ready for this, not yet.

On the way home, Kelly was mostly quiet. Carol entertained Clay by pointing out wonderful places along the road and telling him about her Wildflower Café and his special grandchildren. They stopped to get the anti-anxiety prescription filled. By the time they got home and had a sandwich for lunch and one of the new pills, Clay was exhausted and headed for his recliner to nap.

Kelly sat for a period in the kitchen, reflecting on all the events in their life together that had led up to this moment. All the years while he was serving in Vietnam, she had feared he wouldn't return. Then the years he was the sheriff, she had feared a deadly confrontation. Now, after surviving all of those dangers, she was losing him to his own mind slowly growing dim. Hopefully, the new medication would stall the inevitable, but she knew she needed to start looking at memory care facilities.

With Clay sound asleep in his recliner, Kelly sat at her computer and started searching how to evaluate memory care facilities. She read that she should look for a staff engaging with the patients, providing them with games, music, and conversation, not just leaving them to sit in front of a TV. Of course, the facility had to be secure, which meant that they must lock the doors to prevent the patients from wandering out. It was important that the place have a 'feel like home' atmosphere, not a hospital ward. It warned her to use the sniff test. Did the place smell like urine or some other odor? Also, she should go at a mealtime and see what the patients were eating. It was overwhelming.

The neurologist was correct. There was only one memory care facility in Gristmill. Since she couldn't imagine not visiting Clay every day, maybe twice a day, the option of him staying in a facility in San Antonio was out of the question. She picked up her cell phone and called the Sunrise Senior Care Center of Gristmill. It was an Assisted

Living and a Memory Care Facility. Since Jeryl would come to bathe Clay tomorrow, she made an appointment to visit.

While using her computer, she checked her emails. There was an email from Brenda. She told Kelly that they had really enjoyed the visit and were accepting the invitation to join them in Gristmill for their Easter family picnic. Brenda was eager for her family to meet her half-sisters' families. She said she would get reservations for her family at the Gristmill Bed-and-Breakfast for Saturday night. Her final request was that, since the next day would be Easter Sunday, they would like to attend church with them, if that was possible.

Kelly quickly responded to the email. That would be great, and they would look forward to the visit.

The next morning, Jeryl came and was convincing Clay to take his bath while Kelly cleaned up the breakfast dishes. She waved at Jeryl, letting him know she was leaving and would be back soon. As she headed to Sunrise Senior Memory Care, she had no idea what to expect. She had never visited this place and knew little about it, even though it was located in Gristmill.

The place looked well maintained outside. She entered the lobby, and the receptionist led her in to see the director. Kelly explained Clay's situation, and the woman seemed to understand completely. The director described their program and assured her they could accept Clay whenever Kelly thought it was time for him to enter the facility. And, more importantly, they were equipped to care for him all the way to the end of his journey with Alzheimer's. Kelly thought, "She's right, this is a journey from not-too-bad, to worse, to terrible." As she listened to their programs, she remembered so many things she had learned from her support group. She tried to focus more and more on what the director was saying. Finally, the director invited her to tour the facility.

As they led Kelly through the locked doors, she expected to feel like she was in a prison. But it wasn't that way at all. The facility was pleasant, and she did the sniff test and smelled nothing offensive. She heard soft music playing in the background. The director explained, "They built our facility in a big square so that when patients leave their rooms, no matter whether they go right or left, they will end up back at the nurse's station or at their rooms. Each room has a current photo and a younger photo of themselves on the door. They will not remember their room number, but most will recognize one of the photos."

As they passed the activity room, Kelly saw a group playing balloon volleyball with swimming noodles and balloons. They were fully engaged with their game and seemed to have a great time. The dining room was just beyond the activity room, each table was set with linens and a small vase of flowers. Kelly commented, "This is nothing like I expected. The smells coming from the kitchen are delightful."

The director said that today they were having ham and sweet potatoes for lunch. She told Kelly, "Once a month, we have parties and families are invited to attend. Sometimes it is a Hawaiian party or an Elvis party or a Sixties party; but always there's a theme with decorations." Then, as the director turned from the dining room, she pointed out a side door. "This door leads outside. The patients can walk into the fenced gardens any time they choose when the weather is decent. We fence the back sides of the building in so they can walk completely around the gardens and come back in through a different door. There are benches under trees where they can sit outside. We try to do all we can to give them options, so they don't feel locked in. But the locked main door is for their protection and is absolutely necessary to keep them safe."

The contented looks on most of the patients' faces amazed Kelly. However, she saw some patients who were just walking up and down the halls, looking into every room and mumbling to themselves.

When she asked the director about this, the director explained, "At later stages of Alzheimer's, patients often suffer from a need to wander. Maybe they are looking for their parents who have been dead for years or maybe they are looking for a way to go home. We try to work with them in their reality, not ours. The constant walking and searching is their effort to find what they are looking for. We may try to redirect their attention to another activity, but sometimes it's better to let them keep walking rather than to confront them."

"Let me show you a typical patient room."

The room was nice and simple. A wardrobe for their clothes, a bed, a nightstand, and a bathroom but no shower. As the director began to explain why there was no shower, Kelly said she completely understood. Each room had a single window looking out on the gardens.

The director invited Kelly to return to her office and fill out an application to reserve a room for Clay when he was ready. Kelly nodded yes, accepting the dreaded final step to acknowledging that she would put Clay in a facility at some time, maybe not today, but someday soon.

When she got home, Clay and Jeryl were playing dominoes and discussing baseball. The new medication was working. Clay seemed much more content and not agitated at all.

When Jeryl left, Kelly realized that there would be no more days to socialize, at least not with the freedoms she had previously. Mrs. Brauder had refused to return to sit with Clay; she was now afraid of him. Kelly couldn't blame her! Kelly turned on TV Land, and they sat watching another "Andy Griffith Show."

As the days went by, Clay was happier than he had been in several months. Since Easter was only a few weeks away, Kelly had decided that she and Clay could make cascarones, the confetti stuffed Easter eggs. They were time consuming to make, but the children always had a wonderful time smashing them on heads and spilling all the confetti onto the victim.

Each morning before Kelly made scrambled eggs for their breakfast, she tapped a small hole in each end of the egg and gently blew the yoke and white out into a bowl. Later, she would rinse out the eggshell and set it out to dry. At the end of the week, she had enough eggs to color for the cascarones.

She mixed up the egg dye and encouraged Clay to dip the shells. They worked for several hours dipping the shells and then setting them on paper towels to dry. After the eggshells had dried completely, she glued a small piece of tissue paper over one of the end holes. Then she held a funnel in the other hole, allowing Clay to pour confetti into the empty egg. When the egg was filled, she glued a small piece of tissue over the second hole to enclose the confetti.

Finally, they put all the cascarones into egg cartons to save for Easter. Kelly was enjoying herself so much that she took one of the cascarones and smashed it on the top of Clay's head. He looked shocked, and she was suddenly afraid that she may have upset him, but then he laughed and shook the confetti off his shirt. The day had turned into one of their best in a very long time.

That evening they watched "Bonanza" and ordered a pizza. They then looked through an old scrapbook of their grandchildren, Turner and Kenzie, when they were babies. Clay could name just about everyone in the photos. He enjoyed talking about the grandchildren, when they were born and when they were brought home from the hospital. They joked about how many photos they had taken of them. But just when Kelly seemed to think Clay was better, he started calling Kenzie by their daughter's name, Carol. A reminder that persons with Alzheimer's disease do not get better!

Two weeks before Easter, Jessie dropped by one day. She excitedly told Kelly, "You need a day out of the house. Let's go on a road trip to check out the Catholic church in Cyril Hill. I've talked to Diane, Kathy and Sister Elizabeth. They can all go on Thursday."

Kelly replied regrettably, "I can't leave Clay alone that long. Jeryl only comes for a few hours and Mrs. Brauder won't return. So, you all will just have to go without me."

"That's the good news!" exclaimed Jessie. "I've already talked to Tom and Claude. They have agreed to spend the day with Clay so you can go with us. And I've already talked to the Cyril Hill Catholic Church, and they are expecting us at eleven."

Kelly almost cried with excitement, "That sounds fantastic!"

On Thursday morning, Jessie, Tom, Diane, and Claude all arrived at Kelly's house, soon followed by Kathy and Sister Elizabeth. Tom and Claude approached Clay with their plans for the day. They had found an old "Caddy Shack" movie to watch, and then a new barbecue place for lunch. Then they would watch a University of Texas baseball game on TV after lunch. Their plans thrilled Clay, so much so that he never asked Kelly where she was going or what she was planning to do.

After loading into Jessie's Suburban, the lighthearted women headed across south Texas toward Cyril Hill. There was so much new oil drilling and construction related to the frack wells and pipelines that some land around Karnes City and Beeville was not recognizable from a few years ago.

While they were traveling, Diane said, "Let's examine what we know. We're pretty sure Honey Hickson Moniac was originally RK, but we don't know what RK stands for. We know that Honey Hickson appears in the census in 1880, but not in the previous census; so we don't know where she lived prior to living at the orphanage and marrying Gebhardt Moniac. We know Honey Hickson and Gebhardt had a son in 1873, who is Kelly and Jessie's great grandfather. We know that our murdered dead man is a priest named Anton Bithowski, that he was living in Cyril Hill around 1870, and after that he is never in another census. So, we know he was murdered sometime after 1870 and before 1880. Is that about it?"

Kathy spoke up, "We know that RK or Honey Hickson was a very good artist and that she painted the murals in the bed-and-breakfast, which was the orphanage at that time. We also know she painted the carousel horses."

"There's just such a gap between the murdered priest and Honey or RK. And then there is another puzzle piece: the carousel horses. They must somehow be connected, but for the life of me, I can't figure out how they fit together. I just can't connect the dots," mused Kelly.

Sister Elizabeth contemplated, "Maybe our trip today will provide some clues. I've often read about these painted churches around Schulenburg. I'm excited about finally getting to see them."

"Where did they come from? What's the story on them?" inquired Kathy.

Sister Elizabeth became a teacher. "Well, I did a little research, knowing that we were going to Cyril Hill. The big town in this area is Schulenburg, and it is usually the town recognized as the home of the painted churches. But actually, the churches are in several neighboring towns like Dubina, High Hill, Ammansville, Moravia, Praha, St. John, and of course Cyril Hill. The area of Schulenburg was first established in about 1831 by Kesiah Crier. When the railroad came through in 1873, they changed the official name to Schulenburg. They built some of these other towns in the same period of time. Several Czech families migrating from their homeland established Dubina in 1856. It was a Czech-Moravian community. What's interesting about it is that, according to some Texas historians, this section of the state was at one time hunting grounds of the Tonkawa Indians, who were later overrun by the fierce Comanches. But there were also European people living in the Dubina area before the Czech community."

"There is also an older community called Praha. They established it in 1854, but it was first called Mulberry Creek, then later changed to Praha, for Prague."

"Cyril Hill was established in 1844 as one of the earliest communities, but the church wasn't completed until 1854. Cyril Hill was a Czech community, whereas some of these other communities were German. Much of the church at Cyril Hill was destroyed by a hurricane in 1909, but it was later rebuilt. They preserved small portions of the original church. Today, the church is named St. Cyril & St. Methodius Catholic Church of Cyril Hill."

"The German and Czech immigrants painted their beloved churches to emulate the churches they left behind in

Europe. Many of the immigrants were fleeing religious oppression, wishing to practice their faith in peace. The churches are perhaps the most awe-inspiring example of the rich German and Czech culture in the Texas Hill Country. The Painted Churches feature hand-painted sculptures, angels, filigree, faux-marble, and stencils. Some are even listed in the National Registry of Historic Places."

"Many of the German churches now have stained glass windows, but originally they did not. The Czech churches, such as the one in Cyril Hill, preferred natural lighting. Some churches were damaged in hurricanes and fires. Some were whitewashed and then later repainted from old photos to be exactly like they were originally painted. Cyril Hill is full of delicate floral designs with vines and spring flowers painted on the faux stone walls. The sky-blue domes are covered in metallic stars and harp-playing angels. And that is all thanks to Wikipedia!"

They all laughed at Sister Elizabeth's recitation.

Kelly exclaimed, "I can't wait to get there!"

Arriving at the church in Cyril Hill, they parked the car and were at first disappointed with the outside of the church. It was a lovely, white clap-board church with windows down the side and a tall steeple. Nothing extraordinary.

The inside of the church, though, was a contrast to the outside. The walls were covered in faux cream and tan stones. They were so real that the women had to touch them to believe they were not large granite or marble stones. The filigree on the walls and ceilings were delicate and painted gold. The ceilings surpassed all their expectations from the description that Sister Elizabeth had described. The sky was a brilliant turquoise, and the angels were cherubic and seemed to rejoice in their role as heraldic musicians to the worshippers. No word except "awe" could describe the church interior.

The local priest met them midway to the front of the church. It overjoyed him to be guiding them through his church. He told them about the original church and about how it was constructed. He told them about the hurricane of 1909.

Finally, he led them to the front where there were two statues just beyond the railing. On the left was the Holy Virgin Mary and on the right was Jesus Christ. Christ was reaching his hands out to the congregants. His face radiated and looked compassionate as if extending His welcome to everyone. Farther back, the altar stood as tall as the ceilings. It had a small alcove near the bottom with a golden cross enclosed in the frame. Another statue of Jesus stood above the cross, this one of Jesus holding a white lamb in one arm and His scepter in His right hand. Again, the statue was enclosed in an almond-shaped alcove frame. On either side of Christ were two men. The priest explained that they were not St. Paul and St. Peter but were St. Cyril and St. Methodious.

The priest explained, "St. Cyril and St. Methodious brought the gospel to the Czech people; we regard them the Saints of the Slavs."

Jessie asked, "Do the people of this church consider St. Cyril and St. Methodius more important than St. Peter and St. Paul?"

"Oh, of course not. But St. Cyril and St. Methodious are the patron saints of this church. They were two brothers born about 827 AD in Thessalonica. They were Byzantine Christian theologians and Christian missionaries who translated the Latin Bible into the Slavic language. The Slavic people consider them equal to the apostles."

Kathy, gazing at the statues said to no one in particular, "These statues look like stone, but they are really made of wood. What marvelous craftsmanship!"

The other women stared back at the statues. They had assumed they were stone, but now upon closer inspection, they realized they were wood sculptures. The priest told them, "We saved these statues from the 1909 hurricane. They are from the original builders of the church."

The women had not been forthcoming about their interest in the church, so Kelly began, "We have been trying to solve a mystery about a recent discovery in Gristmill of a murdered man. His remains were found and, according to good records, his name was Father Anton Bithowski. All we can find out for sure is that he was at one time the priest at Cyril Hill. We also believe that there may be a connection between the priest and a person with the initials RK. Do you have any records from about 1870 for this church?"

"Let me see. As a matter of fact, I might have something that would help. In 1954, this church celebrated its one-hundredth birthday. The family of a man named Simon Moravec brought forward a diary that their ancestor had found in the ruins of an old home in Cyril Hill. Supposedly he purchased the home many years ago and found this diary. Well, it turned out this diary held a great deal of information about the beginnings of this church. We had the diary published and copies printed. I think we still have several copies in the church office. I'll go and check. In the meantime, if you are interested in the early, early days of this church, the little alcove off to the side of the main nave might fascinate you. It contains a few icons that were saved after the 1909 hurricane that we decided should be kept as remembrances of our beginnings. I'll go and check on that book."

The five women raced to the alcove. There, before them, was the Anastasis. They knew Honey Hickson had painted the same painting at the orphanage, but this painting had the initials RK. They were speechless. How could this be? How did she get from Cyril Hill to Gristmill?

Peering at the rest of the paintings, they found several more with the initials RK, but also some with the initials JK. Diane took out her cell phone and began taking photos. They would want to look at all of them closer, especially when they had the sketchbook in front of them.

The priest returned and handed a book to Kelly. He said, "We still have several and there's not much demand for them anymore."

Kelly asked, "Do you know who painted these icons?"

"The original architect of the building painted them. Legend says it was a father and daughter. Their last name was Kosovitsky, I believe. If you're interested, I think their tombstones are in the very old section of the cemetery near the back of the church. I'll show you where if you'll follow me."

He took them out the side door of the church, where the oldest tombstones stood nearby. The tombstone was not like tombstones found on individual graves; it was more of a marker. It was obviously ancient. It just stated:

> Josef Kosovitsky and
>
> wife, Suzanna Kosovitsky,
>
> children Konrad Kosovitsky
>
> and wife, Becca

        child, Hanka Kosovitsky

        All went to their Lord, 1869

The priest said, "I'm afraid that is all that I know about the original church. I hope it will help."

They all thanked him profusely, expressing that his information had been very helpful.

Diane continued to take pictures with her cell phone. When she thought she had well covered all the subject, they wandered across Main Street to a little Czech restaurant. They ordered roasted pork and dumplings, as well as some sauerkraut and sausage. They all shared and tasted their various dishes. But the dessert was the highlight. Apple strudel!

Finally, in the car and headed home, Kelly was eager to read the book that the priest had given them. She opened the book and began reading to the group. It was a diary written by Suzanna Kosovitsky beginning in 1842. She read aloud to her captive, but mesmerized, audience. As she finished the diary, she found an addendum that someone had added and read it also.

"Some older members of Simon Moravec's family remembered a story he told years later. He told the tale that Josef Kosovitsky, the architect who built the church and created all the artwork for the church, died before they completed the church. The man's daughter, Ruzika, continued his work and then she disappeared, nowhere to be found. He related that an old Indian man named, Hickory, came to the town and told him that Father Bithowski, the priest, had attacked Ruzika Kosovitsky and that was why she ran away from the church without finishing the painting. He said that Miss Kosovitsky lived with his Indian family for a year and then she moved on to west Texas. He did not know where she moved."

Diane was the first to speak. "That explains so much. We now know that Ruzika or Ruzi Kosovitsky is without a doubt the same person as Honey Hickson Moniac. And we know how she became such a skilled painter. And we know why she left Cyril Hill. We can only guess how she got from Cyril Hill to Gristmill, but we can connect the dots fairly well. And we can speculate with a certain amount of confidence what happened to Bithowski."

"Yeah, and he deserved what he got, if the addendum is true, and he attacked a young girl who had gone through what she had suffered. And good for her that she was able to survive!" exclaimed Jessie.

Kathy pondered, "Everything fits; and it explains a lot, except for the carousel horses. Obviously, Honey Hickson was capable of sculpting and painting them, but why were they in the barn on top of the buried dead man?"

When they arrived home, they found Clay in good spirits. There had been no terrible outbursts from him. Sheriff Russell had come by late that afternoon in his sheriff's car, and he talked to Clay about some cattle rustlers that were giving him trouble. It was a fabricated story, but Clay enjoyed being asked for advice. Afterwards, they all rode in the police car to the Dairy Queen for hamburgers and dip cones.

It had been an exquisite day for everyone, especially Kelly and Clay!

Chapter 14

1872 to 1898

If Gristmill could claim a royal wedding, then Gebhardt's and Honey's wedding would befit the honor. Gebhardt was the son of one founder of the town, Caleb Moniac. Gebhardt was handsome, rich, charming, and genuinely liked by most everyone in Gristmill. Honey was now famous for her paintings at the orphanage that had been roundly celebrated. In addition, Honey was a persona of mystery and legend with no background. It was most definitely a Cinderella marriage steeped in folklore. The whole town was excited about the upcoming hochzeit, the wedding.

The two who were most enthusiastic were the mother of the groom, Elsa, and the groom's aunt, Josefina. Josefina claimed equal maternal rights with her sister-in-law, since she was resigned to never having a wedding to plan for her daughter, since Sister Carlita had become a nun and her son, Francisco, did not yet have a girlfriend. Both women were filled with anticipation as they planned for the couple's nuptial.

They ordered fabric and lace from the best retailers in San Antonio then commissioned seamstresses to sew Honey's wedding dress. More dresses were to be made for Honey, Elsa, and Josefina. The Moniac home was bustling with excitement. They ordered food, beer, and liquor. A dozen cooks and kitchen help were hired to prepare the feast. Caleb and Jacob tried to escape to the ranch, leaving Gebhardt to deal with the female dilemmas *du jour*. Gebhardt, love-struck and jovial, went through the days completely oblivious to any stress about his soon-to-change marital status. He wrapped his mind around one thing: Honey!

They swept Honey up in the excitement. Her emotions swung between thrilled and despondency. One moment she was elated with happiness, her heart filled with love for Gebhardt, and then thoughts that her Papa and Mama would not be at the wedding ripped through her soul causing her to weep with sadness. She was mortified with thoughts that someone might find out about the murder of Father Bithowski and all this could come shattering down around her. Gebhardt kept assuring her not to worry, but it nagged constantly in the recesses of her mind.

Gebhardt and Honey had contrived a background story for Honey's life. They told everyone that Honey had come from Kentucky with her parents to San Antonio. Then both of her parents had died of the influenza, and the Ursuline Sisters brought her to the orphanage. It was all a fabricated lie to deflect attention from Honey's true identity. If no one knew she was from Cyril Hill, then they would not likely connect her to Father Bithowski. Since Honey had been less than forthcoming about her family, with this story she seemed to be safe from any suspicion. Strangely, as far as anyone in Gristmill knew, the Catholic Church dismissed the search for Father Bithowski, assuming that he had abandoned the order of priests. Gebhardt and Honey's secret seemed secure.

They sent invitation letters to Elsa's family in Fredericksburg. Elsa's parents, siblings, nieces, and nephews were making plans to attend. They also sent letters to Josefina's family. Not only would they attend the wedding, but they intended to stay for several days.

As the day approached, the field around Caleb and Elsa's older home near the gristmill was cleared and prepared for the gathering. They braced planks of wood over sawhorses to provide tables where the guests could enjoy a meal. Several cows were to be slaughtered two days prior and slowly cooked over open pits. Huge caldrons of pinto beans were to be boiled. They arranged every other dish imaginable – from cornbread and honey to fresh vegetables from the garden, to delicious German pastries and cakes, and fresh corn tortillas.

At last the Wedding Day June 1, 1872, arrived. The guests showed up early that morning, since the wedding was scheduled for noon. Fortunately, it was not the hottest day of the summer and a gentle breeze blew through the trees. As they gathered beneath an arbor of spring roses, Gebhardt stood with his best man, his cousin Francisco, and the priest, ready to receive his bride. Elsa, Jacob, and Josefina came and sat in chairs at the front. Caleb walked with Honey down the aisle. She was the most beautiful woman that Gebhardt had ever seen! Her flaxen hair and her lovely face were even more striking in her elegant wedding dress, its veil flowing behind her.

The children from the orphanage sang "Treulich Gefuhrt" with Sister Carlita directing them.

> *Treulich gefuhrt ziehet dahin*
>
> *wo euch der Segen de liebe bewahrt*
>
> Faithfully guided, draw near
>
> to where the blessing of love shall preserve you.

They sounded like a chorus of angels.

The couple said their vows with the firm conviction that nothing would separate them forever. Gebhardt gave Honey a flawless diamond ring on a simple golden band. He wanted to give her anything and everything, but Honey had said she didn't want extravagant gifts. She was delighted with him, not his gifts.

After the ceremony, the festivities began. A band of guitars and accordions played German oompah music, followed by a Mexican mariachi band. Before the dancing began, everyone gathered in front of the bride and groom. Each wedding guest had brought a clay pot or a piece of earthenware or a vase, and together they broke them making a loud noise. Everyone cheered, satisfied that the traditional polterabend made a loud enough rumble to bring the couple good luck. The German band played a sweet waltz as Gebhardt and Honey danced their first dance together. Then the entire town of Gristmill and all their family joined and danced. The merriment continued for hours. Gebhardt and Honey tried to visit with each guest before finally sitting down. Elsa brought them a plate of food. Until then, they had not realized they were famished, not having eaten since the night before.

Needing a rest, Honey sat down to relax with Sister Carlita. They had become close friends. Sister Carlita told Honey that they would miss her at the orphanage, but Honey responded that she planned to continue to help with the children. The children had played a large part in healing the hole left from her parents and brother's and sister's deaths.

Gebhardt left them to join his male cousins from Fredericksburg, who were smoking cigars in a group near a campfire. Goodheartedly teasing their cousin seemed to be the fun of the evening. However, Gebhardt couldn't keep his eyes from wandering back to look at his gorgeous bride!

Eventually they dropped the joviality, and the conversation turned to politics and the interests of the time. Several felt strongly about the recent War Between the States and the issue of slavery. Many of them knew of families who had lost sons in the war. Fredericksburg, Gristmill and many other German communities did not support the confederate position on slavery, but the prohibitions imposed by the north were proving difficult even for them.

One cousin, Albert Froede, said that Fredericksburg had organized a turnverein. Gebhardt was keenly curious and asked, "What is a turnverein?"

"In Germany, there was a man by the name of Friedrich Jahn, who started a movement for athletic clubs. In these athletic clubs, the men exercise doing gymnastics. That's why they called them Turn Verein because they are 'turners.' But there's more to these places than just gymnastics and calisthenics. They are really a social club where Germans can discuss freedom and politics."

Another cousin chimed in, "They were an important factor in the revolution in Germany, but unfortunately they were on the losing side. Actually, several turnverein members were bodyguards for President Abraham Lincoln."

"Several of these men and their families have moved to Fredericksburg. They have started a turnverein in our town. We call it Turner Halle. We go there often and do tureining or we call it chin ups–pulling up to our chins to a metal bar. Mostly we do cartwheels and handstands but we're planning to start a basketball team."

"The older men and the women have a Liederkranz Singing Society that meets there."

Albert wrapped it up with, "The best part is that on Saturday afternoons and evenings, there is a dance and lots of beer drinking. Almost all of the families come, but I go because of the frauleins." As he slapped Gebhardt on the back he said, "But you, my Gebhardt, no longer have eyes for the frauleins." At this the group had a hearty, roaring laugh, and Gebhardt blushed a deep red.

Gebhardt returned to Honey, and they danced and talked and laughed late into the evening. They left the festivities in a shower of flower petals and shouts and applause from the guests as they ran across the fields to Gebhardt's childhood room at the back of his family's home. Elsa and Caleb were spending the night at Jacob and Josefina's home to give them privacy on their first night.

Early the next morning they found a basket of fresh pastries and milk on their doorstep. Someone had graciously prepared two horses and a carriage and left it tied outside their room. As soon as they were up, they said a quick goodbye to Gebhardt's parents, and they were off to San Antonio for a honeymoon.

They arrived at the Menger Hotel, the most elegant place that Honey had ever seen! It was like a royal palace! It was two stories high and located just across the street from the Alamo. Gebhardt had been there before, but it was a new experience for Honey, so he reveled in her every comment. She talked incessantly about the architecture, the arched windows, and the open area. Gebhardt had never examined the building in depth but had accepted it as a masterpiece. Honey loved every detail and couldn't stop herself from pointing them out to him.

The dining room was elegant, and the food could be ordered and served already prepared. The hotel amazed Honey. In their room stood a clawfoot bathtub where a chamber maid brought steaming water and good smelling towels. She told Gebhardt, "This is paradise!"

After two days of romantic time together with room service, they finally ventured out to the plaza around the hotel. Honey had heard lots of stories about the Alamo, so she was excited to see it. The stories had made it sound grandeur and large, but it wasn't. It was a small Spanish mission. The columns around the front door reminded her of the columns that she and her Papa had built in the Cyril Hill church. She couldn't believe that such a massacre had occurred here only thirty-six years ago, but it changed everything for the Texians and eventually for her.

They walked down Commerce Street, busy with people crowded in shops. The shops were usually on the first floor with an overhanging cover for the sidewalk and a balcony upstairs, which were boarding rooms or the shopkeepers' homes. The wagons, carriages, and horses turned the dirt streets into sloppy, muddy trenches. Sitting on the sidewalk were pagarias, Mexican women selling bright-colored birds. They had the birds caged and often had their children huddled close by. Gebhardt bought a sack of candy from a Mexican man with a little table covered in a white cloth displaying several choices of candy. His multi-colored serape, which was draped over his upper body, fascinated Honey. Threads were woven in long stripes of red, blue, and green. Honey was wondering which plant pigments they had used to dye the fabric into such vivid colors.

Gebhardt anxiously coaxed Honey into one shop called Doerr and Johnson, Photographers. The shop was full of cards with photographs of San Antonio. Honey had never seen a photograph. She was amazed, but then their biggest surprise came from the stereoscope that was being sold in the shop. Henry Doerr greeted them. "Would you like to look at a stereoscope?" As he handed them the device he continued. "I have photographed scenes all around San Antonio, such as Alamo Plaza, the San Antonio River and Commerce Street. I put the scenes on cards with double photos side by side. When you place the card on the end of the arm extending from the eyeglasses of the stereoscope, you'll be able to see the scene as if it is in real life or in three dimensions." The stereoscope fascinated Honey and Gebhardt, so Gebhardt purchased one as a wedding gift for Honey. They purchased several sets of cards depicting the street life in and around San Antonio to take back home with them.

Gebhardt led Honey to a side street where they entered a hovel, a small Mexican home. Inside they found a long, rough table with wooden benches about it; a single candlestick dimly sent light into the dark recesses of the building where a hard-earth floor exposed chickens, their soft clucking lulling themselves to sleep. Honey asked Gebhardt, "Are you sure this is where we should eat?"

Gebhardt replied, "Absolutely! My cousin Albert at the wedding told me we can get the best stew here. He said it is spicy and hot, but delicious."

Senora Garcita, a large, tawny Mexican *materfamilias,* placed a plate in front of them of various savory compounds swimming in fiery pepper that burned their tongues and made them grab for the nearby glasses of water. She called the stew: *chili con carne.* It was composed of stewed beef, peas, a red gravy and red peppers and ground cumin. As Honey gulped down water, Senora Garcita laughed and said, "This is my Anglo-chili. It has beans in it. If you really want hot chili, then I can get you some Mexican chili." Honey declined the offer, but she was curious about the mysterious chili.

After Gebhardt paid for their meal, they wandered back up to the Alamo plaza and walked along the San Antonio River. There were several brick walls embanking parts of the river where they sat and talked.

Gebhardt told Honey that he was not as keen on ranching as his father, Caleb, and his uncle, Jacob. He said, "I know how to herd the cattle and breed them and get them to the sales auctions. But I don't have the passion for sleeping in a pasture and watching the cattle or for learning the rodeo skills that the vaqueros use to herd. I don't know what I want to do, but it's not ranching all the time. I realize that my cousin Francisco and I have no choice but to carry on the ranching operation. It is our responsibility to our family, but there's got to be more to life than ranching."

Honey listened attentively, and she knew that Gebhardt had a gentler side that he rarely displayed to others. She asked him, "What is it you want to do?"

"My cousins told me about a place in Fredericksburg called a turnverein. It is a social club where people can come and enjoy singing and dancing. But it is also a place where men can come and exercise. They can do gymnastics. That's why they call it a turnverein, a place for turners."

Honey giggled and then quickly apologized. "I'm sorry, I just can't imagine you or your father or your uncle, turning somersaults!"

"Well, I see so much depression and sadness in our world after this War Between The States. People are angry at how the northern states are treating us in the south, even when many of us were not involved in the war and had no slaves. Many people are desperately poor. Our town needs something to bring joy and fun back into their lives. Did you see the happiness everyone was feeling at our wedding? I want to give them that enjoyment more often in their lives than just at a wedding."

"So, how would you plan to do this?" asked Honey.

"I think we could start with a building and call it a turnverein. The men could come and exercise and each week we could have a singing society. My mother already has a small group of people who gather at her house to sing while she plays the piano. But this would be more public, a place where anyone could come and join the singing society. Maybe we could even start a basketball team. Sometimes we could have a dance on Saturday afternoon."

Honey was beginning to catch Gebhardt's enthusiasm, "I could paint murals for the walls that would depict Gristmill, with the mill and with the cattle range and the general store and the wagon trains down by the river. I can see it would be a place that could bring happiness just to come inside."

Gebhardt put his arms around her and said, "I knew you would approve. I will need a lot of help from you, because I can't stop being a rancher. But together we can bring some fun back into Gristmill." And with that he kissed her long and hard, and she returned his warmth.

That night they went to the rathskeller, the basement in the Menger Hotel. After their long day of sightseeing, they found the cold beer to be delicious. As they sat enjoying their beer at the long wooden bar, Gebhardt suddenly got excited and said, "You know what we should have at our turnverein? We should have a bar! A place like this where people can come and enjoy drinking a beer with their friends!"

The man behind the bar joined their conversation. "You know what old Ben Franklin said, 'Beer is proof that God loves us and wants us to be happy.'"

Gebhardt exclaimed, "He was correct – we must have beer at our turnverein." And he laughed heartily.

Honey told him, "When I was growing up, most Czechs preferred lager beer. I think it is cold brewed from yeast that ferments near the bottom of the tank. All I know is that I like it, too."

With that, Gebhardt picked up a conversation with several people in the rathskeller, talking about the breweries in Texas that could deliver beer. They told him about the difficulties of spoilage. It gets hot in Texas and beer does not do well if it sits and gets hot. They suggested that he become a home brewer. As Honey listened, she thought she could probably brew beer if she could learn the procedure. If she could learn to concoct paint from pigments found in nature, then surely, she could learn to brew beer.

They returned to their room late that night, exhausted and excited about their plans for the turnverein. Gebhardt fell asleep almost immediately, but Honey could not stop her mind from cycling through everything that had happened today.

Sometime on their honeymoon, she had started calling Gebhardt, Gebby. It just happened. She didn't plan it; she adored him so much and Gebby just slipped from her mouth. To her it was an endearing nickname. He was so loveable and charming that she decided "Gebhardt" sounded too stern for her feelings toward him. From that point and forever, she would call him Gebby.

When they returned home, Gebby began describing his plans to his father and uncle. Amazingly, they were acquiescent to his ideas as long as he maintained his work on the ranch. They even suggested that the field which had been cleared for their wedding party would be a good place to build the building.

Gebhardt and Honey were now living in the back room of Caleb and Elsa's home. They had plans to build an additional room for their living quarters, and the land for the new turnverein would be near, so Honey could oversee the building project. To everyone's surprise, Honey seemed a natural at designing the building and knowing what had to be done to make the structure stable. Gebhardt arranged for several workers to help her on the project. She directed them to cut timbers and even showed them how to plane the logs. Honey's architectural skills baffled most everyone, especially Elsa, Josefina and Sister Carlita. Where did she learn all this?

Honey had such an authoritative demeanor, and she was so direct and absolute in her direction, that no one questioned her ability. Within months, the building was taking shape. According to her design, the building should sit with side walls to the north and south. Along those walls were large windows shuttered by panels. When the hall was being used, the panels would be raised and braced open to allow the flow of air to circulate through the building. The front had a small office on one side and big doors on both sides. Between the doors was a stage.

At the back of the building she constructed the bar. Curiously, the bar had many of the designs that her Papa had used in the construction of the altar at the church, such as turned columns and decorative arches across the top of the backdrop of the bar. Honey ordered a large mirror to go in the center at the back of the bar, just like the one at the Menger rathskeller. On each side of the mirror were shelves for glasses and bottles of liquor. They milled most of the wood for the turnverein in Gristmill, but Honey ordered mahogany wood for the bar from Cuba. It was very expensive and would take several months to arrive. However, Honey wanted the bar to be the showpiece of the turnverein.

Off to the side of the bar through two doors, she built a kitchen with a large fireplace where pots of food could be cooked. She had not forgotten the delicious, spicy *chili con carne* that they had eaten in San Antonio. She had discussed it with Gebby's aunt, Josefina, and together they had created a similar dish which she hoped would become a highlight of many of the turnverein events.

As the months went by, she realized that she was tired almost all the time, often wanting to sleep later in the morning, and then sometimes feeling nauseous when she got up. This was not like her. But as she began to remember, she had not had a monthly flow for several months. Could she be pregnant? Without a mother since she was fourteen, she really didn't know what to expect or how the whole pregnancy thing worked, but she thought she definitely could be pregnant!

She told Gebby what she suspected, and he was exuberant with happiness. However, he was not much help to her in determining what this meant. He suggested that Honey talk to his mother, Elsa. She confided in Elsa and, within hours, the whole family knew that Honey was going to have a baby! They treated her like a princess. She was told that she should no longer work on the turnverein because it might hurt the baby. She was to rest every day for several hours, and on and on. Finally, Honey decided this had to stop! She was not helpless, and she had seen many women back in Cyril Hill who worked every day while they were pregnant. She might not know much about being pregnant, but she knew she wasn't an invalid.

Honey accepted that she should leave the heavy lifting of timbers to the men working for her. She supervised everything but was now spending her time carving much of the scroll work for the bar and painting the murals on either side of the stage. She captured the gristmill, the river and the bluebonnets on one side, and on the other she painted the vaqueros riding with a herd of cattle across the prairie.

When Honey was eight months pregnant, the turnverein was complete. They called it Gristmill Turner

Halle. Almost a year to the day from when they were married, they opened Turner Halle with a dance to which they invited the whole town. Honey sat off to the side watching the crowd of people. The turnverein was already accomplishing what Gebby wanted. People were happy and enjoying themselves. She thought, "Papa would be so proud of me; he taught me how to do this, and I built this."

As she got up to go to the bar and sit with Gebby, she felt hot liquid run down her legs. Elsa had explained the possibility of her water breaking but she had no idea how that would feel. She saw Elsa and Josefina running toward her as she collapsed back into her chair. The two older women helped her to her feet, and Gebby carried her back to their room.

For two days she suffered through excruciating pain as the contractions came harder and closer together. She could hear the women talking about blood seeping from her womb. They said the baby was under distress, and it might not live. She prayed over and over to God to please let her baby live. Finally, they told her the baby was crowning and when the next contraction began, she should press down as hard as she could. She did as she was told, and the glorious sound of a baby's cry racked the house. She and Gebby had a son! They named him James.

After some recovery, Honey could nurse James, and she learned all the things she needed to know about taking care of a baby. She returned to her job, bringing events to Turner Halle. Their son, James, was always being held and cared for by one of his grandmothers, Elsa or Josefina, or his second cousin, Sister Carlita, or one of the many children from the orphanage. Sometimes, Honey felt like she had to wait in line just to hold him.

When James was only a year old, Caleb invited a painter, Gregory Temple, from San Antonio to come and paint a family portrait. The whole family gathered together and sat on Elsa's fancy couch from Chicago. Everyone was there: Jacob, Josefina, Francisco, Sister Carlita, Caleb, Elsa, Gebhardt, Honey and James. James wiggled and squirmed and the painter complained and ordered them to keep the child still. When he finished the painting and left, Honey raised a fuss. She told the group, "This is the most awful painting that I've ever seen. He painted every one of us with a scowl on our faces and he made all of us women look like we're as dry skinned as the prairie grass. Please let me re-paint our family portrait. I can do it without all of us sitting for hours in one place. I know you'll like it better than this one."

After looking at the disappointing painting, everyone agreed that Honey would do a much better rendering of their family.

Honey began the project at once. She ordered a very large canvas and good oil paints, knowing that this portrait would be with their family for many years. She worked almost around the clock to get it complete. When she finished it, she proudly added her initials in the bottom right corner, HHM. They hung the painting in Elsa and Caleb's front room, and it was admired by all.

James was much like his father, easy going and smart. He was walking in no time at all. He loved the horses, so his grandfather, Caleb, bought him a small pony. Honey was afraid that he would fall off and get hurt, but James seemed to have a natural ability to ride.

Time seemed to fly by for Honey and Gebby. Two years later, Francisco was thrown from his horse, and he died from complications. Jacob and Josefina were so consumed with grief that they could hardly manage their day-to-day life. Shortly after Francisco died, Josefina passed away. This left Gebhardt and Caleb to take care of the ranch without Jacob's help. Elsa had her hands full with the general store. Honey spent much of her day entertaining and teaching James. He was a growing toddler trying to get into everything; and whatever he could find, he threw – usually rocks and sticks. Honey had developed many programs for Turner Halle. They now had a basketball team for the young men of the town, and a lady was teaching dancing lessons.

She had read about a game called ninepin bowling. She decided it was just right for Turner Halle. There was plenty of room to set up two alleys along the side of the building. The bowlers rolled wooden balls of various sizes at nine pins set in a diamond configuration. The object was for a team to knock down the eight surrounding pins, but leave the larger number-five pin, or kingpin, standing, for a strike worth twelve points. Downing all pins resulted in a score of nine. Pins were reset only when an inning was complete – when all members of the team have bowled two balls, when all the pins were downed, or when only the kingpin remained.

The ninepin games were so exciting that matches were set up between teams. Members of the town often came out to bet on the teams. Honey hired young boys to be the pin setters and she provided chairs for the people who came to watch. All the while, they were drinking beer from her bar. Turner Halle had become the social center for Gristmill.

One day Jacob showed up on his horse and announced he was ready to return to work. He didn't smile and laugh as he once did, but he had decided that he must get up and go on with his life. This relieved Gebhardt of some of his ranch duties. He now had time to play with little James. How he loved to watch him run and talk and laugh. Gebby would take the boy fishing and riding on his pony.

It seemed that Gebby had been dreaming much of the time when he had been out on the range with the horses. One night he told Honey, "When we drove the cattle to Fort Worth on the last trail drive, I met a man from England who told me about a thing called a carousel. I think it is something that we should build."

Intrigued, she asked, "And what is that?"

Gebby proceeded to tell her his idea, "A carousel is like a giant merry-go-round. It's all for fun, especially for the children. The base or platform is round like the floor in a room. The center has a large, enclosed column and the mechanical workings are inside of it. There is a round top like the ceiling. The platform holds several wooden horses in place by poles going through their centers in front of their saddles. Between the horses are some benches. People can either ride on the horses or sit on the benches as the carousel goes around and round. We would attach the poles to some pulleys and gear mechanisms in the top so that, as the floor turns, the horses go up and down."

"It's really magnificent with decorative carving all over and it's painted in bright colors. There are mirrors placed on the ceiling to catch and reflect the light of the colors even more. The man said that they are the newest things at European fairs."

"And the best part is that inside the center column is a calliope that plays music. The music is whimsical and fun. It plays mechanically like a little music box, though the music is more polka-like than dainty."

The whole idea sounded overwhelming to Honey. After listening for a while, she asked Gebby, "And how does this carousel turn around and round. Do we have to pull it to make it go around?"

"Oh no, that's the beauty of it. You've heard me talk about a steam engine, like the huge steam engines in the new trains. The carousel would have a small steam engine. It would turn the gears and mechanisms inside the column, which would then make the platform turn and play the calliope music."

"The man I met had a piece of paper showing where we can order the steam engine and the calliope and he sketched what the carousel might look like," explained Gebby. "I know, with your artistic skills, that you can design flamboyant horses, bedecked with jewels and gold and silver leaf. And we can carve the whole carousel canopy with flowers and ribbon trim. I believe I can make the engine work and together we can build the most extraordinary carousel that Texas has ever seen!"

Honey wanted to protest that it sounded like too much hard work, but the idea captivated her as it had Gebby. "I think I could design wooden horses. If I can carve statues of saints, then I guess I can carve horses!"

"These won't be just ranch horses. They will be fairy tale horses – beautiful steeds with colorful bridles and saddles in bright colors. The horses will have vivid-colored blankets and fantasy faces. With your imagination, the carousel will be stunning."

As Gebby spoke, he became more and more animated and excited. He picked Honey up by the waist and spun her around. She had never seen him as enlivened as he was about this carousel.

Gebby ordered the steam engine from England. They ordered gold and silver leafing along with paint and brushes and all the accessories that Honey would need to create the horses, benches and carousel canopy. As she carved and worked, James sat by her side or played nearby. He was as consumed by the project as she and Gebby were. Honey let James name each of the horses. Elsa helped Honey sew the red and white canvas canopy that rose above the carousel top.

By the time that the small steam engine arrived, Gebby had the main structure of the carousel built. The steam engine resembled a giant wooden barrel with a chimney above the engine that allowed the smoke to rise through the red striped canopy. Everyone in town was curious to see what Gebby and Honey were building in front of Turner Halle. So fantastic was the plan that, when Gebby would try to explain and describe the carousel, most people would just raise an eyebrow in skepticism.

Making the carousel turn and the poles glide up and down was a nightmare. Sometimes the carousel would go so fast that if a person were riding the horse, he would be thrown across the lawn. At other times, it would go so slowly that even an elderly grandmother would get bored. When Gebby tried to make the calliope music work, it played so loud that everyone in town complained about the noise. Finally, the carousel with the calliope was working correctly. They announced that the next Saturday there would be a dance at Turner Halle and there would be carousel free rides for everyone.

People from throughout the county came to Gristmill to see the much talked about Moniac's Steam Carousel. After Honey, James, Caleb, Elsa, and Jacob rode the carousel, they retired to the park benches beside the ride to watch. Grown men, who never had a pleasant thing to say, were riding the carousel and laughing with pleasure. Gebby was beaming with pride. He winked at Honey, and she could not have been happier.

The carousel became the attraction of south Texas. Families came to Gristmill to shop at the General

Store and ride the carousel. Gebby hired men to maintain the steam engine and to collect the money for the rides. The carousel was profitable from the beginning.

After that, life for Gebby and Honey settled into a routine. Elsa was getting older, and she needed more help at the General Store, so Honey split her time among the General Store, Turner Halle and caring for James. James was growing up, becoming a young man. Honey began worrying that Gebby was staying later and later at Turner Halle, drinking beer or hard liquor with the men who gathered there. He often came home late at night only to pass out in bed. But her complaints to him landed on deaf ears. He said that as the proprietor he had to be there.

Elsa and Caleb took a trip to Fredericksburg to visit her sisters. Since Elsa and Caleb were getting older, James went along to manage the carriage and help with anything they needed. While he was there, he met Lou. When he returned to Gristmill, he described Lou to Honey as 'the girl I'm going to marry.'

Eventually James followed through on his prophecy, he married Lou, and they made their home in Gristmill. Lou was pretty, kind, and a joy to be around. She was shy but held a quiet strength so common in German women. Honey adored Lou. It wasn't too long before Lou was pregnant and, in 1896, James and Lou had a little boy, Adam.

Honey was sure it was one of the happiest days of her life when she held Adam, her grandson, in her arms. Once again, she wished that her Papa and Mama could have lived to be old and to meet a great-grandson. They would be so thrilled that she had found her destiny in life!

She spent every spare minute singing to Adam and playing with him. James had become the rancher that Gebby never wanted to be. James knew every cow and every cowhand. He knew the price of beef and when to round up the cows to take them to market. He promoted the use of barbed wire fences, saying, "The cattle rustlers are stealing us blind." It seemed there was a constant argument going on between old Caleb and James about barbed wire and branding and breeding cattle. Gebby remained content to let them have the ranching while he spent more and more time at Turner Halle behind the bar.

The Fourth of July was a big celebration at Turner Halle. Gebby roasted meat from two cows that had been slaughtered. His men had stacked wood over eight feet high to be used in the barbecue. He had beer delivered from San Antonio and set inside the bar. Honey was cleaning and preparing the hall for all the expected customers. Gebby and a group of men built the fire behind the hall and were waiting on the fire to burn down to coals. All the while they were drinking and drinking, talking and cussing and telling jokes.

Two-year-old Adam was tagging along with Honey. While she cleaned, she made him a pallet on the floor in the front of the hall. He liked to race up and down the hall floor, riding his stick horse. It was getting late and Honey wanted to head home, but she had just a little more to get finished. She gave Adam a bite to eat, after which he lay down on his pallet and fell sleep. Honey returned to the kitchen behind the bar to finish up.

At first, she didn't think much about the smoke coming under the door, because Gebby and the men were just outside cooking the meat. Eventually, though, the smoke began to fill the kitchen and then, without warning, the whole ceiling was on fire! Before Honey could escape, the kitchen ceiling fell in on top of her. She was screaming, but Gebby didn't hear her! Mercifully, Honey's life was taken by the smoke before the fiery flames wrapped around and consumed her body.

James saw the smoke and raced from his home to Turner Halle. Hearing Adam screaming from inside, he raced into the front of the hall, scooped up Adam, and carried him outside to Lou. James went back into the burning building looking frantically for his mother, Honey, but could not find her in the smoke.

When the fire was finally out, they found Honey's body in the kitchen. Gebby had come from his home, looking hung over, confused, and sleepy. When the scene became clear, he sobbed uncontrollably. James walked up to him and swung his right fist hitting Gebby square in the face. Gebby's nose was bleeding, the blood running down to his chin. James yelled at him, "You stupid old drunk! You let that fire burn out of control; it killed my mother, and it could have killed Adam! I never want to see you again! Stay away from me and my family!" James took Lou and Adam and left Gebby standing by the smoking remains of the hall.

The carousel was still, standing although much of it was covered in soot. What remained was a bitter reminder of what was lost.

For months, Gebby never left his home. He had some of his old friends bring him beer. His guilt and his grief were so overwhelming that he could hardly get out of bed. His didn't eat. He didn't bathe. He was determined to wallow in self-pity and shame. His drinking had caused the fire that had killed the love of his life. He considered taking his own life, but he guessed he was too much of a coward to do it, so consumed was he in self-loathing.

One day he asked a few of his old friends to dismantle the carousel and burn it. Unable to bring himself to destroy

Honey's beautiful horses, he directed they be put on his wagon, so he could take them down to the barn. He knew he couldn't look at the carousel ever again. It would be a reminder of his shame.

He carried the horses into the barn as if they were his babies. He carefully laid them at the back of the barn. As he turned to leave, he went past the stack of old lumber and trash that had accumulated over the shallow grave. His memories washed over him as he remembered all the joy that Honey had brought to his life. Now she was gone. Life as he had known it was over.

When Gebby stored the horses in the barn, he swore to himself never to speak of Turner Halle or the carousel again! The memory was too shameful. He recognized that it was his fault that Honey had died; he had killed her with his drinking. If ever asked about Honey, he would always tell people she was from Kentucky and after her parents died from influenza, she lived at the orphanage. He would tell them that family was everything to Honey and when Honey became a grandmother to little Adam, it was the happiest day of her life. Honey's secrets and his shame hid in the barn forever and no one would ever know.

As he drove the wagon back up to his house, he saw Lou and Adam sitting on their front porch. He waved but went on past, knowing they would not want to speak to him. He went back to his home, and he took every bottle of beer and alcohol from his house and threw them away. He had a family and even if James hated him, he would ask every day for him to forgive him. He wanted back what was left of his family.

Eventually, Lou and Adam started to come by to check on Gebby. Gebby asked James to forgive him, but James' hate for Gebby continued to eat at him, and he wanted nothing to do with Gebby. Over time, James' disgust for Gebby finally softened. Though he still blamed Gebby and his drinking for the death of his mother, time slowly healed some of the old wounds.

Chapter 15

Jessie arrived early on Thursday morning. Soon, Kelly, Jessie, and Clay were sharing the warm blueberry muffins that Jessie had brought. They were discussing all that they had learned the previous week on their trip to Cyril Hill. Voicing what was on their minds, Jessie offered, "I think we can connect the dots on this mystery of the dead man in the barn. He was obviously Father Anton Bithowski, and I'm guessing that Honey, also known as Ruzi, murdered him, probably with the help of Gebhardt Moniac. Does that about sum it up?"

"Yes, except for the carousel horses."

Clay seemed eager to get to his recliner and watch his game shows, so Kelly helped him to his chair and turned on the television to his favorite game show channel. Then she motioned to Jessie to follow her into her office.

"I want to show you something that I found," said Kelly. "This site has scanned-in archived newspapers from all over the country. And these newspapers go back for years and years. It turns out that the San Antonio Express is available back to 1813. I've searched for Anton Bithowski and there are several articles about his disappearance. They all say that he and several high-ranking Catholic officials traveled to Gristmill for the unveiling of a baptismal chapel at the orphanage. I'm guessing that is when he saw the Anastasis, Resurrection, the same painting we saw; and he probably saw Honey, recognizing her as Ruzi Kosovitsky. The article says that when the Catholic officials were ready to leave, Bithowski was nowhere to be found. He had just disappeared, leaving behind his belongings in his room."

"As you say, connecting the dots, that's probably when Honey and Gebhardt murdered the priest. And there's probably a story that would tell us the reason they did it, but that story is left to our speculation."

Jessie stated adamantly, "Whatever their reason, he deserved what he got. I haven't any sympathy for him, maybe some admiration for Honey and Gebhardt though."

"It's amazing that they didn't get caught and that their secret remained hidden all these years," remarked Kelly.

Jessie, excited about what Kelly had found, exclaimed, "Let's search for Gebhardt Moniac or for Honey Hickson Moniac!"

"That's a great idea," said Kelly, as she was already typing in the names in the search dialogue box on the newspaper website.

Article after article popped up on the search listing. "I had no idea we could find all this information. Here's a story about Gebhardt and Honey's wedding and where they were going on their honeymoon. The story makes it sound like they were a royal couple," muttered Kelly as she quickly scrolled through the articles. "Here's another article. It's the birth announcement for their son, James, born May 4, 1873, which we already knew."

"Oh, my gosh! Have you ever heard of a Turner Halle in Gristmill?" blurted Kelly.

"I don't think I know what a Turner Halle is," answered Jessie.

"This article says that Gebhardt Moniac built a Turner Halle in Gristmill. They are having a grand opening of the hall on May 2, 1873. It is also called a turnverein, obviously something that German communities built for social events and exercising. In particular, it says the

German men would do gymnastics at the turnverein, thus the name Turner Halle – where they would do turns." Both women were laughing so hard they almost cried.

"Can you see Tom, Clay and Claude doing gymnastics?" chortled Jessie. "I'd pay to see that!"

"According to this article, the Turner Halle was designed by Gebhardt's wife, Honey Moniac. It goes on and on about the beautiful bar made of mahogany and the murals depicting Gristmill on either side of the stage. They completed it in May 1873," stated Kelly.

"What day did you say James was born?" inquired Jessie.

"May 4, 1873. That's the same month that Turner Halle was completed. Honey had a major part in building Turner Halle; yet she was pregnant most of that time. Wow!"

Kelly continued to scroll but did not find another article about the Turner Halle. So, she decided that she would just google Turner Halle. A wealth of information popped up, and she summarized, "Ah! Many Germans built Turner Halles or turnvereins. There were quite a few in Texas. It was a community center in a German town where people gathered. They used Turner Halles for community events to enjoy dancing and singing and basketball; and an unusual game called ninepin which sounds similar to bowling. And of course, since they were Germans, there was a lot of beer drinking."

Jessie mused, "I like Gebhardt, and Honey too. I wish we knew more about them."

"We can only imagine Honey's artistic skills and maybe her architectural skills involved in building Turner Halle. Why don't we know more about it? I just can't get over that no one ever mentioned this to us, and it wasn't in Granny Franny's book," pondered Kelly.

Kelly went back to searching the archived newspaper articles. Then she exclaimed, almost jumping out of her chair. "You won't believe this! Here's an article about a carousel in Gristmill in 1878."

"What does it say?" Jessie inquired pushing her for information.

"Gristmill, Texas Gebhardt Moniac of the Moniac Ranch announced today that Moniac's Steam Carousel, much like the one on Coney Island, will begin operation on Saturday. The rides will be free to the public at the opening celebration. Moniac feels that the community will enjoy a recreation that will be fun for the whole family. They built the carousel in front of the Turner Halle, which Moniac built several years ago. The citizens of Gristmill already enjoy turning, singing, basketball, ninepin and dancing at Turner Halle. Moniac declares himself a renaissance man at heart. He states that he loves ranching, but his passion is to bring fun and enjoyment to the families of Gristmill. He credits his wife, Honey Moniac, with the sculpting and painting of the beautiful horses and the benches that will be on the dais. A small steam engine that came from

England will power the carousel. They will mount the horses and benches on a platform, which will turn. Fanciful horses will glide up and down on a pole going through their saddle attached to the platform and the ceiling of the canopy. Mechanisms powered by the steam engine will provide for the horses' movements. The steam engine will also power a calliope musical instrument. The citizens of Gristmill can expect to be delighted as they are entertained by the latest contraption for fun in Bexar County."

"Well, that confirms at least something: Honey Hickson Moniac sculpted and painted the carousel horses that we found in the barn."

"I'm still curious. What happened to all of this?" asked Jessie.

Kelly was busy searching the newspapers for more articles about Gristmill. "There are no more articles relevant to Turner Halle or the Carousel until 1898. This article may explain some things." She then began reading:

On the night of July 3, 1898, a fire broke out at the Turner Halle in Gristmill, Texas. It completely destroyed the structure. There were two people in the building at the time of the fire, a young boy, Adam Moniac, and his grandmother, Honey Moniac. The boy was rescued and is safe, but Honey Moniac died in the fire. They found her body in the ashes.

The fire is suspected to have started by sparks from the fire pit in the back of the hall where meat was being roasted in plans for the July Fourth celebration.

The owner, Gebhardt Moniac, was not available for comment."

"That's terrible. But that explains a lot. Maybe Gebhardt never rebuilt the hall because Honey was gone. Or maybe he was part of the reason that the hall burned. We'll never know. But for some reason, he didn't rebuild and must have shut down the carousel after the fire," said Jessie.

"We know the carousel was not burned, because the horses were still in good shape when we found them, a hundred years later. Maybe he was brokenhearted and just never wanted to talk about it again. He might not have even talked about it to Granny Franny so she wouldn't have known about it to put in her history of Gristmill book," romanticized Kelly.

"I love that we've found all this about our past that we would have never known if we hadn't found the carousel horses in the barn, not to mention, the dead body," said Jessie.

"Kelly, just for fun, could you look up the parents of Honey or Ruzi in that ancestry website that you use? What were their names? Maybe, Josef and Suzanna Kosovitsky?" asked Jessie.

Kelly switched over to the ancestry site and typed in Josef Kosovitsky. There in front of her was his information, including where he was born in the Kingdom of Behemia and married Suzanna. It did not list any children, but his record had a little leaf that carried back to his father and mother. Kelly speculated, "This must be where that 16% eastern European part of our DNA comes from."

"Well, this is very intriguing, but we must save it for another day. I'd best be going home. I need to check on Lupe and Melissa. Melissa is doing so much better. She is opening up to Lupe and Sister Elizabeth about her past. It turns out that she is probably from a good family. She was just an ordinary, rebellious teenager using social media to vent; then her messages were caught by traffickers. They enticed her to come to the mall to meet them. There they paid a lot of attention to her. Before long, she was entangled in their web and kidnapped from her home. I hope that someday she can be returned to her home with a success story like Karen's," said Jessie wistfully as she headed out the door.

Kelly joined Clay in the living room to watch "Let's Make a Deal." Clay was nodding off, and Kelly just looked at him and smiled. She imagined that she and Clay had the same storybook romantic life that Gebhardt and Honey lived, at least she hoped their life was a storybook tale of happily ever after.

Good Friday arrived and Kelly had lots to do. She had a ham to cook and a coconut cake to bake for the family Easter picnic tomorrow. Still in her nightgown, she came into the kitchen for coffee, and noticed one of the overhead light bulbs had gone out and left the kitchen semi-dark. Knowing she would be cooking all day, she had no choice but to put in a new light bulb. One thing that she missed was Clay's help doing these little things, but she was in too good a mood to let that bring her down.

Into the pantry, she headed for the stepladder and a light bulb. She climbed up to the next-to top step on the ladder and started to remove the old bulb. Suddenly Clay barged into the kitchen yelling, "What are you doing in my kitchen? I can change my own light bulbs! Get out of my house!" And with that ultimatum, he reached up and yanked her off the ladder. Kelly fell hard toward the floor, first hitting her head on the cabinets, leaving a gash in her forehead. Then she hit the floor on her left arm. The pain was excruciating. Clay grabbed her by her right arm, pulling her toward the back door while continuing to scream at her, "Get out of my house!"

Kelly scrambled to her feet and pulled herself away from Clay. She ran as fast as she could across the street toward Kathy's house. She had to get away from Clay. She did not understand what set off this agitation and confusion. For the past several weeks, it had appeared that the new medication was working. But now, this was worse than before. She knocked and yelled for Kathy, who quickly opened the door. Kelly stood weakly with blood running down from her face and nightgown. Her left arm hung limply at her side. Kathy was stunned and gasped. "On my gosh, what happened to you?" After Kathy helped her into the house and into a chair, Kelly warned, "Lock the door in case Clay follows me!"

Kathy cleaned Kelly's face and got her a robe. Kelly called Russell. "Please come over here. I'm at Kathy's but Clay is still at home, and he physically attacked me. I'm safe, but I don't know where Clay is or what he is doing. Can you come and help?"

In moments, they heard Russel's siren approaching. He pulled his patrol car into Kelly's drive with Carol was right behind him parking at Kathy's. Carol rushed into Kathy's house while Russell went to check on Clay.

Russell found Clay sitting in his recliner looking at a magazine. When he approached, Clay greeted him with a hello. Russell asked him, "How are you?" To which Clay gave his automatic response of, "Just fine."

Russell left Clay sitting in the recliner and proceeded across the street to Kathy's house. He found his mother-in-law, Kathy, and Carol sitting in the kitchen. Kelly was in a robe, holding an ice pack to her badly cut and bruised face. Carol told him she thought Kelly's arm was broken. Kelly's face explained the whole situation; it was full of pain and distress. She knew Clay could no longer live at home. It was not safe for her, and there was no controlling his aggression. Kelly's inevitable day had arrived!

Russell said he would go back and help Clay change from his bedclothes to street clothes, then take him to the emergency room at the hospital to be checked out, in case there was anything physically wrong with him. He asked Kelly, "Have you chosen a memory care facility where you want Clay to stay? I'm sure the hospital could keep him for twenty-four hours if you need, but if you've made arrangements someplace, I'll take him on."

Kelly's voice came out a whisper, so soft and hoarse, even she couldn't recognize it, "The Sunrise Senior Memory Care has a place waiting for him. I'll call them while you go ahead. They already have all of his paperwork."

As soon as Carol saw Russell's patrol car leave with Clay inside, she, Kelly and Kathy walked across the street. Walking into her home, Kelly felt like it was a ghost house. It felt cold and too quiet, like a spirit was haunting the place. She shivered but continued to her room. Carol helped Kelly change clothes, being careful not to move her left arm. Kathy cleaned up the ladder, the glass, and the blood in the kitchen.

When they arrived at the Emergency Room to have Kelly's cut face and arm checked out, they saw Russell's patrol car pull out of the parking lot headed toward the Sunrise Senior Memory Care facility. Kelly's face needed a few stitches, and after they x-rayed her arm and found it was broken, they put a temporary cast on it. She would have to wait until Monday to get a permanent cast, since her arm was too swollen to cast immediately. Fortunately, the break was only two hairline fractures and it would need no surgery.

Several hours later, Kelly was released from the hospital. She, Carol and Kathy headed to the memory care home. Kelly was apprehensive about facing Clay. Would he be angry at her? Would he lash out and try to hurt her? Would he even understand what was happening?

They checked in at the front desk and were told that Clay was in room 131. They also gave her a list of items that she should bring for his room. It felt a lot like taking Carol to summer camp years ago. He needed clothes that were easy to change, his toiletries, a blanket, a pillow, and a bedspread that he was used to having at home. They suggested that she bring family photos for his room and two photos for his door. They also gave her a ten-page questionnaire about Clay's likes and dislikes for food, music and conversation topics. Right now, she couldn't focus on any of it. She needed to see that Clay was all right.

They proceeded through the locked door using a code she would soon be using often. Turning down the hall, they found room 131. Clay was sitting on the bed and Russell was sitting in the only chair in the room. They were talking about baseball as if this was the most normal day in their lives. Clay was calm. He looked at Kelly not showing any sign of recognition, but then he looked at Carol and said, "Hey, Kelly."

Kelly's heart nearly burst. Clay didn't recognize her after almost fifty years of marriage. Maybe he thought Carol was a younger Kelly. She didn't know for sure. Clay seemed completely oblivious to the fact that Kelly's face had a large bandage on it and that her arm was in a sling. To him, she was just a stranger. Is this what it has come to? Is this our new normal?

One aide informed them that lunch was ready and invited all of them to stay for lunch. As they walked to the dining room, Clay seemed pleasantly happy. They sat at a table and were served a nice lunch of meat loaf and vegetables. Russell and Clay continued to talk about sports, but Kelly just sat silently watching Clay and the rest of the residents of the home. After lunch, a nurse suggested that Clay should probably take a nap. They took this as their cue to leave. Clay got up to leave with them, but when the nurse said to him, "After you take a nap, could we get you to help us with something?" Clay said, "OK."

Kelly told Clay she would be back that evening, and he just smiled at her, showing no regret or anxiety about her statement. They left Clay talking to the nurse and exited out of the same locked door with the same passcode as earlier. When they reached home, Kathy offered to stay with Kelly so Carol could get to her café to check on the employees and plan for the day.

Finally, Kelly and Kathy were alone together. No longer able to hold her emotions inside, Kelly collapsed in tears. She knew she had done the right thing, but why did it feel so bad? Kathy held her and probably understood more than anyone else how she felt. Kathy sympathized, "When Joe died, it was a shock. I had no choices to make; it just happened. I can't imagine how you feel. I'm just so sorry."

Kelly sobbed. "My support group warned me about feelings of guilt. They tell me I haven't broken my wedding vows for better or worse, in sickness and health, to love and cherish. I know that what I'm doing is best for him; I know that I'm loving him, even though I can't keep him at home anymore. It's for his safety and mine. But I just feel so guilty – he must think I've betrayed him, leaving him in a prison."

"That's not true. You saw him today. He wasn't particularly upset when we came or when we left. I think you need some rest, and then we'll go back this evening to visit him. I'll come back later, and we'll gather up the things you need to take with you when we go to visit."

Kelly laid down on her bed and, as Kathy left the room, she was already falling into an exhausted sleep.

Later, she selected items that Clay would need over the next few days. She marked his name in all his clothes, again a reminder he was going to summer camp, except he would never come home from this camp. She shook off the feeling. She had to get her mind focused on what was good about Clay's care and quit fixating on the negative. She found a few photos that she knew Clay would like and set them aside. She and Kathy packed the items and headed back to the memory care home. They found Clay in the main living area playing Bingo. They sat down beside him, and each took a Bingo card to play. He showed them his winnings, three candy kisses and said, "The prizes aren't very good, but I think I've got a good chance of winning more candy." They smiled and agreed with him.

Kathy took his belongings to his room, placing them in the wardrobe. She set the photos in strategic places around the room, putting the photo of Clay and herself next to the bed. Kelly had left Clay's meds with the nurse, so Clay should be set for the night.

When she returned to the Bingo game, an aide announced that dinner was ready. Kelly and Kathy escorted Clay to the dining room and sat with him to eat dinner. The aide came and sat with them. She spoke directly to Clay telling him that after dinner they would sing sixties music. She asked which sixties group was his favorite; but, without making him try to think of a group, she suggested, the Beatles, the Beach Boys, or maybe you are an Elvis fan. Clay responded that he liked them all.

During the meal, Clay seemed to recognize Kelly, and he asked her how she had hurt her arm. She just told him she fell. There was no remorse in his eyes; he didn't remember that he had pulled her off the ladder. When they were getting ready to leave, she leaned over and kissed him on the cheek. He turned his head and kissed her back quickly on the lips. The nurses had advised Kelly that when she got ready to leave, not to announce that she was leaving. Just say, "I'll see you later." Then just get up and walk away.

She thought Clay would insist on leaving with her, but he didn't. Kelly and Kathy left through the locked door. Kelly was sad, but no longer crying. When they arrived home, Kelly thanked Kathy for being such a good friend, expressing how grateful she was for her support. Kelly waved goodbye and returned to her home alone.

Kelly awoke early on Saturday morning; she had endured a restless night of tossing and turning and terrible dreams. Each dream was a different scenario of waving goodbye to Clay.

She got up and put the ham on to cook. She would forget about baking the coconut cake; there would be plenty of desserts without it. But they might miss the main course not being there. Besides, a baked ham was easy to make.

Diane and Claude were coming by to take her to visit Clay. Since she couldn't drive, at least not until she got her permanent cast on Monday, she would have to depend on others to drive her around.

When they arrived, they found Clay sitting with several other men watching a tennis match on TV. If you didn't know that the men had dementia, you would have thought the setting was a normal one: three friends just hanging out together, maybe waiting on their wives and watching sports. They sat down with the men and Claude commented on the tennis players. One man said, "The players are very good. I play tennis."

Then another man replied, "Yes, they are good."

Then Clay said, "We can't play tennis today, it's going to rain." Then there was a pause. After which the conversation was repeated among the three men, verbatim, two more times. They didn't seem to notice the repetition. It was odd only to Kelly, Diane and Claude.

Finally, the two other men got up and wandered off, leaving Clay with his friends. They chatted about the weather, how he was doing and what he had been doing, but Clay didn't offer much to their conversation. They completely avoided the mention of Easter and the family picnic. After about an hour of visiting, they got up to leave. Clay got up with them and followed them toward the exit door. This was the moment that Kelly had dreaded. How did she tell Clay that he couldn't come with her?

They hesitated at the door and Clay said, "My truck is out front, I'll drive home in it."

"No, Clay, you can't leave right now. You need to stay here," replied Kelly.

Clearly, Clay was becoming agitated. "I don't want to stay here. I've got things to do."

Seemingly from out of nowhere, one of the male aides appeared by Clay's side, and gently mentioned to him, "Hey, Clay, I thought you were going to help me fix the popcorn machine for our party this afternoon. We need to start fixing it now, so it'll be ready. Can you come help me?"

Clay looked at his friends and said regrettably, "You guys go on, I'll catch up with you later."

Kelly sighed in relief, wondering if every time she would leave, there would be this conflict, which only contributed more and more to her feeling of guilt. Diane and Claude opened the exit door, and they went out to the parking lot. Kelly despaired, "I don't know if I can do this. I'll never not want to come and visit Clay, but if every day when I leave, he's going to want to come home with me, I just don't know if I can survive." Her friends had no answers but gave her comforting hugs.

After picking up the ham from Kelly's home, and getting into the car, suddenly Kelly said, "Wait a minute, I've got to go back and get the cascarones." Soon they were heading to Jessie's home for the family picnic. Kelly tried to put on a cheery face, but everyone could see her sadness and worry. They covered her in a cloud of greetings, each offering concern and sympathy. She answered all their questions about how Clay was doing and how her arm was fractured. She told them that the bandage on her face looked much worse than the cut really was. Jessie led her to a lawn chair and brought her a glass of wine. For once, iced tea was not enough.

Shortly, Brenda and Kenneth arrived with their three sons, Hector, Doug and Danny. After introductions were made all around, Clint and Casey arrived with their four-wheelers and offered to take Hector, Doug and Danny on a ride to see the ranch. The five young men were off in a whirlwind of dust.

Tom made sure that their guest, Kenneth, had a beer and was included in the conversation with Claude, Russell and Gus. Kathy was a little late arriving. She, Sherry, and her son-in-law had closed the Antique store at lunch. They said they saw Carol leave the Wildflower Café when they were leaving. Russell had already brought their children, Turner and Kenzie, so Carol would be here soon. One of the best things about the Easter picnic was that everyone could attend, since all their businesses were closed at noon before Easter.

Sister Elizabeth had been visiting Lupe and Melissa, so they walked from the El Asilo apartment together. Gus rushed to Lupe's side to help her up the steps to the patio. Lupe's knees were getting bad and Gus knew she needed a helping hand to find a chair. Kelly thought: How wonderful it must be to share your life with your spouse way into your older age. Gus and Lupe are a true love story, not a Romeo-and-Juliet type love story, but the steadfast, trusting kind that comes from many years of caring for each other. Do they realize how lucky they are?

Lunch was served outside on a long buffet table. Jessie had decorated the table to be especially pretty with baskets of wildflowers – bluebonnets, buttercups, Indian blankets, brown-eyed Susans, and Mexican hats. In each basket, Jessie had included at least one Pink Bluebonnet, a tradition in their family. Tom led the blessing prayer. Then everyone filled their plates with the delightful Easter food. A broccoli and rice casserole accompanied Kelly's ham, plus a fruit salad, steamed carrots, and of course, macaroni and cheese for the little ones, and deviled eggs. So many desserts were available that no one could have missed the coconut cake that never got baked. When lunch was almost over, Kelly secretly gave Turner and Kenzie the cascarones. They first attacked Russell and Tom cracking the confetti eggs over their heads. Before long, everyone was cracking eggs over someone's head. At first Melissa looked shocked; soon she realized it was all in good fun, and she grabbed an egg and cracked it over Lupe's head. They covered the patio in confetti.

Once they finished lunch, Hector, Doug and Danny were begging Brenda and Kenneth to let them go out again with Clint and Casey on the four-wheelers. Brenda just shrugged and looked over at Clint and Casey to see if it was all right. Doug said, "Mom, we have to go and feed the cows. They eat right out of my hand. And they slobber a lot, but it's fun." Everyone laughed as the boys headed down the dirt road again.

The men strolled over to the chaise lounges beside the pool so they could keep an eye on Turner and Kenzie, who were eager to swim. Melissa asked Lupe if she could go swimming and Lupe told her to go and have a good time.

When she was gone, Lupe told the group, "Melissa is like a butterfly. It is like she was trapped inside of a cocoon and now she is finding her wings and learning, or maybe remembering, how to fly. She is also beautiful like a butterfly when she smiles." Lupe's smile told the story, too, because she was watching a blossoming young lady emerge from the shell of a drug addicted, world-worn prostitute.

As the women sat and watched Melissa sprint off to the apartment to change into her swimsuit, they collectively thought, "Maybe there's hope that her stay at El Asilo will be a new beginning for her."

Kathy turned to Kelly. "How was Clay this morning, and how are you doing?"

"Clay was fine until we started to leave. Then he wanted to come with us. It just broke my heart to leave him there. I don't know if I can survive that guilt everytime I leave him."

Jessie solemnly spoke, "Learning to survive when your whole being is begging to stop and die is the hardest thing that you'll ever face. I remember the night when the accident out on the highway killed our son, Jackson, and his wife. Kelly, you remember that night. Clay was the sheriff, and they called him to the scene of the accident. Then he brought you with him to tell me and Tom what had happened. We had the babies, Clint and Casey, with us while their parents took a short getaway to Kerrville. When you told us they were dead, my entire world just collapsed. It turned dark. My little boy just couldn't be dead. All my dreams for him, for us, were gone. I remember little about the next few weeks. I know people held me and cried with me, but I can't recall much about the funeral except the vision of those two caskets being lowered into the ground.

Then one day, Sister Elizabeth told me I should look for the blessings that was still here. The twins needed me now more than ever. And I realized that my life would be different from what I had planned. I would be starting over. Going to groups for preschoolers, to little league baseball practices every day, to junior high dances and dealing with teenagers – all those things that grandparents have put behind them. I was like a new mother, except with about twenty-five years added to my age. At first, I thought I couldn't survive. But as time passed, I saw that I was blessed with the care of Clint and Casey. They have brought unbelievable joy to our lives. I not only survived, but I've thrived in raising them and giving them a home. But at the time, I felt as if it was the end with no hope."

Sister Elizabeth softly spoke, "You've heard the old saying that when one door closes, another one opens. But that is not exactly the way life happens. Sometimes a door closes and there's a period of time before the next door opens. What happens in that in-between time is when you are just sitting in the hallway outside the closed door before you discover the next door is open. It's hell when you're waiting in the hallway. You don't think there is any way to survive."

As she continued, "You know, today is the day that the church remembers the waiting. It's called Holy Saturday. Most people don't take notice of this holy day. They go from Good Friday to Easter, when the women who went to the tomb were sitting outside thinking Jesus was dead. The tomb was sealed and guarded. All the hopes that Jesus had taught were gone. They were in the hallway waiting. But Jesus was doing important work on this day. You remember the painting by Honey, the Anastasis, the Resurrection. Jesus descended into Hades, and He was freeing the saints from everlasting death. He was making it possible for us to be a part of His resurrection. We can't experience resurrection without having gone to the garden and the crucifixion and the valley of the shadow of death with Christ. Resurrection is the Good News of Easter; we are the resurrected people – Easter people."

Kathy lamented, "I agree, the time between the already and the not-yet can be excruciating and lonely. After Joe's death, I thought I would never survive the all-consuming pain and loneliness. I still miss him, but I've found that I'm still here and new doors are opening. My daughter is here now and we're closer than ever managing the Antique Shop."

"I guess we all experience that hallway after a closed door in our lives," pondered Brenda. "I remember the days after my fourth miscarriage. We so desperately wanted a family, but the doctors told us it would not happen. We could not have a baby. It seemed like I cried for weeks until my mother suggested that we adopt a baby. We never dreamed that her suggestion would open a door not only to six wonderful children, but to a passion to encourage people to adopt rather than just proclaim they are pro-life."

Kelly sadly said, "I'm sure you all are right, but I just feel like I'm in that hallway of hell. I'm bitter and resentful and I can't fix it. And at the same time, I feel guilty about leaving Clay. And yet I know that bringing him back home would be dangerous. I pray for wisdom and comfort, but I feel like God is not listening. He's shutting me out. I hate being in this place."

Diane put her arm around Kelly's shoulders. They all sat there for a moment with nothing to say, just considering in their minds the doors that had closed and opened in their lives.

Sister Elizabeth whispered, "Kelly, be patient. God is there with you in the hallway. Just trust Him, there is more going on than you can see or understand. It's a reminder of God's steadfast love that never ceases. You must stay present, doing what you know is the right thing to do. Then when the next door opens, and it will, you will be there to walk through it.

Jessie exclaimed, "On a lighter subject, I see the boys coming and I think they found some mud!"

Hector, Doug, Danny, Clint and Casey were piling off the four-wheelers and climbing the stairs to the patio. They were splattered and covered in mud. Danny excitedly said, "Mom, we hit some mud. And we found some goats and chased them until the mama goat chased us!"

Jessie told the boys that they could go swimming, but first they had to wash off with the water hose; she didn't want all that mud in the pool. Those instructions delighted them. Squirting water all over each other was as much fun as getting splattered with mud. The women soon heard them doing cannonballs into the pool and the men yelling at them not to splash them or the younger kids.

As the sun was setting, Brenda and Kenneth left with their exhausted boys. They all wished Sister Elizabeth a 'Happy Easter' since they wouldn't see her tomorrow. As they all said goodbye, Diane and Claude offered to Kelly to take her back to see Clay, but she said no, just take me home, I need to get some rest tonight.

Easter sunrise came early. Carol came and helped Kelly get dressed for church. Then they joined Russell and the children at the worship service. Kelly's heart was just not in the day's sermon from Reverend Brown. She sat contemplating her own loneliness and troubles. They stood to sing, "Up from the grave He arose, with a mighty triumph o'er His foes, He arose a Victor from the dark domain, And He lives forever, with His saints to reign. He arose! He arose! Hallelujah! Christ arose!" Kelly's morose feelings began to lift and the gloom started to fade away. Kelly looked around to see her family, Carol, Russell, her grandchildren, and Jessie and her family. She saw Brenda and Kenneth and their three sons, and her friends Kathy, Diane, and Claude. She had not the faintest clue when or which door would open next, but she knew she was not alone in trying to survive. In the past few months, she had learned about an ancestor who had survived the worst kind of losses to find happiness. She, herself, had found a whole new part of her family that she didn't know existed. At that moment, she rejoiced in her blessings. She would find resurrection. She would survive.

They all stood as Reverend Brown proclaimed the benediction and then they sang,

> *Hallelujah Christ is risen,*
>
> *I will shout and sing along.*
>
> *He is the Day of new beginnings*
>
> *Every Day He's my resurrection song.*

Acknowledgments

Thank you to my wonderful three editors: Lois Boles, Cheryl Kensing and Fran Murr. They spent endless hours reading, editing and encouraging me to rework parts of my manuscript. They provided insight into my characters and led me to discover each one's authentic personality. Without them, I could not have completed this book.

A very special thank you to my Tuesday Morning Bible Study, the Alzheimer's Caregiver Support Group and the Girls of 66 who have given me numerous stories to use in my plots and have supported my effort to write.

My family sustains and encourages me to keep writing. But especially I'm thankful for my loving husband, Ted. He makes possible huge blocks of uninterrupted time to give me the freedom to write. He critiques my manuscript and offers fantastic ideas that I have overlooked. Most of all, even after fifty years of marriage, he's still my cheering squad. Always supporting me!

Also by Sussie Jordan

Pink Bluebonnets

Pink Bluebonnets is about the same five extraordinary women in Secrets of the Carousel. Kelly and her four best friends refuse to sit down in their rocking chairs to nod off in retirement. They want nothing more than to live peacefully in a small Texas town and enjoy their grandchildren. They courageously face the challenges of Alzheimer's and widowhood, while still finding fun and humor through their lifetime friendships and family. Their cozy world is shattered when they come face to face with pure evil. Reminded of their heritage of freedom fighters, they are determined to change the status quo. They reject the idea that we're trapped and doomed to repeat the same old cycle of struggles. However, when confronted with a sinister shadow world, they become the target of a corrupt gang of sex traffickers.

Pink Bluebonnets is available on Amazon